# CASK STRENGTH

## AN AGENTS IRISH AND WHISKEY NOVEL

## LAYLA REYNE

Cask Strength

Copyright © 2017, 2023 by Layla Reyne



Cover Design: Cate Ashwood Designs

Cover Photography: Wander Aguiar Photography

1Ed Editing: Edits by Kristi, Deborah Nemeth

2Ed Editing: Adam Mongaya, Sandy Bennett

Second Edition

August 2023

E-Book ISBN: 978-1-962010-02-3

Paperback ISBN: 978-1-962010-03-0



**Content Warnings**: Explicit sex; explicit language; violence; off-page death of a former spouse; instances and/or discussion of homophobia.

# ABOUT THIS BOOK

FBI agent Aidan Talley has been hiding parts of himself since he was a teen. Thirty years later, he's hiding his heart from his partner. He's already lost the love of his life once, and Jamie could be that kind of love again. He won't survive the loss a second time.

Cyber agent Jameson Walker left behind a promising sports career to keep his sexuality out of the spotlight. Now, he must return to his old life, as a coach, to bust an illegal gambling ring. He needs his partner, but after refusing to hide how much he cares for Aidan, they're as far from partners as they've ever been.

Jamie struggles undercover. Not with the job, but with deciding which life he wants when it's over. Aidan wants Jamie to choose the present, but to convince him, he'll have to drop the act and stop hiding. And even if he wins Jamie back, even if he rescues Jamie after the case takes a dangerous turn, the secret Aidan doesn't know Jamie's keeping could blow his world apart.

*Romantic suspense and sports romance collide in this swoony second book of three, now in its second edition with a new cover and formatting and extended content.*

*For anyone who's ever been homesick, then realized your heart
and home lie somewhere else now*

# ONE

The roar of the Vanquish's V12 engine sent a bolt of desire racing down Jamie's spine, warming him from the inside out and chasing away the February chill. The sports car's growl was sexy as hell on its own. The fact that it also heralded his partner's perfectly timed arrival, right on Jamie's heels, magnified the seduction tenfold.

Aidan's gleaming black sports car careened around the corner, wheels squealing on wet pavement. Jamie laughed as he pushed open his front door. He and Aidan were rubbing off on each other, and not just in bed. He had begun twirling his pen around his thumb, and Aidan ignored his brakes with increasing frequency, drifting with unbridled zeal whenever the opportunity presented itself.

Figuring Aidan would need a couple times around the block to get the drift thrills out of his system—and find a parking spot on a rainy Friday evening—Jamie headed inside. He flung his sopping trench at the coatrack, dropped his bag on the floor, and toed off his socks and shoes. He added his crumpled tie to the scattered remains of his work week, then climbed the stairs to the main floor. He was drying his hair with a dishtowel in the kitchen when the front door opened and closed again. The muffled thump of a tumble, followed by a filthy Gaelic curse, floated up the stairs.

Jamie smiled. He'd also learned a few of those over the past five months. They came often, Aidan daily tripping over his messes here or at the office. Tidiness was not a habit he had picked up.

Head in the fridge, scoping out dinner options while music blared, Jamie wasn't prepared for Aidan's sneak attack. His dress shirt was yanked out of his pants, and Aidan pressed something cold and wet against his spine. Jamie hissed his displeasure, cold and wet enough already from his commute home, but then Aidan's teeth nipped his earlobe and desire burned away his chilly irritation. He stretched his neck and fell back against Aidan's hard body, a wine bottle trapped between them.

"What've you got there?"

Aidan trailed his open mouth from Jamie's ear down his offered neck. "We're celebrating." He yanked aside his collar and sucked hard enough to leave a bruise.

"Because it's Friday?" Jamie limited alcohol to special occasions, of which the weekend didn't qualify on its own, but his self-imposed rules hardly seemed the point as he rubbed his ass against Aidan's stiffening erection.

"Because we're officially on top of the FBI's clearance board."

Attention snared, Jamie whipped around, beaming. "We passed Powell and Hazen?"

Aidan wore a smile to match, heat blazing in his autumn eyes. "That piracy case put us in the lead." One-handed, he grabbed Jamie by his open collar and dragged him into a hard, searing kiss, lips and teeth colliding, his wicked tongue invading.

"You're gonna tear another dress shirt," Jamie mumbled while unbuckling Aidan's belt.

With a hard jerk, Aidan ripped his shirt the rest of the way open and scorched a path up his exposed torso. "Then stop taking off your damn tie so I have something else to tug."

Hand inside Aidan's slacks, Jamie palmed through silk an erection he knew as well as his own by now. Liked better than his own. "I'll tell you what you can tug."

Aidan jutted his hips forward and his arousal filled Jamie's hand. "You'll pay for that," Aidan said before hauling him in for another bruising kiss.

Jamie was playing with fire, and he couldn't wait to get burned. He came up for air and threw on another log. "Promises, promises."

In one of those frighteningly fast flurries of motion Jamie still wasn't used to, Aidan shoved the bottle of champagne in the fridge, slammed the door closed, and manhandled Jamie around so he was facedown against the white quartz island. Hands bound behind his back by his dangling shirtsleeves, body trapped between the cold, unforgiving countertop and Aidan's warm supple frame, Jamie gasped. The hold, the contrast, was exquisite, but he wanted more. He wanted all their clothes gone and his hands back on his partner. Aidan, however, held him pinned, one hand on his back and the other braced on the countertop beside his face. Jamie turned his head to the side, as much as Aidan's open mouth on his nape allowed, and the sparkling gold and emerald clover cuff link twinkled back at him.

Aidan drove his dick along the crease of his ass. "Last Friday of the month. Always my favorite."

Jamie shoved back, begging for it. "Payday?"

Aidan snaked a hand around his front, loosened his belt and zipper, and dove inside. "Cleaning day." He swiped a thumb over Jamie's leaking cock and took him in a firm, slick grip. "All month long, I dream about fucking you on this countertop."

"You could just take an arm to it. Wipe it clean yourself."

"Where's the fun in that?" Aidan suckled the sensitive spot behind his ear, warm lips and warm breath overwhelming Jamie's motor functions. His toes curled and his knees turned to jelly. Aidan shoved a hard thigh between his legs, and Jamie ground against it shamelessly. "I see you take my point."

Oh, he took his point all right. But it was time to make his. He was two seconds from exploding, and the countertop was not his intended target. Exerting his core, he levered up and trapped Aidan's dick between their pitching bodies. He leaned back and licked the underside of his auburn-stubbled jaw, the five-o'clock shadow stoking Jamie's lust. "Point taken. Now fucking take me."

Growling, Aidan released his cock and ripped the dress shirt the rest of the way off his arms. Limbs freed, Jamie flailed forward, saved at the last second by Aidan's arm around his chest. Aidan's hand landed atop his interlocking N and C tattoo, fingers clawing at ink and skin. His hand always went there, and each time, Jamie swore he could feel it burrowing through skin and closing around his heart, the grip tight and unyielding. With the other hand, Aidan grasped the back of his pants and briefs and tugged them down, freeing his cock. Aidan took him in hand once more, palm sliding along the underside, thumb circling the tip.

Jamie rocked forward, putting on a show. "Baby, please." He angled his face in, seeking Aidan's lips, as he groaned and pumped into his fist. Aidan bit his bottom lip, sucked it between his teeth, but only for a second before he pushed Jamie away, spun, and lifted him. His ass hit the island top, and Aidan fused their mouths back together.

Lost as he was in the kiss, Jamie vaguely registered Aidan's multitasking—dropping his own pants and boxers, shedding his shirt and tie, scrounging in the island utility drawer for the condoms and lube they had stashed there, among a dozen other places in the house. Five months of the best sex of Jamie's life, each time hotter than the last. He hadn't been so regularly fucked into oblivion like this in years, if ever. But kissing Aidan was still the highlight of every encounter. The way their mouths fit just so. The sensual glide and demanding suction of Aidan's silky lips and rough tongue. The lingering taste of coffee and some-times whiskey. The addictive mix of light and dark. He would never get enough.

Tearing their mouths apart, Aidan put a hand to his chest and laid him out, yanking his ass to the end of the counter and dipping out of sight. Jamie's grumbled objection became a strangled moan as Aidan spread his ass cheeks and applied that rough tongue to an up-close-and-personal tour of his most sensitive areas. A torturous sweep around his hole, the tip diving in to tease, before lapping at his taint, toying with his balls, then tracing the underside of his dick on the way to swallowing him whole.

Jamie gripped the counter's edges and writhed from pleasure overload. From curbing his orgasm, not ready for this to end. "Fuck, baby."

Dark eyes stared up at him through a hank of dyed blond hair. "That's exactly what I intend." Smirking, Aidan slid two slick fingers inside him and sucked his cock back into his mouth, all the way to the root.

*God*, that mouth. Hot, wet, almost as good as he remembered the heat inside Aidan's ass, but he hadn't had the pleasure again since that one night during their investigation in Galveston last fall. Just one of the boundaries Aidan had thrown up since their return. Jamie lived with it like he lived with the other walls. Worth it for the precious pieces of Aidan he did get. There was too much there to walk away from. Too much he lo—

Cool air and emptiness chased away the dangerous thought. Aidan rose from his crouch, pressed Jamie's knees back, pulled his ass the rest of the way off the counter's edge, and thrust inside. A burning sting gave way to glorious fullness, and Jamie had no more thoughts, only sensation.

They both groaned and Jamie curled up, bracing one arm behind him and draping the other over Aidan's shoulder, dragging him closer. "Come here, Irish. Need to feel you."

Aidan clawed at each ribbed ab, at the tattoo, at his heart. "Think you're feeling me just fine."

A wrecked moan rumbled out of Jamie's throat. Fingers splayed on Aidan's back, he contorted so they were skin to skin, his erection wedged between them, rubbing against ridged muscles and coarse hair. He would pay for the acrobatics tomorrow, but *fuck*, the heat, the sweat, the smell . . .

"Come for me, Whiskey," Aidan whispered in his gravel-soaked brogue.

Jamie exploded, coating both their torsos, while Aidan cradled his head and clutched his ass, holding him impossibly closer as he sprinted to his own finish, muffling a final moan in his shoulder.

Arm giving way, Jamie relied on Aidan's tight embrace to hold him up, relishing the quiet intimacy his partner seemed as loath to part with as he was. These were the moments Jamie craved, the pieces he treasured, the reasons he didn't walk away. In these moments, he was sure Aidan felt the same as him. He kissed Aidan's sweat-dampened temple. "I'll clean more often."

"Bullshit. I'll pay for biweekly housekeeping."

"Fine by me." Jamie lowered his legs and pitched forward, letting Aidan help him stand. "Shall we move this celebration to the bed?"

"I don't know . . ." A mischievous glint flared in Aidan's eyes. He grabbed the dishtowel Jamie had used earlier and wiped them clean. "Beds upstairs made?"

Jamie took the rag from him and tossed it in the sink. "You're incorrigible."

"Ooh, seventeen-point word." Aidan slapped his ass and skirted past him. "Grab the champagne."

Laughing, Jamie admired the firm backside and toned legs climbing his stairs. There were two more rooms upstairs with king-size beds, both freshly made and free of laundry. It was going to be a long night.

Of the best possible kind.

———

Jamie's long night ended two short hours later.

Aidan rolled away, and cold air hit Jamie's naked back. He buried his face in the feather pillow and muffled his complaint. Aidan still heard him, judging by his laughter as he ambled to the bathroom to clean up. Cheek to the pillow, Jamie raked his gaze down his partner's tall, lean body, eyes lingering on the scratch marks and bruises he had left. Even in the rain-dimmed moonlight, the marks stood out, red and purple.

Undeniable.

Jamie waited for Aidan to reemerge from the bathroom, then rolled over and stroked himself lazily. "Come back to bed."

Aidan's eyes flashed hot, but the rest of his body was down for the count. He sat next to Jamie's hip, covered his hand, and twined their fingers, stroking him together. Despite the warmth and strength of their combined grip, Jamie wasn't getting hard again either. Still, he arched his back like a dog getting a good scratch and glided a hand up the inside of Aidan's thigh. A tremor passed under his fingertips, gooseflesh rising in the wake.

Aidan bent and captured his lips in a languid kiss. "I can't keep up with a young stud like you."

Jamie inched his hand north, palming Aidan's balls, while licking into his open mouth. "You do just fine."

Minutes of kissing and fondling later, Aidan pulled away with a sigh. "I've gotta go." He stroked him once more, withdrew his hand, and slapped his thigh. "Come on, see me out." He rose and headed for the door.

Jamie flopped back on the bed, staring at the ceiling and blowing out a frustrated breath. He was tired of seeing Aidan out. Galveston was the last time they had shared a bed for more than just sex. Another of Aidan's barriers. It wasn't enough for Jamie. He wanted more than a few stolen hours at the end of the workday. Maybe Aidan would consider it if they went out of town. A place where no one from work was likely to see them together in a less than professional context. Buoyed by the idea, he rolled off the bed and followed the racket downstairs, not bothering with clothes. On the upper levels of his Edwardian, atop the highest hill in Bernal Heights, prancing around buck naked wasn't a concern.

By the time Jamie reached the kitchen, Aidan had his pants and boxers on and was buttoning his shirt. Jamie snagged Aidan's tie and cuff links off the floor and slid in front of him. He looped the navy silk around his neck, then grabbed a wrist to fasten in the jewelry. "Let's get out of here this weekend," he said. "Go up to Napa or down to Carmel."

"Can't." Aidan offered the other wrist. "Birthday party for one of the nephews tomorrow. Going out with Nic on Sunday."

Dominic Price, who Jamie shared a federal building elevator with at least once a week, was the federal prosecutor who had tried a Cyber case they had worked. Case follow-up with Aidan had led to lunch. Lunch led to drinks. Drinks led to semiregular dates. Jamie wondered if Nic knew Aidan was also fucking someone else.

He would if those scratches and bruises hung around until Sunday.

"Nic again? What about Casey?"

They had met Casey in the coffee line one morning. Aidan had gone out with him that same night.

"Casey got too clingy."

*Clingy.*

Aidan's primary reason for casting men aside. Jamie didn't want to be cast aside. He avoided clingy and stuck to casual as they had agreed, but he hadn't realized he'd also agreed to share. *The original Casanova,* Aidan's brother had said. Aidan hadn't denied it either. He'd been a player who had shut it down for his late husband, Gabe. Would he do the same for Jamie if asked to choose?

Aidan was afraid to commit, afraid to lose someone else he loved. While Jamie understood, it hadn't stopped him from falling. If he didn't heed the blinking warning signs soon, hit the brakes and put things in reverse, he would be too far gone, and the resulting explosion would rival the car crash they had barely survived in Texas.

Protesting the others was the opposite of reverse. And what right did he have to object when there was so much he hadn't shared with Aidan? He knew secrets about Gabe that would destroy Aidan. Secrets Jamie could barely stomach now and could in no way hold down if this thing between him and Aidan became serious. Jamie bit his tongue, grabbed the navy ends of silk around Aidan's neck, and carefully tied his Windsor knot.

When he finished, Aidan patted his cheek. "What's up with you, Walker?"

*Walker.*

Another boundary. Since Texas, he had only been Walker or Whiskey. Never Jamie, not even in bed.

"A lot on my mind," Jamie answered.

"Would have thought sex and champagne wiped that big brain of yours clean."

"Afraid not."

"Don't think too hard. You're too gorgeous, and too young for wrinkles."

Jamie's eyes slipped shut under Aidan's dancing fingertips. They coasted over his face and neck, drawing him in for a slow, sweet, unbearably tender kiss. His heart swelled and his mind reeled, more confused than ever. Aidan said he wanted casual, but he kissed like he wanted something more.

He parted with a gentle press to the corner of Jamie's mouth. "Night, Whiskey."

"Night, Irish."

Autumn eyes held his, swirling with that same something more. More than casual. Everything. But only for a moment before Aidan shuttered the slip and descended the stairs, the front door closing behind him.

Maybe Aidan would eventually stable the playboy for him, but now wasn't the time to ask. He would have to be satisfied that Nic, no matter how good a prosecutor he was, couldn't dispute the physical evidence on Aidan's body that another man had claimed him.

Grin smug, Jamie pulled on his boxer briefs and eyed the stack of mail on the far end of the counter. At the bottom of the teetering pile was a padded envelope. He pushed the other mail aside, turned over the package, and glimpsed the postmark.

*Houston.*

He dropped it like he'd been burned.

Nothing good ever came in envelopes from Houston.

Their boss, SAC Melissa Cruz, had received a package like this eight months ago. Inside had been the first of many bombs. A mysterious flash drive with files connected to the crash that killed Gabe and Tom Crane, Aidan's former partner, plus a picture of Aidan's dead husband with Pierre Renaud, the terrorist who had tried to kill thousands, including him and Aidan, with a very real bomb in Galveston.

Aidan knew about the flash drive, not the photo. And for every day that passed, another ton of guilt over the omission weighed down Jamie's shoulders. Cruz had demanded his silence, and he'd followed orders. He had also decided not to tear Aidan's world apart until he had the full story. Until he could explain why Gabe had betrayed him. It was Jamie's only hope for softening the blow of his own betrayal.

And now another envelope. From Houston. Were there more bombs inside, real or otherwise? Renaud was still on the loose after all.

He picked up the package by one corner and held it to his ear. Nothing ticking, no noise of any sort. He carefully felt out the contents. A stiff card or note, and at the bottom, a solid mass a few inches long.

Another flash drive.

*Fuck.*

Using a knife, he pried open the flap and spilled out the envelope's contents. A plastic jump drive matching the one Cruz had given him tumbled across the counter. Jamie's heart raced. He swallowed hard around the rising fear and flipped over the card, dreading the worst.

*We're even. —KP1013*

Scrawled in doctor's chicken scratch, the short message calmed Jamie's heart. The package was from Kevin Currie, a hacker he and Aidan had questioned in Texas. Jamie had helped Kevin rebuild a hack he had deleted, and Kevin was returning the favor. After months of hitting a brick wall on Renaud, the break couldn't come at a better time.

In the office nook, Jamie fired up his computer, inserted the flash drive, and accessed his encrypted remote server. Work and case files littered the computer desktop. Before opening the drive, Jamie clicked on the Project Angel folder and scanned the directory. Every piece of damning evidence was still there, untouched and unopened by anyone other than him. This was the reason Aidan wouldn't commit and the reason Jamie didn't pressure him to do so. If Aidan ever learned his secret, they would be over, professionally and personally.

He closed the folder and opened the flash drive. It contained a single file. A string of numbers, letters, symbols, and commands Jamie recognized as a decryption key.

*Bingo.*

He crossed the room to the Dean Dome panorama on the far wall and slid his hand along the bottom edge of the frame, flicking the hidden latch. The picture swung outward, revealing an in-wall safe. He entered the unlock code, the little metal door opened with a pop, and he retrieved the flash drive Cruz had given him. A more complete copy than the one she had given Aidan, a duplicate of which also sat in his safe. He plugged the second stick in, opened the file directory, and applied Kevin's unlock key to the encrypted files.

Five files in, the key worked, and cascading PDFs filled his screen. On each of them, a hauntingly familiar name.

And the bombs kept exploding.

# TWO

Aidan loitered at the busy corner of Seventh and Bryant, coffees in hand, his red-and-white Stanford umbrella balanced on one shoulder. Today was the first time since Friday the downpour had let up, but even a drizzle in the Bay Area extended his forty-minute commute to ninety. He had left early to make it on time. He had counted on their targets not to. The question of the morning was whether he had left enough time for his partner.

On cue, a packed Muni bus stopped at the curb, and among those jostling to exit, Walker stood taller than the rest. He wore a broad smile and Aidan conjured his smooth Southern drawl, dropping "excuse me, ma'am" and "pardon me, sir" as he shuffled to the door.

That smile had been Aidan's private hell the past five months, a dangerous double-edged sword that hovered over his chest. He couldn't get enough of it or the man it belonged to, and with each upturned corner, each brush of their lips, Aidan soared . . . and damned himself further. Worse was watching that gorgeous smile die each time he mentioned another man. Walker's visible disappointment stung, but the burn was a necessary reminder not to get attached. No attachment meant no loss. Aidan was having a wee bit o' fun and aligning a blockade of other men—his last line of defense—against anything serious, anything heart and life shattering, with Walker.

Casual. They were just fucking around.

*Liar.*

Walker ducked his head and cleared the door. Sans umbrella, he lifted his handsome face to the gray sky and stood there, smiling face to the misty drizzle, as commuters split on either side of him.

"Hey, Walker! Don't act like you've never seen rain before."

Walker righted his gaze, and his bright blue eyes lit on the coffee cups. His smile widened, and Aidan's heartbeat tripped over itself.

Awful. Wonderful.

"We've only got a couple months of weather left," Walker said. "Gotta enjoy it while it lasts."

Aidan wouldn't begrudge him the indulgence or his caffeine. He held out a cup, their fingers brushing over each other's in their usual morning greeting. Heat sparked and Walker's eyes warmed, same as Aidan's cheeks. He covered by taking a sip and starting down the sidewalk toward SFPD's giant cement headquarters. "The year we emigrated from Ireland, we arrived in March, the rain stopped in April, everything was brown by mid-May, and it didn't rain again until December. I'd come from the land of green. I was so confused."

"How long did it take to get used to it?"

Aidan considered the question, then closed his umbrella

and turned his own face to the rain. Walker laughed, deep and attractive, and Aidan joined in. A good start to the gray day.

The light mood lasted barely a block.

"How'd your date with Nic go?"

Good manners or morbid curiosity? Aidan wondered what drove Walker to ask. He usually answered "Fine," but this morning, after gulping down the rest of his coffee, he switched it up. "He may be reassigned to San Diego."

"Shame," Walker said, not sounding remorseful at all.

Aidan was about to call him on the half smirk when Walker suddenly picked up the pace. Aidan followed his line of sight and spotted their targets approaching from the other side of the street. "Think this meeting will be any different than the last one?" Aidan asked.

SFPD Detectives Ben Nelson and Jeff Rollins had investigated the car crash that killed Gabe and Tom. They had ruled the accident a random hit-and-run, but Walker's review of the crash data pointed to a targeted hit. They'd previously questioned them about the inconsistencies and the veteran Nelson had brushed it off. *Above our pay grade,* he'd said.

*You're fucking detectives,* Walker had countered furiously.

In the months since, Walker had channeled his rage into examining every cyber nook and cranny of the detectives' lives. Aidan had investigated the old-fashioned way, a combination of surveillance and tapping contacts. Unfortunately, they hadn't found much. Until today, judging by the confidence in Walker's step. He had caught a trail and it was a sight to behold.

"What'd you find?" Aidan tossed his cup into the trash bin after Walker's.

"Follow my lead." Walker didn't break stride as they closed in on Nelson and Rollins. "Detectives, happy Monday."

"Agents," Nelson replied. "Gotta say, not a happy day seeing you here. Rotten start to my week."

"This week's gonna be worse than usual, Nelly."

Glaring, the bald, rail-thin Nelson rested back on SFPD's cement monument sign. Rollins, a bruiser in every way—buzz-cut brown hair, hard brown eyes, muscles too big for his short frame—stood beside him, arms crossed. "What speculation and rumor do you have for us today, G-men?"

"EH Consulting."

Neither Nelson nor Rollins reacted.

Aidan, on the other hand, had to force himself to stay calm despite the familiar initials.

*EH.*

*Eric Hamilton.*

Renaud's mercenary henchman who had engineered the attack in Galveston and had died by Mel's hands during the takedown.

Walker continued to press the detectives while Aidan's head spun with questions. They had investigated Hamilton and Renaud separately and apart from the accident here. Were they connected?

What link had Walker found?

The car crash in Houston?

Were the similarities between that crash and the one that killed Gabe and Tom more than mere coincidence?

Eric Hamilton and EH Consulting. No way that was a coincidence. And apparently neither were the similarities between the two accidents.

Walker's derisive laughter snapped Aidan back to attention. "Really?" Walker said to Rollins. "Because you and Nelly here each received ten grand from EHC last March."

"March?" Aidan said.

Walker glanced at him, concern momentarily eclipsing confidence. Aidan gave him a stiff nod, and he resumed the interrogation. "That's right. Same month SFPD officially ruled the car crash that killed your husband and former partner an accident. Also the same month SFPD paid bonuses and made pension contributions. Someone deposited that ten grand into your accounts at just the right time. A blip. There one day and gone the next. Accounting errors happen all the time, don't they?"

Nelson grew red-faced, Rollins paced, and Aidan had heard more than enough. "Now, as my partner asked, are you familiar with EH Consulting?" He stepped forward and leaned over the shorter man. "Or Eric Hamilton?"

Rollins rounded on Nelson, voice frantic. "You said we wouldn't get caught. That it was routed through the pension fund so no one would find it."

"Here's the thing," Aidan said. "My partner can find anything."

"Shit, shit, shit." He shook Nelson's shoulder. "If he found this—"

Nelson knocked off the younger man's hand. "He'll find that girl you date-raped in college who your parents paid off."

"That's how Hamilton forced you to cooperate," Aidan said.

Nelson rose slowly and looked every bit his age, a mere two years from retirement with his full pension. Likely gone to shit now. "We don't know any Eric Hamilton."

"Bullshit." Walker dug out his phone, loaded a picture

of the dead merc, and shoved it under Nelson's nose. "You know this man."

Nelson's eyes flicked down and back up, giving Walker the same tired look he had given Rollins. "We don't know your man. We were approached by a person claiming to be Mason West."

"Lawyer type," Rollins added.

"But the only Mason West registered with the California Bar is eighty-two years old," Nelson said. "The man who approached us was white, midthirties, average height, dark hair, brown eyes. No record anywhere."

"West had something on you as well?"

Nelson remained tight-lipped.

"You might as well spill." Aidan cut his eyes to Walker. "He'll find it."

"I was having an affair," Nelson admitted to his shoes.

"And that was worth risking your career? Asshole frat boy over there"—Aidan jutted his thumb at Rollins, who shot forward, his puffed-out chest meeting Walker's hand—"doing crime to cover his crimes makes sense, but really, Nelson, you'd risk it all to cover up an affair?"

"You'd be surprised . . . The secrets people keep for love."

Walker flinched, Rollins pressed forward into his hand, but then Walker locked his arm again and held the meathead back.

"If you loved her, why'd you cheat?"

"I may be old, but the plumbing still works."

Walker scoffed and Aidan moved things along, sensing his partner's growing frustration. "Anything else you recall about West? Scars, accent, clothes?"

"New England accent," Rollins said, retreating. "And

dressed like you. Expensive suit, shoeshine, gold cuff links."

"What exactly did West order you to do?" Walker asked.

"They wanted us to—"

"Nothing further, Jeff," Nelson said, cutting him off. Then to Aidan, "Unless you charge us, and only with our attorneys and union reps present."

Aidan raised a brow. "You want this on the record?"

"I don't want anyone else having leverage over me."

"Too late. Now you're going to get pressured from both sides."

"If we talk, we get protection," Nelson bargained.

"You think you're still in danger?"

"Why do you think we stonewalled you?"

"Figured you were protecting your asses," Walker said.

Gray eyes cut to Walker, then back to Aidan, revealing the absolute fear hidden behind weariness and affront. "Not from you."

———

Aidan swung closed the glass door of their main floor office and held out his hand. "Give me your coat, then spill."

Walker tossed him the dark trench and stepped between their desks. They had arranged them back-to-back. More often than not, they needed to look at each other's monitors. In this arrangement, a spin in the chair was quicker than a walk around the desk. It also kept longing stares at a minimum.

Aidan couldn't help but stare now. Walker had bumped their chairs out of the way and was bent over, ass in the air, as he rooted in the bottom desk drawer. The black hole,

Aidan called it. He frequently called all of Walker's area the black hole, but that drawer of electronics detritus was the worst.

At the moment, they had more important things to do than go on a scavenger hunt. "Now, Whiskey."

"Hold your horses." Cords, empty jewel cases, and an ancient battery pack were tossed out before Walker reemerged with a small handheld device. He flipped it on, and a high-pitched beep pierced the air.

"What—"

Walker angled away from the bullpen outside their glass walls and held a finger to his lips. "Can you make us some coffee?" he asked as he swiped the device over the phone on his desk—one beep—then over the keyboard—another single beep.

Catching on, Aidan moved to the coffee set up in front of the bullpen walls while Walker swept their office for listening devices. "Decaf for you?" he asked, carrying on the mundane conversation, just in case.

"No way in hell, Irish."

Lots of one beeps, no twos or threes. Their coffee finished dripping through just as Walker tossed the sweeper back in the drawer.

"All clear?" Aidan asked.

"Clear." Walker wheeled their desk chairs back into place and plopped into his. "We don't talk about this investigation here, so I wanted to be sure."

"You drop a bomb on me like that," Aidan said as he slid into his chair, "I'm not waiting for answers."

"I'm sorry I didn't tell you in advance. I spent all weekend processing the data and tying it together. I wanted to approach Nelly and Rollins without your bias."

"My bias?"

Walker speared him with a knowing look. "You would have gone at them like an angry, angry hippo. I needed our approach to look routine so the curveball would knock them off balance."

"Fine," Aidan conceded. "What've you got?"

Walker reached into his coat pocket, pulled out a flash drive, and spun in his chair toward his desk.

"Nuh-uh." Aidan spun him back toward his. "Yours is a mess."

Grumbling, Walker rolled closer and bumped Aidan out of the way. He plugged in the flash drive, called up the haunting file directory in which every file was dated the date of the accident, and opened a terminal window.

Aidan hated this part—waiting to see what that damn black box revealed once Walker entered the decryption commands. Walker had been slowly cracking files, but without context and a connecting thread, they made little sense. Had Walker finally uncovered the piece that would tie them all together?

"I've been digging into KAG Holdings," he said.

Aidan leaned closer, anticipating the reveal, knowing full well he probably wouldn't like it. The flash drive files they had initially hacked were bank records for a Caymans account owned by KAG Holdings, a Bahamian company whose website remained "Under Construction."

"It's not a dummy corporation so much as a shell." A few more keystrokes and the black box disappeared, the screen filling with PDF and Excel files. "These are corporate formation documents and bank records for at least a dozen other companies owned in part by KAG Holdings. Any names look familiar?"

Scanning the open PDF, Aidan read the corporation's name—EH Consulting—then the Authorized Representative's signature, expecting Eric Hamilton's. Instead, in chicken scratch, was Mason West's.

"You knew Mason West was the guy?"

"Yes, but in digging, I found the same thing as Nelly and Rollins."

"A whole lot of nothing," Aidan said.

"Exactly, so I had to determine if Mason West was Eric Hamilton."

Aidan inhaled a shaky breath, preparing to click through the other files, wary of what else he would find.

Walker placed a hand on his thigh beneath the desk. "That's the worst of it." He had recognized the signs of impending panic and moved to calm him.

Roughly exhaling, Aidan forced air in and out of his lungs and unlocked his muscles. "And the bank records?"

Walker left his hand on Aidan's thigh and leaned forward, pointing with the other at the Excel files. "EH Consulting's bank records."

Aidan expanded the spreadsheet with two highlighted entries.

"I went back to the date of the accident and searched forward," Walker said. "I found these two transfers to a pension fund manager."

"Same manager of the SFPD fund?"

Walker squeezed his leg, drawing Aidan's gaze. "Smart man."

Then why did he feel so stupid? For not making the connection to Hamilton. For not taking Walker up on every advance. He shook off the temptation and refocused. "So you weren't sure when we questioned Nelson and Rollins?"

"I was ninety-five percent of the way there." He stole the mouse from Aidan and clicked through several other spreadsheets until he displayed one with highlighted deposits matching the first.

"Those were on the flash drive?" Aidan asked.

"Not exactly."

"I don't want to know. What about the other five percent?"

"Rollins's and Nelson's names were on the pension fund accounts but not on the accounts in the Caymans. However, the dates lined up and the financial and corporate trails led back to KAG Holdings."

The unknown again, only now connected to Hamilton. "And to Renaud's MO," Aidan said, reasoning it out. "Leverage." Renaud identified a person's weakness and manipulated it to his advantage.

"It's looking more and more like he's involved. The accident in Houston, the vibe when we interviewed Hamilton at the Port." During the brief, intense interrogation, Aidan had felt like the merc knew him, like he had been trying to tell him something with his steely eyes and cryptic comments. Because his boss, Renaud, was behind the crash that killed Gabe and Tom? Because Aidan was a target?

Walker had pieced all this together. "You were already thinking this?" Aidan asked him.

He nodded slowly, eyes downcast, and Aidan's gaze drifted outside the glass walls, his mind reaching for any link to a prior case, anything that made him or Tom a target of Renaud's. Had Gabe died because of a case they had worked? Someone they had put away? A criminal enterprise they had taken down? Texas had been the first Aidan heard of Renaud, but now the international terrorist was infecting every part of his life. Maybe he had infected his past too.

"I'll start searching old cases," he said. "See if I can find a link to Renaud."

"Anything on his whereabouts?" Walker asked.

As the one tasked with tracking Renaud's movements, Aidan felt like even more of a fool. He opened his desk tray drawer, withdrew a key from inside a hollowed-out eraser, and unlocked the bottom drawer of his desk. He retrieved his file on Renaud and opened it to the picture of Renaud standing in a North African bazaar. Walker shifted, removing his hand and withdrawing to his space.

"He's a ghost," Aidan said. "The picture is from Morocco. I had an analyst try to date it." Walker looked askance. "Minimal details given. Summer, during the past five years, was the best she could do."

"I could have told you that from the dress and cars."

"Thought I'd give someone else a chance."

Walker chuckled, breaking the weird tension that had crept in with the photo. "Any other sign of him?"

"None. There's no record of him even entering Morocco the past five years."

"Under a different alias, then." Walker spun to this desk and, with a few keystrokes, opened the bases of operations map from Interpol. "Because we've confirmed he's got a base there."

"His passport only shows quarterly trips between France and Switzerland."

"Which clearly that"—Walker nodded at the picture—"is not. And quarterly to Switzerland, nothing funny about that."

"I've got a meeting with Interpol in an hour. Today puts a new spin on things."

"I'm due in court on another case."

"I'll fill you in. Oh, and Mel wants to see you before you leave."

The corners of Walker's eyes and mouth creased. Despite what they had gone through with the bomb scare in Texas, despite the closeness between Aidan and Mel, or maybe because of it, Walker remained guarded around their boss.

Aidan stretched out a leg and ran the top of his shoe along the back of Walker's calf, attempting to tease him out of his unease as he had done for him earlier. "Don't worry, Whiskey. I'll tell her to go easy on you."

# THREE

Minutes after Aidan left, their office door swung open, and SAC Cruz waltzed in. There was no other word for it. Dark curls loose, dressed to the nines in a pencil skirt, silk blouse, and designer heels, she gave the first impression of a runway model. Until you noticed the badge and gun clipped at her waist. Or the way she cased a room, cataloguing humans, contents, exits, and blind spots. She did it now, even though the space was familiar and three out of the four walls were glass. Jamie wondered if his boss was ever "off."

"SAC Cruz."

She lowered herself into Aidan's chair. "We talked about this, *Jamie*."

"Mel," he said with a polite smile. He hadn't been raised to call his superiors by their first names. Then again, Mel wasn't any boss. She was the best friend and former sister-in-law of the man he fucked. She was also his accomplice in hiding a terrible truth from the same man.

"I saw Aidan on his way out. He said there'd been a breakthrough?"

"Of a sort."

She glanced around the room again. "We're secure?"

"I checked for bugs. We're clear."

"Report."

He recounted the meeting with Nelson and Rollins and the debrief with Aidan, then showed her the highlighted bank records. He hesitated to disclose what else he had pieced together—the worst of it he hadn't told Aidan.

The latest bomb to explode.

She picked up on it right away. "There's more?"

"Another record of interest." He accessed his remote server through an encrypted portal and opened the Project Angel file. He clicked through until he reached the financial record he had buried apart from the rest.

"It looks like the others," she said.

He nodded. "It's a third deposit made by the same fund manager."

Her manicured nail tapped at the transaction date on the screen. "But that's a week before the crash that killed Gabe and Tom."

"Because it was made for Agent Crane's account."

She shoved away from the computer, the rolling chair ramming into the other desk. While she had advised checking into Tom, she clearly hadn't expected this.

"I haven't found any other evidence he was involved." Jamie left the "yet" implied.

She covered her face with her hand and mumbled a curse behind her fingers. "He could have tipped them off that night," she said, voicing the horrible thought that had plagued Jamie all weekend.

"Someone did. The SUV that struck their car was waiting on Geary Boulevard for them."

"Tom." She dropped her hand, allowing a rare glimpse of vulnerability in her dark eyes.

"I requested his phone records. We'll see if there's activity preceding the accident." He didn't hesitate implying his other suspicion. "I pulled the FBI file on the accident. It's pretty thin, given that there were two FBI agents in the car."

"You're not wrong. I was blocked from the investigation because of my personal connections to the victims. As soon as SFPD ruled it a hit-and-run, my predecessor closed the case. With the promotion pending and Aidan's injury rehab, I backed off. They questioned Aidan extensively."

"I read the transcripts. There were interviews with Tom's wife too. They asked her a lot of questions about high-risk cases. She didn't have any answers."

"Tom didn't tell her anything. Against the rules, and he sheltered her from everything. Aidan too, given their childhood friendship. They didn't let the outside world touch Isabella."

He pointed at the screen. "No one questioned her about *that* deposit."

"I'll talk to her. There's less chance of it getting back to Aidan if I tell her to keep mum."

Aidan would remain in the dark while he and Mel brought another person close to him into their circle of secrets. Another ton of guilt settled on Jamie's shoulders. The weight must have shown.

"You didn't tell him about this?" Mel asked.

"He doesn't know anything more than what he put together this morning. That Renaud is involved. He thinks it's tied to one of his and Tom's old cases. He doesn't realize Gabe is the link. Maybe Tom too."

She tilted her head, gaze assessing. "I'm surprised."

"You expected me tell him?"

"Frankly, yes."

"You ordered me not to."

"Would that have stopped you?"

She called his bluff, and he hung his head, folding. "I consider it every day. I hate lying to him. He's my partner. He's my—" He cut himself off from saying *lover*, not wanting to compromise Mel's ever-thinning veil of plausible deniability. "This is not the way to build trust."

"But?"

"But I don't want to give him half a story, especially one that will destroy him, when there may be more to it."

"What are you thinking?"

Jamie paused to collect his thoughts, wanting to lay his theory out right and tie together the pieces he had recently discovered. "In Galveston, Renaud leveraged his pawns. Here, Renaud leveraged the detectives. The flash drive and photo you received came in an envelope with a Houston postmark. If Renaud sent it, he also tried to leverage you."

"You think he leveraged Tom and Gabe." She tapped her trigger finger against the armrest. "Were there deposits to Gabe's pension account?"

"Private. I don't have access. But ten to one, he had something major on Gabe and Tom. And if I have to tell Aidan the man he loved most in the world and the man he trusted to watch his back betrayed him, I need to be able to tell him why."

————

Four days and Jamie was no closer to discovering Renaud's leverage over Agent Tom Crane. Besides the errant bank deposit, there were no other anomalies in Tom's records, financial, travel, or otherwise. Stuck in neutral, Jamie was frustrated, but on the flip side, Aidan got to keep his memory of Tom as a trusted friend and colleague a little while longer. The prospect of shattering that mirage only strengthened Jamie's resolve to get the full story before lowering the hammer.

"Earth to Walker." Ahead of him, Aidan held open the equipment room door. "Let's get these vests off and get back to work." They had been roped into a training exercise that morning, Kevlar included. "I've got a fresh box of old case files to dig through."

Jamie's stomach churned. His partner wouldn't find a link to Renaud in his and Tom's old files. Not when Aidan was looking for case connections and the link was Tom himself. Yet Jamie remained silent, letting his partner continue the futile exercise.

Aidan's phone beeped, and he paused, midrip on his Velcro strap, to pull the device out of his pocket. His eyes flickered down, reading a text, then back up, widening. "We've got Nelson and Rollins."

The detectives remained their best leads. They had tried to track them down to get a sketch of Mason West, but Nelson and Rollins had actively avoided them. "Where?"

"Court of Appeals, across the street." Aidan let the door close and refastened the Velcro strap. "They're finishing testimony on a case. Leave the vest on. Nic said time was tight."

Jamie's lip curled.

Aidan, halfway to the elevators already, didn't notice.

"Grab a sketch artist and meet me in the building lobby." He punched at the call button repeatedly. "I'm going to go on down and text Nic back."

"Have him herd the detectives out the back doors," Jamie said. "It'll be easier for us to corner them there."

"Good thinking," Aidan said as the elevators doors slid open. He disappeared inside, and minutes later, Jamie took another cab down with Scott, the on-duty sketch artist.

The three of them pushed out the doors, onto the narrow, shadowed street between skyscrapers.

"Walker! Talley!"

Jamie's gaze landed on Nic exiting the opposite building. The prosecutor's brown hair flecked with gray was perfectly coiffed, and his bright blue eyes were locked on Aidan.

Aidan waited for him to jaywalk, then handed Jamie his umbrella and darted under Nic's, hand extended. "Thanks for the tip."

Nic drew Aidan in for a buss on the cheek. "Happy to help."

Jamie muffled his scoff and hung back.

Scott drew alongside him. "I thought we didn't like the federal prosecutors?"

"Some are friendlier than others."

"I'd say."

Fist clutching the umbrella handle, Jamie's blood simmered. "Where are Nelson and Rollins?" he asked through gritted teeth.

"Couldn't divert them," Nic answered. "They'll be out front in five."

Cursing, Jamie turned on his heel and jogged down the street, the others trailing.

"What'd you tell them?" Aidan asked Nic.

"That we needed to speak on a different matter. Make yourselves scarce"—Nic aimed a pointed look at Jamie—"if that's possible."

Jamie rolled his eyes and wandered toward the curbside coffee truck.

"So, it's just you Nic doesn't like?" Scott said.

A smart retort was on the tip of Jamie's tongue when awareness prickled the back of his neck, foreboding creeping up his spine. He scanned the surrounding buildings, looking for anything amiss. The courthouse steps were completely exposed, with clear lines of sight from any direction across the open plaza. He spun once, twice, looking for rooftop movement or sniper rifle flares.

Nothing.

Maybe it was just the wavering barometric pressure of the drizzly gray day giving him vertigo. But his sense of unease grew heavier, like the other shoe would drop at any minute.

Aidan ducked under his umbrella. "You don't like this?"

"Not one bit." Jamie handed him the umbrella and shifted open one side of his trench, hand hovering by his sidearm. He turned in another slow circle.

Aidan did the same, the red-and-white umbrella rotating over his shoulder. "I don't see anything."

"Those your detectives?" Scott stretched out an arm toward the courthouse.

Nelson and Rollins, in uniform, were walking down the steps toward Nic. "Go," Jamie said. "I'm going to hang back and cover."

Aidan's gaze locked with his, communicated "Be safe" without speaking a word. Jamie nodded and Aidan corralled Scott. They had almost reached the gathered group when something red tripped the periphery of Jamie's vision.

Head whipping around, he frantically searched the street, the crowd, the buildings, until he picked up the broken red line in the drizzling rain.

The beam of a laser sight.

Foreboding sharpened into certainty and Jamie's breath hitched, held, as he followed the red line from the rooftop of a building across the plaza to the courthouse steps.

To a spot in the middle of Nelson's chest.

The exact spot Aidan was about to step in front of.

Fear lanced through him, stopping his heart.

*Not again, not now, not yet.*

"Gun!" Jamie shouted, drawing his own. "Talley, get down!"

Aidan turned, wide-eyed, a split second before the shots rang out.

Rapid fire, automatic, one after another.

*Tat-tat-tat-tat-tat* . . .

Nic tossed his umbrella and ducked for cover.

Rollins and Nelson ran up the cement stairs.

Screaming pedestrians darted every direction, arms over their heads.

And Jamie watched in horror as Aidan's body jerked once, twice, and fell forward on top of Scott, taking them both to the ground.

He'd been hit. He was wearing a vest, but Aidan had been hit. *Fuck.* Blood rushed in Jamie's ears, his heart pounded in his chest, and there was a sea of chaos between him and his partner.

"FBI! Get down!" Jamie hurried ahead in a crouch,

desperately trying to wade through the panicked crowd. His heart revolted, propelling his feet forward, while his mind went into crisis mode, shouting for bystanders to stay down and trying to control the scene.

More gunfire rent the air—*tat-tat-tat-tat-tat*—from the same direction as the last round.

Jamie hit the deck, arms thrown out over pedestrians, holding them down until the gunfire ceased. "Everybody stay down!" he shouted.

He counted the seconds it took to reload, waited for the gunfire to resume, and when it didn't, he slowly lifted his head. He searched for the glimmering red laser beam, saw nothing but gray sky and an empty rooftop, and cautiously stood.

A long second of silence later chaos resumed.

Bystanders rose from their hiding places, yelling for loved ones. Sirens wailed. Cops and armed guards poured out of the surrounding government buildings.

Jamie shoved his way toward Aidan but was intercepted by the officer in charge. He held up his badge. "Special Agent Jameson Walker. FBI. I've got an agent down. Shooter is on the roof." He indicated the building from which he had seen the laser sight's beam. "Get me medics here and a team up there, now."

Orders were shouted down the line—secure the building, set up a perimeter, no one in or out—but Jamie had moved on, his world tunneling in on his partner.

Aidan lay unconscious on the sidewalk, an officer working over him, Scott crouched at his side. Heart in his throat, stomach on the ground several feet back, Jamie skidded to a halt beside them. Kneeling, he gazed in terror at Aidan's pale, blank face.

"Move, move!" Jamie pushed the other officer off and palmed one side of Aidan's face. "Come on, Irish, wake up." He ripped open Aidan's coat, hands skittering over the vest. No bullet had come through.

"He must have hit his head when we fell," Scott said.

"Help me turn him."

Scott nodded, and Jamie levered Aidan onto his side. He pushed his coat aside, searching. Metal glinted, and he pulled two bullets from the center of the vest over Aidan's back.

If they hadn't been wearing the Kevlar . . .

Aidan's limp body twitched in his arms, and he groaned low. Jamie returned him to his back and held his face. "That's it, Talley, wake up."

Aidan blinked his eyes open and gingerly pushed himself to seated. "Fucking hell," he rasped.

"You were hit," Scott said.

Aidan's eyes flickered down to his chest.

"In the back," Jamie added. "The vest stopped it."

Wide autumn eyes shot to his, and the reality of another near miss hit Jamie full force. He shook his head, breaths coming short, vision blurring, as fuzzy memories of waking up in a smoking car flooded him.

*Blood dripping down the side of Aidan's pale slack face.*

*Autumn eyes dimming.*

*Body listing forward into his chest.*

*A hand on his face,* then and now.

Aidan's voice drifted through the haze. "I'm fine, Whiskey. Vest did its job."

"Agents," an officer called.

Jamie couldn't move.

*Not again, not now, not yet.*

Aidan patted his cheek more firmly. "Jamie, snap out of it."

His name in Aidan's voice for the first time in months jolted him out of the mire. He stared into Aidan's clear alert eyes, took in his blood-free face, and sucked in a shaky breath.

"There he is." Aidan's fingers coasted down his cheek. "You need to go lock down the shooter site. I'll coordinate here. Stick to the story." Jamie nodded. "Now stand me up before you go."

He threw Aidan's arm over his shoulder and rose, Scott supporting him on the other side.

"Medic!" Jamie shouted, as Nic's voice rang out from several steps up. "Talley!"

Turning, Scott inhaled sharply, and Aidan listed against Jamie's side, giving him more of his weight.

Aidan had narrowly escaped. Nelson and Rollins hadn't been so lucky.

Nic inched back, sidestepping the pool of blood oozing from the detectives' lifeless bodies. "They're dead."

# FOUR

Sticking to the story proved harder than Aidan anticipated. First had been the investigating officers at the scene and now SFPD Chief Williams stood across his hospital room, grim-faced and in a grilling mood. "I need a better explanation for why two of my men were gunned down."

Aidan winced as he shrugged into a clean scrub top. He adjusted the shirt on his sore torso and sat on the end of the bed. "As I told your officers at the scene, we arranged with Assistant US Attorney Price"—he tilted his head toward Nic, who stood by the window on the phone—"to meet with Nelson and Rollins about a person of interest in a cybercrime case."

"I saw you and that partner of yours hanging around the station this week, waiting for Nelson and Rollins."

Aidan straightened, his tone sharp. "Because your detectives were less than cooperative."

"Maybe if you'd brought the matter to SFPD through proper channels."

"Chief." Nic held the phone away from his ear, finger hovering over the mute button. "They cleared it with me."

"Yeah, a *federal* prosecutor."

Delightful. A jurisdictional pissing contest. Just what Aidan needed at the end of an already too long day.

"Chief," Aidan said. "It's just as likely this incident was connected to one of Nelson and Rollins's other cases, if they were intentionally targeted at all."

"Looks pretty damn intentional to me. This was not a random act of violence."

Aidan shrugged. "It's as good an explanation as any until we know more."

"And you? Wrong place at the wrong time? Bad habit of yours, Agent Talley."

Aidan rocketed off the bed, aching back protesting, but the chief's words had hit too close to home. "What the hell are you implying?"

"I'm not implying anything." He closed the distance between them, an accusing finger prodding Aidan's chest. "People around you have a way of dying, Mr. FBI, and you just took down two of my best detectives."

"Best?" Aidan scoffed, anger warring with the biting truth. Before he unwisely waded further into the mud, a commotion erupted outside.

"Where's my partner? Where's Aidan Talley?"

All Southern pleasantries gone, Walker sounded strung out and exhausted, with zero patience for the nurse's visitation rules. They had been separated at the scene. Walker had joined the unsuccessful chase for the suspect, then returned to the shooter's perch to oversee evidence collection. Aidan, with Nic and the local police, had processed the gruesome scene on the courthouse steps.

"I don't give a flying fuck about your rules," Walker barked outside. "I'm going in there. He's my partner."

Nic pocketed his phone and moved toward the door. "I'll let him know you're finishing up."

Aidan threw out an arm, blocking his path. Sending Nic out to calm Walker would only add fuel to the fire. "Are we done, Chief?"

The older man looked far from done, but the younger one beating down the door seemed enough to dissuade him from further questioning. "I want the details of the case you were working."

"Of course," Aidan lied as he resettled on the end of the bed.

With an incredulous huff, Williams pushed his way out and Walker barged in. His frantic gaze bounced from Aidan's face to his torso to Nic at his side. Worry vanished and anger flared. "You too. Get out."

"Hey now, I just covered for you," Nic said, revealing himself to be smarter than Aidan gave him credit for. The prosecutor stepped closer to the bed, and Walker's entire frame went fighter-ready. "That story about a cybercrime case crossing paths with one of Nelson and Rollins's is utter horseshit. And I lied through my teeth to back it. So if I want to be here, I'll fucking be here."

"Irish, get him out of here." Walker glared at Nic like an unwelcome intruder, not like someone who had risked his reputation to do them a favor. But that didn't register for his overprotective partner right now. Aidan had to persuade Nic to leave before Walker burned a bridge they might later need.

Aidan angled toward Nic and put a hand on his arm,

drawing a menacing growl from Walker. "Nic, we appreciate your cooperation."

The prosecutor staggered back, baffled and affronted. "My cooperation?"

"You should go," Aidan said. "I promise I'll explain later."

Walker leaned against the end of the bed, his thigh brushing Aidan's hip. "You don't have to explain shit to him."

"Please go, Nic," Aidan urged.

Nic glanced between them, his eyes widening the instant he put it together. "Fuck, Talley, I didn't think you were this reckless."

"Get out," Walker snapped.

"You leave those marks on him last weekend?"

Walker inched closer, pressing his side along Aidan's back and laying a claiming hand at the nape of his neck. "Damn straight I did. Want to see the ones I got to match?"

"Enough!" Aidan clipped over his shoulder, before turning back to Nic.

"He's why you won't—" Nic started, and Aidan cut him off. "Later, please."

Nic shook his head. "Fuck you, Talley, and fuck later. We're through, here and elsewhere. And don't count on me to cover for you again." He stalked out of the room with a muttered, "Fools."

The door swung closed behind him and Aidan rounded on Walker. "That wasn't smart. He—"

The rest of his words were silenced by a searing open-mouthed kiss that was anything but smart and everything Aidan needed after the day they'd had.

After another close call.

Walker moved between his legs, the hand at his neck drawing him up while the one on his ass lifted him against his strong, hard body. Powerless to resist, Aidan curled his legs around the backs of Walker's thighs and, despite the pain in his back, curled his arms over Walker's shoulders, locking him in a tight embrace. Fingers tunneling through silky locks, Aidan scraped his nails over Walker's scalp, eliciting a growl of a different sort. He licked into Walker's mouth, tongues tangling, tasting, savoring, swept under by the force of everything in his partner's kiss.

Relief, life, need, love.

*Terrifying love.*

Aidan wrenched their mouths apart and gasped for breath as he rested his forehead against Walker's.

"You okay to leave?" Walker asked.

Aidan nodded, bringing their lips in brushing distance again. "All clear."

"Good. Let's go home."

Aidan's panic ballooned, making him lightheaded.

*Home.*

His mind instantly went to the three-story Edwardian in Bernal Heights. Walker's house, not his. Aidan knew the place as well as his own. Just like his intimate knowledge of Walker's body. How fingers trailed over his scalp guaranteed a moan. How he liked fingers and teeth sinking into the tattoo on his chest. How he preferred to be taken hard and rough. Walker had the same knowledge of his wants and desires. How he liked to be kissed hungrily, blanketed by a big body, and touched possessively.

Home, body, life, love.

All of it could have been torn away today.

The chief wasn't wrong. People had a nasty habit of

dying around him.

Nelson and Rollins weren't the only targets. Aidan had the mottled bruise on his back to prove it. Three attempts on his life. Two that could have also claimed Walker's and the tattered remains of Aidan's heart. He couldn't go there again.

Time to throw up blockades.

"I can't," he said. "I need to go talk to Nic."

Walker tore out of his embrace. "Are you fucking kidding me? I could have lost you today and you're gonna go fuck someone else."

"I said talk, not fuck."

"Bullshit!"

"You lost focus in the field today." Aidan gestured between them. "Because of this."

"Oh, so you're admitting this"—Walker mimicked the motion—"is something?"

"Something casual. We talked about this, Ja—"

"Don't," Walker snapped. "Don't you dare fucking 'Jamie' me right now."

"Whiskey," he tried again, only to be cut off by Walker's hands on his face, hauling him in for another kiss.

"I could have lost you today. My partner, my lover. Someone tried to kill you. Again. So yes, baby, for two seconds I lost focus because I care about you."

"You agreed—"

"I'm changing the terms." Walker's gaze shone with love and determination. "I'm done fucking sharing. I want all the time I can get with you. Today just proved how short that could be."

Aidan closed his eyes, unable to watch the light, the love, die in Walker's. "That's why this has to end."

# FIVE

Aidan arrived late the next morning. To an empty office.

Pens and colored file folders still littered Walker's desk, but his laptops were gone, the coffeemaker cold, and the silence unnerving. He stepped between the desks, glancing at Walker's phone display. Calls were being forwarded—to an extension in the cave, the interior boardroom Cyber Division had converted to its office, the one Walker worked out of before they were partnered.

Panic rising, Aidan shuffled through the folders and papers, looking for a transfer request. Nada. He checked the printer next. Likewise cold and silent.

Indecision rooted him to the spot. What was he supposed to do? After yesterday's scene at the hospital, he couldn't blame Walker for distancing himself. But distance at the office spelled ruin for their professional partnership. He had killed the personal one, but he hadn't meant to slaughter this one too. Walker was talented, a damn fine agent. His instincts yesterday had saved Aidan's life. He owed him a thank-you if nothing else. He would beg for more if he had to.

He turned for the door, only to meet the dubious brown eyes of his boss.

Mel stepped inside and closed the door. "Fine mess of things you've made."

There would be no going anywhere until she said her piece. "Which mess are you referring to?"

Her gaze bounced around the room. "Where's your partner?"

"Cave. Next mess."

She raised a brow. "Is he still your partner?"

"Yes," he answered automatically.

She raised the other brow to match.

He collapsed into his chair. "I hope so. He's a good agent, and I trust him."

Some unidentifiable emotion passed through her eyes, but before he could sort it, she claimed Walker's chair and asked, "How serious are your injuries?"

"Back's bruised." He lifted his left arm then winced as pain shot up and down his limb. "Rattled some of the repaired bits when I fell."

"Probably rattled something else too."

"No worse than Texas."

She looked like she had as much confidence in his answer as he had in his fragile partnership. She wasn't wrong. The crash in Galveston had thrown him for a loop because it was so similar to the accident that killed Gabe and Tom. Yesterday, death had seemed even closer, only a Kevlar vest away. Renaud was closing in, but so were they. He had to find the connection and stop this before anyone else died. "We need to kick the Renaud investigation into high gear."

"That's what you were doing, and now your two best leads are dead. I spent all morning on the phone with SFPD and the US Attorney's office trying to steer the matter to us."

"Thank you for that. The last thing we need is another agency involved or this case to get shut down again."

She shook her head. "You're getting ahead of yourself, *hermano*. I'm here to tell you to hit the brakes."

"Not now, Mel," he urged, leaning forward. "We're too close. Renaud wouldn't have made a move if we weren't on his trail."

"And he's on yours, leaving a pile of dead bodies in your wake."

The too-accurate image socked him in the gut. He sank back in his chair and clutched his arm to his body. "I can't let this go. Nelson and Rollins lied on those accident reports. They were leveraged by Renaud, Hamilton, and whoever the fuck this Mason West person is. I don't know why yet, but they died for it and so did Tom and Gabe. Renaud's still after me and now I've dragged Walker into this mess, as you rightly put it. We have to shut this down."

She wasn't fazed in the slightest, except for her tapping trigger finger.

"Mel, please."

"A compromise," she said. "I'll find a case that gets you and Jamie out of town. Let things cool off."

How the hell was that a compromise? It was as good as surrendering, especially when the trail was blistering hot. "We can't drop this. Not now."

"I'm not asking you to. We just need a smokescreen."

———

Jamie was hiding, and he didn't give a rat's ass what it said about his personal or professional demeanor. He had come in early, grabbed his laptops, and reclaimed his corner desk in the cave. He hadn't had the resolve or energy to face curious bullpen eyes or his partner.

He had played his hand sooner than intended, without the answers he had wanted to give Aidan. But after surviving another brush with death, only to find Nic by Aidan's side, in the place where he should've been, Jamie hadn't held back. He had dodged actual bullets only to have the verbal one fired by Aidan take him out.

"Should I expect a transfer request on my desk in the morning?"

Jamie glanced up from the decryption running on his laptop. His boss stood at the opening of the server racks, a case file in her hands. "In the morning?" he asked.

"It's almost ten—at night."

"Shit." He propped his elbows on the desk and scrubbed his hands over his face. "I forgot how easy it is to lose track of time in here." So deep in code and his own head, he hadn't noticed the rest of the Cyber agents clear out.

"Are you relocating?"

It was a valid question. In a day, he had made himself at home again. Laptops open, case files scattered, two empty Big Gulps and Kit Kat wrappers strewn across the desk. The state of things could give a person the wrong idea. "Not permanently," he said. "Just needed a break."

"Your mission holds, Agent Walker."

Find the connection between Gabe and Renaud and

keep Aidan alive. That's what she had tasked him with. Easier said than done, and more difficult by the day.

"I'm still on mission." He closed both laptops and slid back in his chair. "But I would've killed Casanova myself if I had to sit in that glass cage with him today."

Her face softened. "Ah, he's reverted."

Jamie debated whether to say more, given the deniability she clung to, but she had opened the door with that comment. "I'd heard. I just didn't think . . ."

"Aidan's not good at lonely. Before Gabe, he was a player. No other word for it, and I say that with all the affection of a sister."

"He committed to Gabe."

"He loved Gabe. He was worth giving up all the others."

*And you're not.*

His stomach heaved at the implication, and he eyed the trash can. Mel shifted his focus, tossing the case file on his desk. He swallowed hard and forced the upset down. "New case?"

"I talked to Aidan this morning. I suggested you pump the brakes on Renaud."

"You just said my mission holds."

She surprised him with a laugh. "I didn't expect either of you to agree, but you need to fly under the radar for a bit. Things are too hot here."

"Here?" As in the FBI or San Francisco?

"I suggested a case out of town."

On assignment with Aidan, with no place or way to escape, was the last thing Jamie wanted. Hearing a hotel room door open and shut, wondering who Aidan was taking into his bed instead of him, was the definition of misery. Not to mention he wasn't keen on setting aside the Renaud case. Not when they were closing in.

"You can continue to investigate Renaud," she said, as if hearing his thoughts. "But your primary focus needs to appear to be on a different matter."

Emotional discomfort aside, it made sense. Get them out of San Francisco, where Renaud was likely following their movements. Make it look like their investigation into him was on the back burner while working behind the scenes. But she was being cagey about the details. "It's a good plan," he said. "Why are you beating around the bush?"

She smiled. "You really are his match."

Not what he needed to hear. How good he was for a man who didn't want him. "Mel . . ."

Canting forward, she nudged the file off his desk and into his lap. "You're going undercover."

He caught the file before it slipped to the floor. "You know my history, right? Hell, everyone knows my story. I'm not exactly easy to disguise."

"I don't want you to hide. You're going undercover as your old self." Brow furrowed, he opened the file as she continued. "Charlotte University. NCAA Division II. Online sports betting used as means of identity theft."

"What do you need me for?"

"The local officer who brought the case to the FBI's attention suspects someone connected to CU's basketball program is behind this."

Bile resurged, stinging the back of Jamie's throat. People bet on sports all the time, but as a former athlete and team captain, the fact that someone on the team was involved made him sick. "You want me to go in there and make an appearance? See if I can sniff it out?"

"I want you to go in there and coach."

"Coach?" His voice came out mortifyingly strangled. He wasn't prepared, professionally or personally, for such an assignment.

"There's an assistant coaching position open. You're hired."

"I've never coached."

"CU is Division II. And you were a student coach for UNC's Resident Camp when you played there. CU is thrilled to have Whiskey Walker on their bench."

"Just like that, without an interview or anything?"

"Last page of the file," she said, and he flipped there. A travel itinerary from a week ago showed him on a flight into Charlotte and out the next day. A trip he never made. "If the press looks, they'll find a trail. CU wanted to keep things quiet until the official announcement. Press conference is on Monday."

The press. The truth. The very thing he had run from eight years ago. "I left the game. I've been an FBI agent. The press knows all this."

She braced her wrists on her crossed knees. "You were a two-time NCAA champion and contender for NBA Rookie of the Year before your injury. Anyone who watched you play knows you loved the game. No one will question your return to it. And if you want that injury story to hold, coaching is your only option."

*That injury story.*

Mel had a way of putting the finest points on lies. Of every variety.

He closed the file and set it back on the desk. Mundane movements to hide his trembling hands. "CU is on board?"

"The chancellor and head coach know about the investigation. That's it, since we don't know the extent of the team's involvement."

"And the NCAA?"

"The Charlotte-Mecklenburg police officer who brought the case to our attention, Renee Paulson, urged us to hold off on notifying them. Her brother's a player. They're a week from playoffs. If you can solve the case before then, prove no on-court misconduct, and remove the perpetrators . . ."

"Then maybe the rest of the team can play." He would have to make a hell of a plea to the NCAA. And solve the case in time. "You think that the people running this scam won't put two and two together? That they'll really believe I had a sudden change of heart, left the FBI, and just happened to show up at their school as a coach?"

"I guess that depends on how good an actor you are. On multiple fronts."

Oh, he was a good enough actor. Until yesterday, he had hidden from Aidan how not fine he was with casual. And he had spent his entire career on the court hiding who he loved. While he had been discreet since leaving the NBA, he didn't hide his sexual orientation. Could he go back to doing so now, in the place he had fled for fear of exposure? Could he go there with the man he loved but who wouldn't love him back?

"Jamie." Mel's hand closed over his. "I came to you first. You left that life behind for a reason. Before I take this case to Aidan, I need to know you're on board."

"You're my boss. I wasn't under the impression I had a say."

She squeezed his hand. "My brother was a collegiate then professional Afro-Latino athlete, and he was gay. He stayed in the closet until he retired, and for a man who loved clothes, he hated that fucking closet." They both chuckled. "I understand why you left, and I know what I'm asking isn't easy. You have a say."

He bowed his head, considering. What made him sicker —the possibility of being very publicly outed or illegal betting on the game he loved? Worse yet, gambling as a means of identity theft? There was the press to deal with, but he had managed to keep his personal life out of their lens before. They had only closed in at the end because of his injury and his ex's constant presence during his rehab. He would be more careful this time.

There was one other matter, though . . . "How does this protect us from Renaud? The sports media will broadcast my return, even if it is only DII."

"Hide in plain sight," she said. "Yes, it's DII, and your return will get some initial airtime, but CU's games aren't broadcast wide like Carolina's. Keep your head down and the attention will pass. If Renaud buys that you've left the FBI, good. If he doesn't, you're obviously engaged in a different matter. And with the press watching, it'll be harder for him to make a move against you."

"All right, I'm in." He stood, case file in his hand.

She nodded and moved toward the door. "Good."

"Mel," he called, and she waited over the threshold. "If I'm going undercover as Whiskey Walker, what's Aidan's role?"

A smirk turned up one corner of her mouth. "Let me deal with Casanova."

# SIX

Jamie tossed his boarding pass on the bed by the open suitcase, snagged a towel from the primary bathroom, and opened the sliding glass door to his ground-level patio. It wasn't the big, open backyard he was used to, but he had made the relatively-large-for-San-Francisco space his own. He wiped down the patio couch, grabbed a few fire logs, and stoked a blaze to life in the fire pit. He had just arranged himself on the couch with a soda and leftovers when his phone rang.

Shifting his plate and wedging the bottle between his knees, Jamie pulled the phone out his pocket, saw his best friend's handsome mug on the screen, and swiped his thumb to answer.

"I picked up." He placed the device on the seat back cushion near his head and resettled to talk and eat. "No more bitching."

"Brother . . ." Cam's Boston brogue sounded tinny on speakerphone. "Saw the incident report on the shooting yesterday."

"You keeping tabs on me?"

"Of course," Cam answered, voice implying Jamie was a fool for asking. And he was. He had an alert on Cam too. "You okay?"

"Fine." Knowing Cam wouldn't accept his vague response, Jamie cut him off with a question of his own. "It's late there. What're you doing up?"

Cam's muddled "Couldn't sleep" was a one-eighty from his previous teasing tone. He was the Bureau's top kidnap and rescue agent. With so many successes, he took the failures hard, especially the ones involving children. This unfortunately sounded like that kind of call.

"How old?"

"Eight. Not likely to end in a rescue."

Times like these, Jamie hated living three time zones away. "I'd say fly out and visit, but I'm actually headed east tomorrow."

"Case?"

"In Charlotte. Listen, Cam, I need to give you a heads-up about this one. I'm going undercover and may need your help."

Jamie waited out his friend's laughter, glad to have shaken Cam out of the dark mood, even at his own expense.

"How's that gonna work?" Cam asked between gasps. "Hate to break it to you, but you're kinda hard to hide."

"I'm going under as Whiskey Walker."

"How do you mean?"

"Charlotte University. Members of the basketball team are suspected of running an online gambling ring that's a front for identity theft. I'm the new assistant coach."

"I see," Cam said, all trace of humor gone.

Jamie set aside his empty plate. "The press knows I joined the FBI. It won't be hard for them to find the best friend who recruited me."

"If they ask, I'll play along. I'll tell them you changed your mind and missed the game. I've got your back, always. You just tell me how you want to play it."

"Thank you," Jamie said, relieved. "It's nice, someone having my back."

"You've got a partner for that," Cam said, and Jamie couldn't suppress his frustrated grunt. "That doesn't sound good. What else is going on? I've never seen two new partners so in sync as you and Aidan."

"Things are definitely no longer in sync."

"Rule number one of UC work, you and your partner have to be on the same page, one hundred percent, or one of you will slip up. Something will go wrong while you're distracted dealing with whatever shit is between you."

Jamie palmed his forehead. "There's so much shit, Cam."

"How? You've only been partnered five months."

Jamie remained silent and Cam got there on his own.

"Jamie, no—"

"Don't give me the lecture. Besides, it's over."

Without warning, the sliding glass door across the patio banged closed, and Jamie flew out of his seat. In the shadow of the upstairs deck, pale face lit by the flickering flames, stood his partner.

———

*Over.*

Hearing it out of Walker's—*Jamie's*—mouth stung worse

than the bullets that had slammed into Aidan's back yesterday.

Another thing that stung, his partner's name echoing in his head. Getting used to the name change shouldn't be hard—he had worked undercover before—except he had forced *Jamie* out of his vocabulary after Galveston. A pitiful distancing mechanism. With *Jamie* came warm, alluring, heartbeat-tripping memories of an intimacy he hadn't shared with him since. Or with any of the other men he had dated the past five months, despite what Jamie thought about his promiscuity.

Now, he was forced to close the distance against his will.

"Gotta go, Cam. Call if you need me, anytime." Jamie tapped the screen, tossed the phone onto the couch, and disappeared behind the flames. Rounding the pit, Aidan found him crouched in the narrow space between it and the couch, cleaning up the plate that had slid off the sofa.

"You worked in the cave today."

Jamie tossed the detritus into the fire, and the flames burned brighter, enhancing his striking features. "Seemed like the best thing."

"Temporarily."

"How'd your date with Nic go?" Jamie countered, a bucket of ice water despite the fire's heat.

"It wasn't a date. I needed to explain things and make sure he held to the story."

"Is that all it was?"

"Yes, that's all it was." He leaned a hip against the end of the couch. "Why do you even care if it's over?"

"I don't."

Arms crossed, Aidan grasped his elbows, hugging himself, trapping in the last vestiges of fleeting warmth.

The ice in Jamie's eyes, in his voice, chilled him to the bone. He should leave, right now, but he hadn't come here to fight about Nic or rehash his foolish decisions. He had come here because he was concerned for his friend and partner. That's what he needed to focus on. "Mel filled me in on the new case."

Jamie moved to the far end of the couch, tucked one leg under him, and stretched an arm out across the cushion top. His calm apathy was forced as hell. "It's fairly straight-forward."

Aidan's laugh tasted as bitter as it sounded. "Don't lie to me, Whiskey."

"I can handle it."

"You may have Cam fooled, Mel too, but you told me what it cost you to leave that life."

Jamie braced a foot on the fire pit ledge, the absent bounce a dead giveaway of his buried apprehension. "Derrick is at Bob Jones. Not Charlotte."

"An hour and a half away." Aidan sat, angled toward him. "And I'm not just talking about proximity to your ex. You're out, Jamie, but you've not made a public declaration of it, which is perfectly fine and your prerogative, but the sports media is not exactly known for its discretion. They'll latch on to your return, and if they find out . . ."

"Are you worried about me or you?"

"This has the potential to blow your life apart."

His hardened eyes shifted to the fire. "Didn't know you still cared."

*Fuck it.*

Aidan slid closer, a dagger piercing his chest when Jamie tried and failed to move in the opposite direction, blocked by the sofa's arm. Within reach, Aidan curled a hand around Jamie's neck and leaned his forehead against his temple, breathing in the smell that had become his favorite in the world.

"Of course I care." No matter what happened between them, Aidan would always care, would always be his friend, even if he couldn't bring himself to be more. "You're my partner, Jamie, and you're a damn fine agent with a long career ahead of you. I don't want to see that jeopardized because the media can't stay out of your bedroom."

"Maybe they won't find out."

"We talking pipe dreams here?"

Jamie smiled, small and resigned. "Seems to be my specialty lately."

"If you don't want to do this, I'll tell Mel to find us another case."

"No, it makes sense." Straightening, he broke Aidan's hold and resumed his lounged position, albeit more relaxed. "I know the game, and I can work the cyber angle. What about you? Mel didn't give me the details."

"I'm your sports agent." He held out a hand and unfurled his full Irish accent. "Ian Daley, at your service."

"Fuck." Jamie ignored the offered hand and aimed his gaze back at the fire.

Aidan tried not to take it personally. "It's close enough that if you slip up, anyone will think they misheard you." When Jamie still didn't respond, he worried the brief reprieve had vanished. "Jamie?"

He flinched. "Why do you keep calling me that?"

"Would you prefer 'Mr. Walker'?"

Jamie's surprised laugh eased the tension.

"As your agent, it would be odd for me to call you by your last name."

"Anything else I need to know?"

"There'll be a few more changes." He grinned at Jamie's curious side-eye. "You'll see in Charlotte."

"How do we infiltrate the team?"

"Without having met our local contacts or reviewed the file yet, I can't say for sure. Initial thoughts . . . I'll assess administration, you assess players, and we'll come up with a suspect list. You stay clean while I play the crooked agent trying to get in on the action. Let's not give the press added ammunition against you."

At his mention of the press, tension crept back into Jamie's frame.

Aidan laid a hand on his shoulder. "No matter what, you're my partner, Jamie. I've got your back."

"Can't get used to that. You calling me 'Jamie.' "

"You've heard it before." The words were out before Aidan thought better of them.

Jamie's eyes swung his way, and they were no longer cold, his partner's mind no doubt awash in the same intimate memories Aidan shared. Memories his body and heart wanted to relive, but that his mind cautioned against. He needed to shore up his defenses before being swept out to sea. "I've gotta go," he said, standing. "Drinks with Scott."

Jamie shot to his feet, the heat in his eyes morphing from desire to anger. "Christ, Talley. You'll fuck anyone, won't you?" He stalked toward the house and Aidan grabbed him by the arm, spinning him back around.

He needed distance—he would let Jamie continue to think he fucked other men, if that was what pushed him away—but Aidan also needed him to understand not just any man would do. "You haven't noticed a trend?"

"What the hell are you talking about?"

"My choice in men lately. Six foot plus, ripped bodies, light brown hair, bright blue eyes." He gave his partner a significant once-over.

Wrenching his arm free, Jamie stumbled back. "I don't understand."

"What's not to understand?"

"Why you want them when you can have me?"

Aidan closed the distance between them, hating the forlorn look on Jamie's face. He caressed the lines away with his fingertips and Jamie's eyes fluttered closed under his touch. "Because when I'm with them, I can fool myself into believing they're you, but then I can walk away."

Jamie nuzzled a palm. "I don't need forever. I just don't want to share."

"It's not that." Aidan dropped his hands.

Jamie caught them in his big, warm ones. "Then what is it? Guilt over betraying Gabe's memory? You're allowed to move on."

Aidan stared at the fire and swallowed hard around the lump in his throat. "At first, but not anymore."

Jamie pulled him closer, those big hands a hook reeling him in. "Then what is it?"

"God forbid something happen to them, but if it did, I could move on." Aidan returned his gaze to Jamie's and bared the burning hunger and blinding fear that held him back. "But not if it was you. I can't let myself fall for you, because if I do, and something happens . . ."

"Baby," Jamie whispered hoarsely.

It took everything Aidan had not to lean forward and kiss the painful sound away. Instead, he lifted their clasped hands to his chest, dipped his head, and kissed Jamie's knuckles. "I survived the last time by the skin of my teeth, but there's a hole in my chest where my world used to be. If I let you fill it, and I lose you too, I don't think I'll survive this time. I can't do that to myself or my family."

Jamie gripped his hands tighter and pressed chapped lips to his temple, his warm breath bathing Aidan's face and soul. "I get you want to protect yourself and your family, but do you want to spend the next forty years of your life alone, jumping from one meaningless fuck to the next? You and Gabe were settled; you were happy. You like that life. It looks good on you." He leaned back, withdrew one hand, and cradled Aidan's face. "Do you really want to give that up forever?"

*No*, but that answer wasn't fair to Jamie. Neither was so blatant a lie as *yes*, so Aidan settled for silence. Gazes locked, he allowed himself the indulgence of kissing Jamie's palm, one last intimacy, then turned on his heel and left before he drowned.

# SEVEN

While his mom finished putting together her breakfast pie for church the next day and his sister tucked her twin daughters into bed, Jamie snuck outside and took a deep breath of the cold, salt-tinged air. Like many of the beach houses on Oak Island, his mother's home was an inverted floor plan. Stilts, parking, and storage on the ground level, guest bedrooms the next story up, then the living area, kitchen, and primary on the top floor.

From his perch on the uppermost deck, Jamie had a view of the starry sky and the gently rolling ocean stretched out beyond the sand dunes covered with sea oats. It was peaceful here, especially in the winter when the tourists were scarce. Just the waves lapping at the shore, the occasional foghorn from a ship far out, and the sounds of his family puttering around in the house behind him.

He missed this. But he also missed the freeway noise, the hum of the city, loud punk rock, and Irish curses.

Jamie pulled the nearest rocker closer to the rail and sat with his feet propped up, remembering the last time he'd been at the beach, with Aidan in Galveston. Then and now couldn't be more different. The summer's sweltering heat versus winter's chilly sea breeze, the opulent Talley condo versus his mother's cozy home, the sounds of his partner's moans versus his nieces' sleepy voices.

The start of something with Aidan versus the end.

"Why do you look like that time Uncle Charles told you the highway reflectors we ran over were frogs?" His sister, Stacey, crested the patio stairs from the lower level, bottle of Cheerwine in hand, dressed in Batman flannels and an oversize USMC sweatshirt.

Jamie chuckled at her clothing and at the memory. "That was almost as traumatizing as your outfit."

She slapped him in the face with her overlong sleeve, then dropped into the rocker beside him. "I was gonna give you this Cheerwine, but I don't know now." He swiped it from her before she could extend it out of his reach. "Hey!"

He twisted off the cap and took a long swallow of the cherry soda. "Where were you hiding these during dinner?"

"Spare fridge." She braced her feet on the balcony rail beside his. "If the girls see 'em, they beg, and it was hard enough to get them asleep with you here."

"Sorry I riled them up." He wasn't really sorry at all. He'd had fun giving them a "fictionalized" account of the car chase in Texas, complete with sound effects and hand motions.

"They've heard worse from Ty. I swear, I'm gonna have two little girls who would rather watch Michael Bay movies than Disney flicks."

Jamie grinned. "Nothin' wrong with that." He took another sip, then asked, "When is Tyler due back?" His sister's second husband and the only father the girls had ever known was a Marine. They lived on base at Camp Lejeune, an hour and a half north of Oak Island. Stacey brought the girls down most weekends when he was deployed.

"Next month," she said, her whole face brightening.

"I'm sorry I missed him."

She cut him a side-eye. "Really? 'Cause I've never seen him terrified of anyone but you."

"Older brother duty." Laughing, Jamie ruffled her tangle of caramel curls, the same light brown shade as his. "I don't get to see him enough, so I have to give him shit when I do. I like him, Stace. And he's good with the girls."

"Yeah, he is. I got lucky."

Her first husband, the twins' father and a good man, was also a soldier. He'd been killed in the line of duty shortly after the girls were born. Stacey had been devastated, but she'd found love again with another good man, risking her heart on a soldier once more.

If only Aidan were as open to second chances as his sister.

"There's that look again," Stacey said. "And don't think I didn't notice the deflection before. What's going on, J?"

"I'd like to know the answer to that too." The screen door behind them opened, and their mother stepped out with a blanket around her shoulders. She pulled the screen and glass doors shut. "I'd also like to know when my grown children will learn to close doors when the heat's on."

"Sorry, Mom," they said in unison, then burst out laughing. It was a familiar gripe that never got old and always reminded Jamie of home.

His mother claimed the third rocker and the bottle of soda right out of his hand.

He gasped in mock offense, and Stacey shoved his shoulder. "Serves you right."

When their laughter subsided, his mother picked up where she'd left off before the snatch and grab. "You said there was something you had to tell us after dinner."

He wasn't sure which conversation he dreaded more: the one with Stacey about his crash-and-burn love life, or the one he needed to have with both of them about the case. He decided to start with the latter, praying his sister would forget about the former.

"I can't give you all the details about the case I'm working, but I'm going to be coaching basketball at Charlotte University. There will likely be media attention, at least initially. I'll be back in the press, so you might be too." Any time he drew media press coverage, so did his family and their history, Jamie's father's death a matter of public notoriety. They'd all had enough press attention; he worried about it even more now with his nieces in the picture. And if his sexual orientation ever came under the spotlight . . . "I wanted to tell you both in person. I can still pull out. I will pull out if you want me to."

"Why would we want that?" Stacey asked.

"The girls," he said with a glance toward the lower level. "And you've got a good job on base now," he said to Stacey, referring to her HR position. "And you at the Baptist Assembly," he said to his mom, who was an event coordinator at Fort Caswell, the Baptist retreat at the other end of OKI. "You've both got good lives, and I don't want to upset them."

"Jamie," his sister started.

"I'm not oblivious," he said, cutting her off. "I've seen the news. I know this isn't the most progressive state."

"Son," his mother said. "You already gave up your life for us once. You'll not do it again."

"Mom."

She laid a hand on his arm, pausing his rocking motion that he realized had picked up speed with his agitation. "This is your job, Jameson, and it's your life. If the press decides to make a big deal out of either, or if those old bitties at church say you're not doing one or the other right because of who you love, well, all those naysayers can just go to hell."

"Mom!" Stacey hooted, then covered her mouth to muffle her laughter. Jamie bit his lip, doing the same and holding at bay the grateful tears pooling behind his eyes.

"I'm proud of my son." His mother lifted her hand to his cheek. "I'm sorry you thought you had to leave before."

He covered her hand with his own. "I needed to do that for me too."

"And for Derrick," Stacey added, voice flat.

His mother's upbeat tone couldn't have been more different. "Does he know you're back?" She'd always liked his ex.

Stacey not so much. "I don't see why it's any of his business." Though his back was to her, Jamie imagined her expression was similar to the angry bulldog's on her sweatshirt.

He lowered his mother's hand and held it in his lap. "I know you liked him, Mom, but it was never going to work. We'd be in the closet forever."

The corners of her mouth dipped from smile to frown, and her shoulders lowered too, but she nodded, resigned to the fact that Derrick had been out of his life for years. "A mom can dream. I just want you to be happy." She squeezed his hand, then withdrew it and slid back in her chair. "Seeing anyone else then?"

"I was." He shifted in his own chair and stared back out at the ocean, something that would now always remind him of Aidan. His partner's long, lean frame cutting through the waves, those damp swim trunks from the first morning in Galveston, the smoldering kiss they'd shared on the ocean view balcony. Where that kiss had led then . . . and now. "It didn't work out."

He could practically feel Stacey's narrowed eyes boring a hole through the side of his head. His mom, however, thankfully didn't pry. "I'll say a prayer. Ask for someone to sweep my boy off his feet."

"Thanks, Mom."

"Speaking of prayers, I'm going to go say mine and head to bed. It's getting late." She stood and kissed each of them on the head. "Good to have you both home."

"Good to be here," Jamie said with a smile.

Stacey only waited long enough for the door to close behind their mom and for Jamie to put his feet back on the rail before she pounced. "What happened with you and Aidan?"

He whipped his head to the side on a gasp. "What?"

"Oh, don't play dumb. It was clear as day when I was there for fleet week last fall that you two were fucking."

Jamie's heart raced. "Was it that obvious to everyone?"

She shook her head and his pulse slowed, a little. "You're my brother, I can read you. You had that same look about you when you were with Derrick."

"And what look is that?"

Her smile was small and sad, full of the pity—and the truth—he didn't want. "That you'd fallen. Hard."

He dropped his feet and leaned forward, elbows to his knees, head hung in his hands. "For someone I can't have."

"Because of work?"

"Because he lost his husband a year ago." She inhaled sharply, no doubt recognizing the parallel. "He's not like you, Stace. He's too afraid to love again."

She exhaled slowly, then reached out and clasped his shoulder. "I don't believe that, J. He looked at you the same way."

He had thought so too, seen flashes of it in Aidan's eyes, felt it in his kiss and the way his fingers would dig into his tattoo when they . . . He shook his head. "He wanted casual. I thought I could do that."

She chuckled low and threw an arm around his shoulders, hugging him sideways. "Oh, my bighearted brother, you don't know the meaning of that word. You meet, you fall, you love. You were all in with Derrick like that, right until the end. That's your thing."

"You sound like my shrink."

"Who you paid God only knows how much for the same bit of truth."

He hugged her back and used the closeness to knuckle her head, further tangling her curls. "You always were the smart one."

She shoved him off with a righteous nod. "Damn straight."

"What do you think Mom's church ladies would say if they heard how much we curse?"

"You played sports, then went into law enforcement. Both my husbands were military." She shrugged. "And I work on base. Fuck 'em if they have a problem with it. And fuck 'em and anyone else who has a problem with your sexuality too."

He grinned and pulled her back into a hug. "Thanks, Stace."

Before they could relax back in their chairs, twin calls of "Mommy!" drifted up from downstairs.

"So much for them staying down." Stacey pushed out of her chair. "You coming in?"

"I'm going to sit out here for a bit. Enjoy the peace and quiet a little while longer."

Smiling, she turned to go, then paused and turned back to him. "I want you to be happy too, Jamie, and I can see whatever's going on with Aidan isn't easy. But don't give up on him."

"Stace—"

"It took me two years. It's only been one for Aidan."

"I can't watch him be with other people." He forced the words out around the lump in his throat.

Her smile turned into a full grin. "I don't think you'll be watching for long."

He was still contemplating her prediction, an echo of Ellen Talley's months ago, when his phone vibrated in his pocket. He withdrew it and read the text on-screen.

His stomach sank.

Whiskey Walker was needed tomorrow. And Agent Walker needed his partner.

———

Knee bouncing, thumbs swiping over his clover cuff links, Aidan fidgeted in the stylist's chair, debating whether to have Cory cut his overlong hair. The long strands made it easier to separate and treat, but it was well beyond its normal length. There was no reason not to cut it. Except Jamie liked it long. He had never said *Don't cut it*, but the way those deft fingers dove into his hair whenever they kissed, the way they clenched around the strands when he came, Jamie liked something to hold on to.

And Aidan liked the firm grip.

Missed it already.

"Earth to Ai."

His brother's raised voice and windmilling arms jerked Aidan out of his melancholy-laced thoughts. "What are you doing here?"

"Mel texted. Said you were getting back to your roots. Had to see and hear it for myself."

"It's fucking weird," Cory said.

"What's weird?" Aidan asked.

Danny sank into the chair beside him. "The accent."

"You've heard it every day of your life from Mom and Dad."

"Yeah, but never on you, at least not that thick. Jamie's gonna lose his shit."

Aidan twisted toward him, and Cory corrected with a tug. Aidan gritted his teeth against the flood of memories and resumed his wooden position, glaring at Danny via the mirror. "I'm his partner. His sports agent for this assignment. Nothing more."

"Since when?" Danny asked, eyes narrowed.

"He couldn't keep it casual."

"Or *you* couldn't keep it casual."

"Are you and my boss keeping it casual?"

Mel and Danny had been in each other's orbits for

years. Danny flirted mercilessly; Mel always blew him off. Until Texas. By the time they had left, more than mere flirting had transpired between his brother and sister-in-law.

Danny looked him right in the eye and answered, "No."

Aidan clutched the armrests to keep from jerking in surprise. "Wait, what?"

"I'm not shopping for rings or anything, but I'm also not shopping for anyone else's bed."

"What happened to a 'wee bit o' fun'?" Aidan drew out the accent and Danny laughed, his sharp features transforming into a dopey smile.

"I am having fun, with her." Danny eyed Cory. "All done?"

The stylist laid his tools on the vanity. "He needs to bake. I'm going to make a coffee run while you two gossip. Three lattes?"

"Make 'em ventis." Danny pulled several bills from his wallet and handed the cash to Cory. Danny waited for him to exit before spinning Aidan's chair to face him. "You're not ready to commit again after losing Gabe. He was the love of your life. I'm not in your situation."

Aidan swiped his thumbs over the cuff links again. He missed his husband every day, but the pain of loss and sense of betrayal had faded. Looking at his changed appearance in the mirror, feeling a different sort of pain in his chest and his balls, both there because of his own fear and foolishness, Aidan wondered if he wasn't now closer to Danny's situation.

Aidan's phone vibrated on the vanity.

"Speak of the devil." Danny reached over him, grabbed the phone, and dropped it in Aidan's lap.

Jamie's face smiled up at him. They had exchanged a few terse texts this morning about the case and his arrival Monday. Jamie was supposed to be visiting his family today, and Aidan had a bad feeling about why he would be calling him. "Jamie, what's going on?"

"Can you catch a red-eye out tonight?" His partner's voice was tense, agitated.

Aidan straightened in his chair. "Of course. What's happened?"

"The press conference got moved up to tomorrow."

Jamie was nervous about making his return statement, but he wouldn't call him out early just for that. "What else?"

"Our week time frame to solve this case . . . It just became three."

"Weeks?" Aidan asked, confused.

"No, days."

# EIGHT

Jamie checked Aidan's flight status on his phone.

*Landed*, the app told him.

He checked the escalators and baggage claim.

Jam-packed with overnight travelers and morning commuters, but no Aidan.

He snagged a chair in an out-of-the-way row and waited, turning his phone end over end on his knee, anxiety ratcheting up with each passing minute. Yesterday, there had been no question in his mind when he had asked Aidan to fly out early. Their case timeline had been significantly compressed, and he hadn't wanted to tackle today's press conference alone. But as he waited for Aidan's arrival, Jamie reconsidered whether they should have worked apart another day. He could have used it to rein himself in. He wanted to be the consummate agent who could separate their professional and personal relationships, but after Friday night, after learning Aidan wanted him but stayed away out of fear, the personal had dominated his mind, making him want to fight harder for Aidan.

But what if he won the battle, only to lose the war when Aidan learned of his betrayal? He had never intended to move past casual until he told Aidan the truth about Gabe, and now Tom. He didn't have all the story yet—he had to be patient and calm—but he was closer. That was the other reason he had called Aidan out early. He had learned the identity of Mason West and wanted to deliver the news in person.

"I know our schedule's fucked, but that face of yours is awfully grim."

Startling at the full-blast Irish accent, Jamie's head shot up and the phone slipped from his fingers, clattering to the ground. *Pick it up,* some instinct ordered, but he was too busy losing the rest of his fucking mind. The veneer of calm shattered and any hope of patience took a flying leap out the window.

Because standing in front of him was his stylishly dressed partner, a messenger bag over one shoulder, a coat tossed over the other, and silver-rimmed aviators nestled in waves of auburn hair. More times than he could count, Jamie had imagined Aidan with his natural hair color, and *damn* if the reality didn't surpass each and every one of his fantasies.

Mouth dry, heart racing, cheeks burning, Jamie's fingers twitched with the urge to weave through the long red strands. Reaching down instead, he grabbed his phone, held it between his palms, and wedged his clasped hands between his knees, forestalling his impulse. He tried to force out a "Hel-lo," but his brain refused to cooperate, all the blood in his body having raced south where his jeans became painfully tight.

*Fuck.*

He was gone. So far gone. Past casual, past a crush, past simple attraction.

This was Aidan, sans disguises, and Jamie wanted him more than he had ever wanted anything.

"Is it that bad a dye job?" Aidan asked, interrupting his mental breakdown.

"Ai—" he started, only to be corrected with a brogue-laced "Ian."

Jamie blinked, reminded that this was a disguise. It sure as hell didn't feel like one. "I wasn't expecting this." His eyes raked over Aidan again, taking it all in. Dressed in jeans and a navy V-neck sweater, the dark blues set off his pale skin, the freckles, his autumn eyes, that hair . . .

"Fuck," he muttered out loud.

Aidan shifted on his feet in front of him. "I said I was making a few more changes."

"Yeah, but this"—he spread his arms wide, the motion totally inadequate—"is more than a fucking few."

Their gazes locked, heat sparking. "Problem, Jamie?" Aidan's eyes flickered down to the very obvious problem.

"You gotta stop that."

He dropped his messenger bag and shrugged the coat off his shoulder. "Stop what?"

"Saying my name in that accent."

"Mr. Walker, then," he said with a smirk.

Way too smooth.

Jamie propped his elbows on his knees and covered his face with his hands. "God no," he groaned. "Not that either."

Aidan laughed as the buzzer went off on the conveyor behind them.

Leather smacked the backs of Jamie's hands, and he snagged Aidan's coat before it hit the ground.

*Leather?*

"Cover that up," Aidan said, eyeing his crotch. "And get yourself together. Debrief in the car." Turning, he headed for the spinning luggage carousel, giving Jamie a prime view of his sinfully fitted jeans.

Get himself together . . .

*Yeah, right.*

# NINE

Hands at ten and two, shoulders locked, eyes forward, Jamie looked like a startled colt about to flee. Aidan reconsidered whether he should have warned his partner about the makeover. But Aidan had wanted to surprise Jamie and get his unguarded reaction. And what a reaction it had been—muttered curses, flaming cheeks, tented jeans. The urge to tease was damn near impossible to resist, but Aidan wasn't ready for where that might lead, and they had bigger problems than unrequited libidos.

"Tell me why we have three days instead of a week to solve this case?"

Jeep still in park, Jamie slid his gaze sideways, over him again. He blinked slowly, like he still wasn't sure he had retrieved the right person from baggage claim.

"Focus, Whiskey."

He stared a moment longer, then gave his head a hard shake, eyes squeezed shut. When they reopened, the haze had lifted. "I screwed up," he mumbled, voice gruff.

"It's fine. I shouldn't have surprised you."

"Not that." He waved a dismissive hand between them. "I found the illegal gambling site on the dark web."

"The one the CU players are using to steal user identities?"

Jamie nodded. He cranked the car and steered them out of the parking garage and toward the freeway.

"I fail to see how that's bad. I thought we needed an invite."

"You actually read the file?"

"On the plane, until it put me to sleep. So you found their secret site on the secret internet. Where'd your hacker cockiness go astray?"

One corner of Jamie's mouth tipped up, a trace of a smile, and a weight lifted off Aidan's chest. This morning could have gone wrong in so many ways, but after the initial awkwardness, they were settling into their usual working banter.

"I tried to hack my way past the invite-only login. Tripped a hidden watchdog that activated an accelerated kill switch."

"When's the system go offline?"

"Tuesday night. Ticker clock and all."

Aidan rolled his eyes. "Overkill much?"

Jamie shrugged. "College kids."

"Why Tuesday night? Why not take it offline immediately?"

"My guess, to clear the bets placed on Tuesday night's games. I can't get in, so I can't see the volume of betting activity, but if it's significant . . ."

"They don't want to lose the money. Tell me about the setup. How's it work?"

"According to our source, when a user gets an invite, it

includes a unique ID. On first login, the site uploads an encrypted access portal on the user's computer or device. We can't gauge the full scope without an invite."

"Which is where Ian Daley comes in."

"If I'm going to appear clean, then yes, you have to score the invite."

"Done." Aidan slumped in his seat, thumb tapping the armrest. "Besides the dark web, we're talking RICO, not Cyber."

"That's the insidious thing."

"Sports betting by the athletes themselves isn't?"

"It is, and that's what convinced me to take this case, despite the risks."

Aidan held up a finger. "We'll get back to that in a minute. For now, connect the dots to Cyber. The case number is for identity theft."

"When a user downloads the gambling program, it also installs spyware that skims the user's personal information." One hand came off the wheel, flailing as Jamie explained, and Aidan smiled wider at his enthusiastic habit. "You're on another site and make a purchase, a copy of the financial information is stolen and transmitted through the spyware."

"And no one reports it because they'd have to admit to the dark web and the gambling," Aidan said. "Fuck, it's genius."

Jamie nodded. "Mutual assured destruction."

"Do you have any suspects?"

"I've got some front-runners, but I want to hear what our local contacts say. They're meeting us at the house."

Momentum slowing, they exited the freeway onto a busy surface street. The area reminded Aidan of Ireland, the overall impression of greenness striking, even in winter. Jamie hung a right after about a mile and slowed to a stop in front of an ornate iron gate. It inched open slowly and they drove through, the uniformed rent-a-cop at the stone guardhouse giving them a friendly wave.

As they wound deep into the neighborhood, towering pines and mature birch, maple and oak trees dotted the acre-plus lawns surrounding gigantic mansions—brick, stucco, stone—all of them minicastles. Including the one Jamie pulled into the driveway of. The gray stucco house was cleanly designed, with touches of elegance in the sweeping portico over the front door, the copper top on a front bay window, and oval windows at the top of the house's two front peaks.

"I can make housing arrangements too," Jamie said as they parked in the basement garage, next to a tarp-covered mystery.

Jamie grabbed his bags out of the Jeep and headed for the stairs while Aidan circled the covered mass. Long, low, wide-bodied . . . "Whose old muscle car?"

Jamie missed a step. "Owner's," he said, recovering.

Aidan would sneak down and take a peek later. He caught up at the top of the stairs, where Jamie pulled a worn key chain from his pocket and let them inside. In the big open foyer, Aidan stared up at the crystal chandelier hanging from the vaulted ceiling. It had to be at least twenty feet high.

Jamie stepped around him and dropped his bags at the bottom of the interior stairs. "I took the primary down here. There are two guest bedrooms upstairs for you to choose from."

"I'm sure either will be fine." He would check them

out later. One floor at a time. He followed the back wall of windows past the gleaming showcase kitchen into a large living area divided in two by columns that sat on a mid-rise row of marble topped cabinets. On the one side, over-size couches were angled toward a granite fireplace under an origami-like ceiling. On the other, a six-leg monster pool table and fully stocked wet bar rounded out the great room. And all around the giant space were more windows.

"You want to shower and freshen up?" Jamie asked.

Aidan held his sweater away from his body, sniffing. "Do I stink?"

His partner's face finally broke into a full grin, and Aidan's chest warmed. And tightened.

"No, was just offering."

"I'd take a coffee, though."

"That I can do."

Aidan strolled through the galley kitchen, bisected by a long island, to the attached dining room. This area looked like Jamie's workspace. At one end of the glass dining table sat open laptops, an empty Bobcats mug, scattered pads and pens, and a rainbow of file folders. Ever since Jamie had picked up the trick of organizing suspects and informa-tion by colored folders, their office in San Francisco was covered in them. He had made himself at home here already.

*At home.*

Barefoot, dressed in jeans and a tee, Jamie moved famil-iarly around the kitchen. Around the entire house and area now that Aidan thought about it.

Realization dawned.

The muscle car. The house keys on an old worn key

chain. The security guard letting them right in. The Bobcats mug on the table.

Aidan kicked himself for not putting it together sooner, seeing as he had done the same thing in Galveston. "This is *your* house."

Jamie's step faltered, as it had on the stairs. "I bought it after I was drafted. It's too much space, but a good investment. It's doubled in value."

"It's gorgeous, Whiskey."

Jamie's eyes met his, reflecting gratitude and pride.

"You rent it out?" Aidan asked.

He nodded. "Corporate tenants. The last rental expired in December, so it was open."

Aidan ran a finger over the smooth white marble and held it up to Jamie. "Sparkly clean too. How long until you destroy it?"

Jamie cut his eyes to the table. "That's less than a day's worth."

Aidan rounded the island and jostled his shoulder. "End of today, then?"

Chuckling, Jamie jostled back, and Aidan grinned, grateful his friendly jab hadn't been rebuffed. Maybe they would be okay.

"So, Mr. Owner, tell me what's under the tarp downstairs and when I can drive it."

"A 70 Chevelle SS, pearlescent black with white racing stripes, and never."

"Aww, c'mon, why you gotta be so mean?"

Smiling, Jamie poured their drinks and handed him a mug, their fingers brushing, and thoughts of mere friendship went up in flames. *Fuck*, he had missed that simple contact, the single gesture that started every day off right.

Glancing up, Jamie stared back at him with so much heat in his eyes Aidan gasped. The live wire that had sparked to life in the airport flared again.

Before either of them could act on it, the doorbell rang and startled them apart.

Coffee sloshed over the rim of Aidan's mug. "Shit!" He flicked off the scalding liquid. "Local team?"

"They're early." Jamie sounded as pleased as him at the interruption. He set aside his mug and tossed Aidan a dishtowel.

Aidan wiped off his hands and the counter, then waited in the kitchen as Jamie ushered Officer Paulson and Agent Grant inside. When they appeared in the dining room, Aidan was glad his mug remained on the counter. Otherwise he would have spilled his coffee again.

Mel was probably the tallest woman he had ever seen stand next to Jamie. Renee Paulson had to be the shortest, five feet at best. If he passed her on the street on her day off, dressed casually, he would think her a pixie white teenager. In her uniform, her bearing Academy-training-straight, her blond hair pulled back and her brown eyes sharp, Aidan thought better of that assessment.

"Renee, Grant, my partner, Aidan Talley."

He extended a hand to Paulson first. "Officer, pleasure to meet you."

She smiled, her freckled face transforming from severe to warm so fast Aidan felt whiplashed. It was a Southern trait he had never gotten used to. "Likewise."

"We look forward to working with you."

"I'm just glad Beau listened to me and got the FBI involved."

"Beauregard Grant," the suited agent said, offering his hand.

Twenty-seven according to his file and a friend of Paulson's as Mel had said, Grant was a Black man of average height and build, dark brown skin, and brown eyes that were cataloguing every detail of the room.

*Good agent.*

Aidan led their guests to the clean end of the table. "Paulson, why did you take this matter to the FBI instead of CMPD?"

"RICO, gaming laws, and identity theft fall under your jurisdiction."

A cop who didn't want to piss all over his jurisdiction. Would today's wonders never cease?

"I'm also not certain CMPD can remain impartial," Paulson added.

Jamie set the coffeepot and a tray of mugs, cream, and sugar on the table. "You mean besides yourself?"

Aidan split a look between them.

"Renee's brother has a career outside of basketball when he's done," Grant supplied. "That's part of the reason he came forward."

"Riley Paulson," Jamie said. "Junior, backup point guard." Meaning he mostly rode the bench. "He's going to work for the State Department after graduation."

"So he's working through credentials," Aidan said. "And he can't be implicated. He came to you?" he asked Paulson.

She nodded. "And then I took him to Beau."

Aidan wanted to rewind to her impartiality comment, but Jamie jumped on a different comment from Grant. "You said that was part of the reason Riley came forward. What's the other?"

"He's concerned some of the older players are pressuring the younger ones to participate in the illegal activity. His best friend, a freshman on the team, told him about it."

Face hard, Jamie braced his forearms on the beveled edge of the table. "Throwing games?"

"Recruitment," Grant replied. "They're athletes, big men on campus, especially the starters."

"But this is DII," Aidan said.

"Yes, it's DII," Paulson said. "But Charlotte's been trying to field a legit college team for decades. It's hard to get attention in the same state as Tobacco Road."

Aidan angled toward Jamie. "Could the players involved be throwing games without the others realizing it?"

"It's possible. Once we get full access to the gambling site, I can check bets against outcomes to see if there's a correlation. I'll be able to tell a lot more on the court. It may not look like much—a foul here, a walk there—but knowing what we do, I'll be attuned to it."

The Bureau couldn't ask for a better inside man on this assignment. Jamie, of all people, knew exactly what to look for on the web and on the court. What had he found already? Who were his suspects? But before those questions, he had another for Paulson. "You said you didn't think CMPD could be impartial. Why?"

She curled her hands around her mug and stared down into the dark liquid. Aidan could guess at her distress. Insubordination was a hard pill to swallow for most LEOs. "The police chief is a CU alum. So are several other officers on the force, including one whose nephew is a member of the team."

"Blake Whitehead." By his partner's terse tone, Blake was near the top of Jamie's suspect list. And he was none too fond of him already.

"That's the one." Grant's voice was likewise dour. Not a fan either.

"Does your captain know about this?" Aidan asked Paulson, gesturing to the four of them.

"Not from me. If my cap got wind, I'd bet on a leak from CU."

"Renee came directly to me," Grant said. "Only Coach Turner and Chancellor Polk at CU were briefed."

"They're not likely to say anything," Jamie said. "The less attention the better, as far as NCAA violations are concerned. Do we know if the chancellor or coach are implicated? What about the athletic director?"

"We don't know anything for sure yet," Grant said.

"Riley doesn't think Coach is," Paulson added. "Not sure on the others."

"You're officially on loan to the FBI for this investigation?" Aidan asked.

"Part-time, case undisclosed to my superiors." A sideways grin turned up one corner of her mouth. "They ain't too pleased about it."

Right on cue, Dispatch squawked from the radio on her shoulder. "Paulson, what's your twenty?"

She signaled silence and pressed the mic. "Fifteen minutes."

Outside, Aidan glimpsed a black F-150 and a Bureau-issue sedan, no police cruiser. Her location wouldn't be tracked.

"Cap wants you here in ten," Dispatch said.

"Roger that." She turned off the radio with a sigh to the heavens. "Like I said, ain't too pleased."

Everyone chuckled as they stood.

"You'll be by the field office later today?" Grant said.

"After practice." Jamie nodded at their coffees. "Want those to go?"

"A morning free of station sludge? Hell yes," Paulson agreed eagerly.

"Give Renny my share, not that she needs the extra caffeine."

She slapped the grinning Grant's shoulder, and Aidan smiled at the two, who were clearly good friends. They would be an asset on this case once he and Jamie got their arms around it.

To-go coffee prepped, goodbye handshakes given, Aidan waited for Grant and Paulson to get halfway down the front steps before closing the door. "You didn't tell them about the accelerated time frame."

"I need to know more and see if I can turn off the kill switch."

"You think you can?"

Jamie fell into his chair with a huff that was more show than burden, that attractive half smirk giving him away. Aidan shifted, wishing for dress slacks instead of jeans. "Fine, dumb question," he conceded.

"I may need direct access, though, which means we need to solve for who as fast as possible so we can get into their computer."

"Press conference and practice today will give us a good look. And I've got a meeting with the AD after. I'll try to meet with the chancellor too. This Blake kid's your top suspect among the players?"

Jamie dug through his folders, found the one he was after, and handed it to Aidan. Blake Whitehead was scrawled across the top sheet in Jamie's barely legible handwriting. "Shooting guard and computer science major with a 4.0 GPA."

Aidan eyed his partner over the top of the folder. "Sounds familiar."

"I went to a DI school."

Aidan rolled his eyes and continued to flip pages. "Okay, overachiever, besides the obvious, what makes you think this is our guy?"

"Keep going until you get to his social media accounts."

Pages of biographical data and transcripts later, he reached the printouts from Blake's Twitter, Facebook, and Instagram. Posts about a night out on the town. Pictures of his new car. Tweets about parties.

Jamie reached over the top of the folder and pointed at the car. "That's a sixty-thousand-dollar ride." Then at the night-out post. "That's the most expensive restaurant in Charlotte. Blake's family is firmly middle class, the cop uncle is the most successful of the lot, and there are strict NCAA rules on income and gifts. Where's all that money coming from? According to his transcript, he has the computer science skills. Judging by those tweets, he's also a punk."

As Aidan read on, he tended to agree. This operation was more than one kid, though. They had a whole team, coaching staff, and administration to assess. He placed the file back on the table. "It's a good start, but we've got a mile-long suspect list to narrow down."

"Which is why I bought a whole box of multicolored files."

Aidan tilted back his head on a dramatic sigh.

Jamie's laughter filled the room, and it was like the first rain of the season, washing away the buildup of messy grime on the road. It was also just as dangerous, a slippery hazard that could so easily send Aidan into a tailspin. Righting his head, Aidan locked gazes with Jamie, that same live wire sparking between them, and he didn't know whether to hit the brakes or step on the gas.

A chime from Jamie's phone made the decision for him. His partner's easy manner vanished as he pushed back from the table like a man headed for his execution. "Press conference at CU in an hour. I need to get ready."

Now more than ever, Aidan wanted to reach out and haul him into his arms. He settled for a hand on his arm. "You can still pull out of this."

"The press has been alerted. The wheels are in motion."

"I don't care. If you want out of this, we're out. No questions."

"I can't keep running. I've got to face this. Might as well be now."

"Okay, but if at any time you decide otherwise, just say the words."

Jamie nodded, eyes downcast. "Thank you."

Aidan dug his cuff links out of his pocket, having traveled with them on his person, and dropped them into Jamie's palm. "Luck o' the Irish," he said, folding Jamie's fingers over them. "Now go charm the pants off 'em."

# TEN

Jamie buttoned his suit coat, adjusted Aidan's cuff links, and ran both hands over his hair, making sure the unruly waves were relatively in place. Standing in the auditorium wings, he half listened to Coach Turner's introductory remarks while counting the rows of gathered reporters. Better than average turnout for a Division II coaching announcement. There shouldn't have been a press conference at all for an assistant coaching hire in any division, but in the booster-driven game of collegiate sports, his hiring was a coup for CU. No matter that he had been out of the game for eight years.

No matter that it was a lie.

While Turner and Polk knew the truth, CU's athletic director and public relations department hadn't gotten the memo, letting it be known far and wide they had snagged Whiskey Walker. He appreciated Turner's and Polk's discretion for the sake of their case. He hated what it was about to mean for his life.

"And without further ado," Turner said in his Southern

drawl, "I'm pleased to welcome Jameson Walker to the CU family."

Jamie took one last breath of freedom, then plastered on the public smile he had perfected during his playing days and stepped out of the wings. Blinded by camera flashes, he walked in the general direction of Turner and Polk, assuming one of them would grab him by the arm and direct him. As expected, he was corralled into a round of handshakes, smiles, and more photos. By the time his vision cleared, he was positioned behind the podium to which half a dozen microphones were attached. He counted another dozen aimed his direction by reporters in the auditorium seats.

Adrenaline flooded his body, racing through his heart and straight to his feet, preparing him to flee. Mind as blank as his vision moments ago, he clutched the sides of the podium and fought the overwhelming instinct to run. Eight years ago, he left behind his career, his home, and his lover to escape this very situation. He ran first to grad school, then to the FBI, requesting an appointment clear across the country to evade these reporters, certain they would discover the truth and turn his life upside down.

A truth that was both closer to and further from the surface than ever before.

He scanned the crowd, searching for blond and landing on auburn. Truth and lies, embodied in the six-foot frame of his partner at the back of the auditorium. The contradictions didn't knock him sideways. Instead, Aidan's intense autumn eyes anchored him, steadied his mind, and muted the buzzing voices and clicking cameras.

This was his job. He was a good agent; better than good. He was one half of the top investigative team in the FBI, and his partner had his back, no matter the other shit swirling around him. He could do this. He had to do this, to solve the case and to throw Renaud off their scent. Everyone had to believe he had recommitted to his old life. He would use the press to his advantage, not the other way around. He was in control this time.

He pressed his heels to the stage, imagining them rooted to the hardwood planks, and relaxed his fingers one by one from their death grip on the podium. He conjured a new Whiskey Walker persona, one with Agent Walker's backbone and Agent Talley's unwavering support. His smile transformed from picture perfect to genuine, and Aidan's face broke into a matching grin.

*Charm the pants off 'em*, he'd said.

No problem.

"Good morning, y'all." Jamie drawled in his deepest Southern accent. "If you lovely folks don't mind, I'm going to say a quick word, then I'll be happy to answer your questions. I want to thank Coach Turner and Chancellor Polk for the chance to return to my first love. The past eight years away from the court have been rewarding, professionally and personally, but the lure of the game can't be denied. While my injury keeps me off the court as a player, I'm excited to return to the sport as a coach here at CU. I look forward to mentoring this talented group of young men and helping the Ravens bring home a championship. All right, then, your questions, please."

They came at him from all directions, and Jamie was grateful for the mock press conference Aidan had insisted on during the drive to campus. Answers rolled easily off his tongue.

"Whiskey, how's it feel to be back in North Carolina?"

"Like coming home."

"Why not apply for a DI coaching position? Why not Carolina?"

"I'm pretty sure there's a waitlist for those coveted Tar Heel coaching chairs." He waited for the laughs to subside before continuing. "There was a real need here and a real shot at a championship. And I missed Charlotte."

"Did you contact the Hornets?"

"As a coach, I think—*I hope*—I can be more of an asset at the college level. The best years of my life were spent at Carolina. I'd like to be a part of these students' best years at CU."

"Why are you leaving the FBI?"

"Like I said, the lure of the court was too much. My years with the Bureau exceeded my expectations. I wouldn't trade them for anything. But my place, my true talent, is on the court."

"You said the past eight years were personally reward-ing? Anyone special back in San Francisco?"

From the *Observer*'s gossip columnist, that was not a question he and Aidan had rehearsed. He swiped a thumb over a cuff link to keep himself from glancing at Aidan. "If there was someone special back in California, I don't think I'd be here now, would I?" More laughs, including a grat-ing, high-pitched giggle from the columnist who had asked the question. Self-interest, then. He smiled wider, selling the cover.

Questions went on a short while longer until Coach Turner joined him at the podium to wrap things up. They posed with Polk for more pictures, then the public relations team shooed people out.

He and Turner followed Polk down the stage stairs. "You always were great in front of a camera."

"Thanks, Coach."

The older man leaned in and lowered his voice. "Damn convincing too. Almost believed all that."

Jamie came to a stop, realizing there'd been a lot of truth to it. He had a job to do for the FBI, but that didn't lessen his love of the game or his eagerness to mentor these players.

Turner slapped him on the back. "We're counting on you, Whiskey." He left to join Polk halfway up the aisle where she waited with Ethan Reynolds, CU's Athletic Director who'd orchestrated today's event.

Rotating, Jamie found his partner rounding the front row of seats, wearing a proud smile. "You were amazing."

"Amazing, okay." Jamie lowered his voice, stepping close. "But believable?"

"Completely," Aidan murmured. "This might be the only UC gig you're cut out for."

"Walker," Turner called. "Practice in twenty."

"Yes, Coach." Jamie waited for the group to depart, then shrugged out of his sport coat and handed it to Aidan so he could undo his tie. "Time to really put it to the test."

"And I've got to dust off my law degree and hammer out your contract."

"Can't say I'm sorry to have an agent to take care of that for me." Laughing, he deflected the jacket Aidan hurled back at him. He didn't care that it landed on the floor. He was too happy with the easy back and forth that had carried over from the morning.

Happiness that vanished when the last voice he expected called out behind him. "Jamie? Is that really you?"

Aidan must have seen the shock on his face, seen his muscles tense, and realized he was seconds from flight. He stepped past him, hand brushing his arm.

"Ian Daley. Can I help you?"

"I'd like a word with Jamie."

"And you are?"

"Derrick Pope."

The one person who could blow apart his cover and his new persona.

Aidan's sharp inhale jolted Jamie free. Turning, he laid eyes on his ex for the first time since he had limped away on crutches eight years ago.

Derrick's five-eight frame was thinner than Jamie remembered, but his chestnut curls were the same wild mess and his hazel eyes, fringed by thick burnished lashes, were as breathtaking as ever. Gone, however, was the Bob Jones uniform of dress khakis, white button-down, and bland tie. In its place, black jeans, a fitted green sweater, sleeves pushed up to his elbows, and black combat boots. The most striking change of all were the words tattooed on his inner forearm.

*To thine own self . . .*

Be true.

Questions fought for breath and words. Was Derrick out? Would someone find pictures of them together from eight years ago? Would they put two and two together? "What the hell are you doing here?" won out.

Derrick shoved his hands in his pockets and smiled shyly, his cheeks rosy. "Not the greeting I'd hoped for."

Aidan stepped to his side, waves of tension rolling off him. "Excuse us a moment," he said to Derrick, all business, not an ounce of cordiality in his voice. Planting his hand in the crease of Jamie's elbow, Aidan led him up the aisle, out of Derrick's earshot. "I thought he was at Bob Jones."

"Last I checked, eight years ago. I don't keep tabs on him. I didn't want to know where he was or what he was doing."

Jaw clenched, Aidan glared daggers over his shoulder. "Ethan's waiting."

"I'd prefer you stay." Aidan's gaze shot back to his. Derrick's presence compromised their mission, and it compromised him. He needed his partner to have his back. He trusted Aidan got all that in his four harshly spoken words but added a strained "please" in desperate emphasis.

Aidan nodded without hesitation. "You want to lead or me?"

"Me, no reason my agent would jump down his throat. I left him."

"Because he took a job where your relationship could never be public."

"So did I." As much as Jamie appreciated Aidan's defense, as much as he wanted to lay his failed relationship with Derrick at his ex's feet, he was the one who'd left.

The muscle in Aidan's jaw ticked. "Tread carefully."

Jamie didn't think Aidan's warning was limited to their cover. He stayed close on his heels as they walked down the aisle.

"What are you doing here?" Jamie asked Derrick again.

"I'm a professor here at CU."

"Since when?"

"Last September."

"You left Bob Jones?"

"Geez, investigator much?" Derrick was being cute, trying for laughs, his default nervous setting. When neither he nor Aidan played along, he reverted to shy, shrugging one shoulder. "CU offered me tenure track."

It was what Derrick had always wanted, what a gifted teacher like him deserved. It had also contributed to the demise of their relationship.

Derrick stepped forward and held out a hand to Aidan. "We should start over. I'm Derrick, an old—"

Aidan ignored it. "I know who you are."

Derrick's green-gold gaze darted to Jamie.

"Ian's my agent."

Those same eyes narrowed. Nothing would have given Jamie greater pleasure than to let Derrick believe handsome, stylish "Ian" was more than a friend and sports agent, but it was a petty instinct and to do so would almost certainly blow their cover, especially if any press were lurking about.

"He's also a friend," Jamie added. That would have to do.

"It's nice to meet you," Derrick said.

Aidan addressed Jamie instead. "You need to get to the arena, and I'm due in the AD's office." He stalked several rows up the aisle and waited.

Jamie turned back to Derrick. "I'm sorry, but we need to go."

"Can we . . ." Derrick hesitated, biting his full lower lip. "I'd like to catch up."

"I don't think that's a good idea."

"You're going to be around campus, and so am I. We're bound to run into each other. Let's meet and clear the air." When Jamie didn't respond, Derrick's gaze drifted to Aidan. "As friends. I'm seeing someone."

Jamie worried again for their cover. Maybe he should

meet with Derrick to set him straight about "Ian" and to cement their story. "Fine."

"A drink this evening, then?" Derrick said, and Aidan's ire slammed into Jamie's back from five rows away.

"Just coffee. I should be home by six."

"Great." Derrick's boyish smile grew wide. "There's a Starbucks near your house. I can meet you there."

"At the house." Still on high alert after the press conference, Jamie was reticent to meet in public.

"See you then." Derrick's gaze lingered a long moment before he left out the auditorium side door, a gust of cold air rushing in behind him.

Avoiding the chill, Jamie started up the aisle toward Aidan and they headed for the main exit. "Thank you."

"Don't thank me yet."

"Why not?"

"He wants you back."

"He's seeing someone."

Pushing out the doors, Aidan shot him a heated look over his shoulder. "There's no substitute for the real thing."

———

Aidan scaled the stairs of the administration building, hoping exertion would burn off his anger. Jamie's ex was not a complication they needed. Derrick's presence at CU threatened their cover and their case. But those weren't the only reasons Aidan's blood boiled.

No, what blasted his anger into the red zone was the look of open adoration on the other man's face and in his stunning hazel eyes. And the way *Jamie* rolled off his tongue in a seductive low-country purr. Natural, as if he had said it a million times. Over the course of their relationship, he probably had. And Jamie responded to all of it. A sharp intake of breath, riveted eyes, a racing heartbeat Aidan swore he had heard.

Aidan had no right to be angry. He had thrown away that privilege by denying Jamie the same. If Jamie wanted another shot with Derrick—and there was no question Derrick wanted another shot with him, even if he was seeing someone else—Aidan couldn't hold Jamie back.

His mind worked overtime to silence his rebellious insides. He was forty-two—gray hairs would tarnish the dye job by week's end. Jamie was thirty. It would be another five years before a gray hair appeared on his head. Derrick was free of dead husband baggage and didn't have an international terrorist gunning for him. With his boyish smile and gorgeous eyes, his curly hair that was just the right length for Jamie's fists, and his freckled cheeks that blushed an attractive pink, Derrick was a safer bet, hands down.

But there was one major strike against him. Yes, Jamie had been the one to walk away, but Derrick had taken a job that compounded Jamie's already considerable fear of exposure, forcing him to leave the home, man, and career he loved. He loved this sport, had taken this case to protect its integrity. It enraged Aidan how Derrick had played a hand in Jamie having to leave it and how he showed up today, resurrecting Jamie's fears of exposure. Not that Aidan hadn't put him in a similar situation. Risking exposure and a career he loved without so much as a commitment on the table.

He crested the third-floor stairs, and a woman waited at the end of the hall. "Mr. Daley?"

"That's me." He followed her outstretched arm into the last office on the right. Ethan's name was etched on the door's brass nameplate, but behind the desk sat the sharply suited Chancellor Elizabeth Polk.

Strike that visit off his to-do list.

She waited for the assistant to close the door, then gestured with a polite smile to the guest chair. "Agent Talley, please have a seat."

So the secretaries were out of the loop. Good. Polk was following orders.

"Chancellor," he said. "I had a meeting with Mr. Reynolds."

"Ethan stepped out for a moment. I wanted to properly introduce myself and see how the investigation was going."

Properly introduce herself . . . by not standing when he had entered, not offering her hand, and not calling him by his cover name. She was letting him know who was in charge. While he didn't doubt the reminder was too-often needed, he suffered no such blindness. She had the title and distinguished bearing of a woman in charge—he had seen it up close and personal with Mel—and he respected Polk for it. But there were rules, and this was his and Jamie's investigation.

"I'm not at liberty to discuss our case."

She smiled, somewhere between a seasoned politician and Southern belle. "But I'm the one who called the FBI."

"Technically, it was Officer Paulson."

"Yes, but I'm cooperating."

Not exactly a jurisdictional pissing contest. Polk didn't want to be kept in the dark about what was going on at her school, and Aidan could respect that, if he trusted her.

"You considered covering it up?" he asked.

The corners of her mouth tightened, but otherwise she remained eerily still. "That's not what I said."

"Other NCAA programs have hidden worse."

"We could play for the championship this year. I'm trying to save that."

"We're going to do everything we can to solve this case before the tournament, but keeping any title you may win is a stretch."

"Not if they aren't throwing games." Her calm was cracking, anger and resignation warring in her expression. She was grasping at straws, afraid of angry boosters with flaming pitchforks.

Aidan tried to offer consolation. "CU is cooperating. The NCAA should take that into account. That said, I'm FBI, not the NCAA. I can't promise anything."

"I understand." Her ramrod-straight spine curled, defeated, and she slouched back in the leather chair. "Do you have any leads?"

"Like I said, I'm not at liberty to discuss that." He was leaning toward trust, believing that Polk just wanted what was best for her school. He mentally moved her into the clear column, with an asterisk to confirm with background searches. "We're working hard, and we will resolve this matter as quickly as possible."

"It could be worse." She glanced out the window, and Aidan followed her gaze to the red brick building with Gilbert Arena etched in stone over the doors. "The publicity from hiring Whiskey Walker will bring in more fans and boosters. Hopefully, they'll realize we're a good team and stay even after he leaves."

"The press conference was well-attended, especially for DII."

"Ethan's got his staff working overtime, and he's very good at his job."

A knock on the door and the man mentioned sauntered in, smiling wide. "Sorry to keep you waiting, Ian."

White, with brown hair and blue eyes, Aidan couldn't help but notice the AD's resemblance to Jamie, though Ethan was closer to his own age. And according to Jamie's preliminary file, he was also openly gay. A fact borne out by the way his gaze landed briefly on Polk, then lingered on him. Aidan could use that interest to their advantage, to get close and assess whether Ethan belonged in the clear or suspect column. He made a show of checking the other man out, letting his eyes coast up and down his figure, and when their gazes met again, Ethan's was sparking hot.

*Hooked.*

Chancellor Polk cleared her throat as she circled the desk. "It was a pleasure meeting you, Mr. Daley. Please enjoy your time at CU."

"Thank you, ma'am."

"Ma'am?" Ethan said once the door closed behind her. "She's going to love you." Rather than sitting behind the desk, he claimed a chair at the small round table beneath the window.

Aidan sat opposite him, crossing his legs toward Ethan. "Not all agents are without manners."

Ethan burst into laughter. "I'll take that bet."

At the mention of *bet*, Aidan leaned forward. "How do you mean?"

"Show me your manners over dinner."

Ah, a different sort of bet, but one that could lead to information on the betting Aidan *was* interested in. It was exactly what he had been after, yet the dinner date gave

Aidan pause, same as drinks with Scott had in San Francisco. There was no attraction, even if both men were Aidan's type. Ethan, real date or not, would only be a substitute for who he really wanted.

The man who was having coffee with his ex tonight.

At the house.

*Fuck.*

"I'm sure Jamie won't mind if I steal you away," Ethan said with a wink. "Negotiations."

Aidan could spend the night waiting outside Jamie's house, wondering if his partner was doing more than talking with Derrick, or he have dinner with CU's athletic director. A person, a potential suspect, who was well-connected to the sports programs, including the basketball team.

No debate.

The job, he told himself, ignoring the voice that echoed the misery.

"I'd be delighted."

# ELEVEN

In his new office, Jamie changed out of his suit and into khakis and a Ravens polo. He stared at his reflection in the glass cabinet behind his desk, finger tracing the team's fierce black mascot and the word *Coach* stitched below it. An excited shiver ran up his spine, and the chaos of the morning—culminating in his first love squaring off against his last love—faded in the face of his true love.

Basketball. The court. The game.

Something felt right about rejoining the sport as a coach, even if it was just a show. He swapped his dress shoes for tennis shoes and let that sense of belonging carry him to the gym. He waited for Coach Turner to finish addressing the team, then stepped onto the parquet court, drawing everyone's attention.

"Ravens." Coach held an arm out toward him. "I'd like to officially introduce our new assistant coach, Whiskey Walker."

Most of the players cheered, clapping loudly, while the doubters among them, including Blake, put on an air of disinterest, their welcome subdued. It made spotting potential suspects easy. Jamie added their names to his mental list, then clicked back into coach mode.

"Please, guys," he said, shushing them. "I should be applauding you. You're doing great this season. Tied for division lead in the conference."

Coach clasped his shoulder. "With your help, we'll break that tie."

"And win the tourney," a student shouted.

Jamie zeroed in on Marcus Smith. Team captain, senior point guard, and a possible draft pick, despite his DII status. "You keep handling the ball like you're doing, Marcus, and we'll get there."

The captain's teeth gleamed in a wide smile.

"I look forward to being a part of this team and getting to know you all." Jamie met each player's eyes, including Riley Paulson's. He shared the same blond-haired, brown-eyed coloring as his sister, though he had clearly inherited all the height genes. "Thank you for welcoming me into the CU family."

"We're happy to have you," Coach said.

"I'm happy to be here."

Coach handed him a shiny silver whistle attached to a Ravens lanyard. "Why don't you do the honors?"

Smiling, he blew the whistle, and practice was on. They ran the players through warm-ups and circuit drills—Coach, a former point guard, on ball handling, Jamie on shooting, and the two other assistants, Kyle and Neil, on free throws. During the scrimmage that followed, Jamie hung back and observed, watching for unusual activity. Nothing was readily apparent, though Blake led the team in fouls, demanded the ball more than any other player, and ignored Jamie's shooting advice. Bad team player all around. Neil was also standoffish, but from what Jamie could tell, the assistant gave everyone the cold shoulder. Jamie added him to his list for further investigation.

Coach and Riley were near the bottom of that list, their cooperation so far and clean background checks making them low priority follow-ups. Marcus too. Jamie's prelim search on the team captain showed his nose was clean, and on the court, his enthusiasm, humor, and patience with the younger players impressed Jamie. If a teammate was having a hard time, he was there with a distracting joke or helpful suggestion, expertly defusing the situation. He didn't seem the sort to pressure others into illegal betting schemes.

Pressure Jamie into a game of horse . . . Now, that was a different story. "C'mon, Coach," Marcus said, blue eyes full of mischief. "Afraid I'll beat you?"

With practice wrapping up, others looked to them, intrigued. He was the new guy; a little hazing was to be expected. He pulled his phone out of his pocket and checked the time. He and Aidan were due at the field office in an hour. Too tight to play a game of horse, change back into his suit, and make it to their meeting on time. He was about to bow out when Blake joined the gathering group.

"Got room for another?"

The chance to knock Blake down a peg or two—and to observe his prime suspect more closely—was worth the tardiness. "Sure," he said. "Who wants to make it an even four?"

Presley Jackson stepped forward. "Press," as the team called him, since he was a beast on defense, and because he hated the name his Elvis-obsessed mama gave him, was all arms and limbs. Jamie had given the freshman shooting guard numerous pointers during practice, and unlike Blake, he had listened, made adjustments, and at the end of two hours, his shots were already falling more reliably. He and Riley were also tight, another good sign.

Blake glared at Press. "Bring it, kid."

Riley not so quietly whispered, "Take his ass down," and Jamie covered his laugh with a cough. Less diplomatic, the rest of the team cheered loudly for Press as he stood next to Marcus at center court atop the giant black raven decal.

Coach clapped Jamie on the back. "Don't embarrass me."

"I'll try not to."

Much to Jamie's satisfaction, Blake was eliminated first, earning his *e* by failing to replicate Press's simple corner jumper. He stormed off the court, his crew in tow, to the rest of the team's applause. Grinning, Press took a bow. The freshman lasted three more rounds until Jamie's underhand, around-the-basket layup ousted him. Jamie, with his "injury," shouldn't have been able to make that shot, or numerous others he had made during practice, but no one said a word.

With Press out, Jamie faced off against Marcus and things got trickier in the insane shots department. Over-the-shoulder tosses, spinning layups, blind heaves. Trick shots Jamie had made as a kid from his gravel driveway into the chain link net over their garage. Fifteen minutes of spectacle later, Marcus beat him on an eyes-closed, half-court, overhead, backward granny. Marcus's shot swished through the net; Jamie's rimmed out at the last second. A chorus of groans went up from their audience. As players, they had all had shots look like a sure thing only to have the basket cough them back up. In this case, however, Jamie was happy to applaud his competitor, who was doing his best *Rocky* impression at the top of the bleachers.

"Smith!" Coach Turner barked. "Get down from there before you break a leg and ruin our championship season."

Jamie admired Turner. Not once today had he let on that his team's season was on the line, in more than the must-win-the-conference way. Jamie hoped the NCAA would let the innocent Ravens play; they'd worked their asses off this season. But could they win without the guilty ones, whomever they proved to be?

Marcus read his contemplative silence as defeat. "Don't take it too hard, Coach." He stepped off the bottom bleacher. "Not too bad for an old dude."

"Hey, I'm not even ten years older than you."

Marcus rose on his toes and eyed a spot on Jamie's head. "Is that a gray hair? You're gonna be in competition with Coach Turner soon."

Jamie swatted his hand away, and Marcus doubled over in laughter. "Get to the showers already."

Beside him, Coach ran a hand over his thinning gray hair. "Don't worry, Walker. You got a long way to go before you reach this level of winter." Jamie almost doubled over himself but stopped when Coach added, "Not so long on other fronts. You're good with them. Jackson's improving already."

"The talent's there. He just needs help honing it."

"I'm guessin' coaching was never in your plan, but you've got a gift. Try it on while you're here, see how it fits, and if you ever get tired of your current gig, you let me know."

Turner left him center court, mind reeling. He shouldn't like the notion. Part of him recoiled at the idea of leaving Aidan's side, but the part of him that was lured by the court warmed to it. For now, though, he was here to work a case. To that end, he needed to change and get to the field office.

As he passed the locker room on the way to his office, angry voices welled from inside and Jamie changed course. He slammed open the door just as a body smashed into a locker across the large black-and-white-tiled room. On the heels of the body-to-metal thud, Blake, angered at being shown up by Press, shouted homophobic obscenities at the freshman along with threats to put him in his place if Press didn't learn it.

Jamie hopped two rows of benches and landed between Blake and Press. He held Blake back with an outstretched arm, ordering him to stay, as Riley and Neil peeled Press off the crumpled locker. Once they were clear, Jamie turned his tightly reined anger on Blake. "That language is unacceptable."

Blake looked smug. "Don't mean it ain't true."

"It doesn't matter if it's true or not. You do not threaten your teammates, you do not assault another player, and you sure as hell do not demean anyone's sexual orientation, whatever it may be."

The punk wrinkled his nose. "Fuck, you one of them too?"

Jamie loomed over him. "Same answer. Doesn't matter. What matters is that you respect your teammates, coaches, and players. That language doesn't respect anyone. Neither does threatening a player who beat you fair and square."

Someone made a sizzling noise behind them.

"That's enough," Jamie clipped, then addressed Blake again. "Next game, Press will start in your place."

"You've been here one day. You can't do that!"

"See that?" Jamie pointed at the *Coach* stitched on his polo. "That means I can and did. Anyone else want to object?"

The locker room was stone-cold silent, until Marcus, from the other side of the room, hollered, "Hey, Whiskey, you sure you ain't coached before?"

Muted chuckles broke out, then quieted again when the door swung open.

"Problem here?" Turner asked.

"Nah," Marcus said before Jamie could reply. "Coach Walker handled it."

Turner grunted. "Blake, AD Reynolds wants to see you in his office."

Blake's face reverted from outraged to smug. "I'm the face of this team. Five bucks says I don't sit out an entire half."

"Ten says you do," Jamie countered.

Some of Blake's arrogance faded as he followed Turner out, and Jamie counted it a win. He thanked Neil and asked Riley and Press to come with him. "I heard that crash against the lockers from out in the hallway," he said to Press once they were in his office. "You need to see the trainers?"

Head bowed, Press ran a hand over his shaved scalp. "Nah, I'm fine, Coach."

"He comes at you again, physically or with that slander, you tell me."

Unusually shy, Press avoided his gaze. "Not slander if it's true."

Riley jostled his shoulder. "Shut up, Prelaw."

Jamie bit back a surprised gasp. "Does the team know? Does Coach?"

Press dropped his hand, took a big breath, and met his eyes. "DII, Coach, no one cares. I don't make a big deal of it, but I don't hide it neither. I got a boyfriend," he said with a shrug, like it really wasn't a big deal.

It was to Jamie, though. Press was brave. Far braver than him.

"Okay, so it's not slander," Jamie said. "But your sexual orientation is also not a source of insult."

"It's just words. Not like I haven't heard it before. I know who I am."

"A damn good shooting guard is who you are," Riley said. "You just keep showing him up."

Pride, at Press's bravery and Riley's friendship, turned up the corners of Jamie's mouth. "I meant what I said, Jackson. Next game, you start in Blake's place. You up for that?"

Press stood taller. "Won't let you down, Coach."

"I know you won't. Now go on. I need a word with Riley." Press shot his friend a cautious look, but Riley waved him off. Once the door closed behind him, Jamie took his seat and gestured for Riley to take the visitor's chair.

"He's the friend who came to you about the gambling ring?"

Riley gaped at him, brown eyes wide.

"I'm with the FBI, Riley."

"Still? You're not a coach?"

Jamie shook his head.

Riley gave a surprised huff. "Could've fooled me."

"I'm undercover. Coach Turner and Chancellor Polk know, and your sister of course. Now you do too."

Riley nodded slowly. "Did you get an invite yet?"

"Not yet. My partner's working that angle."

"Your partner?"

"Ian Daley," Jamie said. "Tall, red hair, Irish accent. Real name's Aidan Talley. If you see him around, he's on our side. We've got your back, Riley." Jamie grabbed a stack of Post-its off the desk. "If you hear or see anything"—he jotted his and Aidan's cell numbers on the top sheet and ripped it off—"or if Blake gets in your and Press's faces again, you call us." He handed the slip of paper to Riley.

The younger man stared at it, flicking the edges. "Even if we go to the tourney, we're not keeping our championship, are we?"

"It's possible it'll be stripped, even if we make a recommendation otherwise."

"I figured. I just couldn't stand by and do nothing."

Jamie came around the desk and put a hand on Riley's shoulder. "You did the right thing. And I am going to try to save this season for you, but no guarantees."

Riley pocketed the note and stood. "I understand, Coach." He turned to go, hesitated, then turned back around. "What you did for Press today . . . He plays it off like it doesn't matter, like it doesn't bother him, but it does."

"You the boyfriend?"

"No. My girlfriend's at Duke. Press and I grew up together. He's like a little brother. I'm the first person he came out to. I do what I can to support him."

"He's lucky to have you."

Riley smiled, relaxing for the first time since Jamie

dropped the FBI bomb. "Glad we have you on our side too," he said. "And for the record, whatever your orientation, don't matter either. You were a great ball player, and you seem like a pretty good coach too, even if you aren't a real one."

# TWELVE

Jamie's **Ready to go** text came a half hour late. And less than a minute after Ethan's assistant buzzed to remind him of an appointment with Blake Whitehead. Blake was Jamie's prime suspect; Ethan was his. After only a few hours with him, Aidan was convinced the AD knew about and was possibly orchestrating the gambling and identify theft. Aside from the fact the guy rubbed him the wrong way, Ethan was meeting with Blake today and, according to his desk calendar Aidan had peeked at, had daily met with other basketball players the past few weeks. Not members of other teams; just the basketball players.

"Blake, he's on the basketball team, right?" Aidan asked Ethan. "Do you meet with the players often?"

"Last year, not as much." Ethan said. "The season before that, hardly ever. But with a shot at the tourney and title this year, they're getting more attention, on and off campus. From teachers and students here"—he made an encompassing gesture toward the campus outside the window, then waved the opposite direction—"to boosters, agents, and the press."

"Is that all the action you run interference for?"

"What are you implying, Mr. Daley?" By the leer in his gaze, Ethan's mind had taken a nosedive into the gutter.

Aidan dragged it out. "I'm not talking about that kind of action. I'm more interested in the kind of action involving game stats."

Eyes narrowed, Ethan pushed aside the contract they had been negotiating and leaned forward. "Betting on college athletics is against NCAA regulations."

"I'm aware," Aidan said. "I wouldn't bet on the Ravens, of course."

"What makes you think I know anything about sports gambling?"

"Everything's a bet with you. Whether or not I had manners," he said with a sly grin, laying on the charm. "How long it takes us to negotiate a contract provision. And over there"—Aidan cut his eyes to the corner table— "is a stack of betting squares from the office Super Bowl pool. You organized that?"

One corner of Ethan's mouth twitched. "And a fantasy football league."

Aidan spread his hands. "All I'm saying is, I wouldn't mind a piece of that action."

"What about the other kind of action?"

And back into the gutter they went.

Aidan silently prayed for forgiveness and canted forward, matching him leer for leer. "I agreed to dinner tonight, didn't I?"

The tips of Ethan's fingers brushed his. "Jamie know you gamble?"

"No," Aidan replied as Ethan's hand slid farther into his. "I do pick his brain from time to time about stats. The man's a walking computer, and damn good with one too."

Ethan's thumb trailed over the back of his hand. "You don't say?"

A knock on the door sent them reeling into their respective spaces. Ethan's secretary stuck her head in the office. "Blake Whitehead is here."

"We're just finishing up. Tell him to give us a minute."

She ducked out, leaving the door ajar. Aidan stood and gathered his things. "I'll expect the final contract later today."

"I have a better idea." Ethan stepped behind him and ran a hand over his backside. Stomach revolting, Aidan forced his muscles not to clench and strike in defense. "I'd like to throw a welcome party for Whiskey. Tomorrow night at my place. I'll invite the chancellor, Coach Turner, and some of the boosters. We'll have the official contract signing there. Think you could talk him into that?"

From a legal perspective, he had hoped to avoid any signing, and Jamie wouldn't want to be trotted out to boosters under false pretenses, but it was a chance to get inside Ethan's home.

To get inside his computer.

"I'll talk to Jamie about it."

"Good, I'll get back to you on the other matter of action." Ethan squeezed his ass, then moved away. "I look forward to dinner," he said with a wink.

"Me too," Aidan lied with as fake a smile as he could muster, feeling dirtier by the second. He couldn't get out of Ethan's office fast enough, nearly running into Blake in the hallway.

"Hey," Blake said, "you're Coach Walker's agent?"

"Yes, Jameson Walker's my client." Aidan held out a hand. "Ian Daley."

"Blake Whitehead." He winced a little at the grip, and Aidan tried not to smile. "How well do you know Coach Walker?"

"He's a friend."

"Your boyfriend?"

*Whoa.* Where the hell had that question come from? Had Blake overheard him and Ethan? Even if he had, why did Blake also assume Jamie was gay? Unless something had happened at practice . . .

*Fuck*, he needed a debrief, ASAP. First, though, he needed to protect Jamie and protect their cover. "Not his type," he said.

Blake harrumphed, as if stumped. After a moment, he shrugged and held out a hand. "You got a card, Mr. Daley? Might need an agent of my own soon."

An agent or another unwitting victim to his gambling and identity theft scam? Either way, it was another in. He withdrew one of his custom Ian Daley business cards. "Here you go."

Blake pocketed the card. "I'll be in touch."

Aidan waited for him to close Ethan's office door before he smirked.

*Gotcha.*

———

Jamie braced for Aidan to tear out of the administration building and harangue him for being late. His partner's mood had been decidedly dark following the run-in with

Derrick this morning. After extra time with Ethan, he could only imagine it was darker now. But the man walking toward the parking lot was anything but surly. Aidan's shoulders were relaxed, his step confident, and that damn attractive smirk graced his face.

"Why do you look like the cat who ate the canary?" Jamie asked as Aidan climbed into the Jeep.

"Ran into Blake just now. He asked for a business card. I was happy to give him one."

"I'm sure you were." Jamie chuckled. "You remember how to activate the tracking and cloning app on your phone?"

"Think so." Hunched over, head down, Aidan was already tapping at his phone. Jamie answered a few how-to questions as he hit the gas.

"I think that's got it," Aidan said a couple minutes later. "Not cloning yet, but it's tracking." He set the phone in the cup holder and sank fully into his seat. "So, interesting conversation this afternoon."

With Ethan? Jamie doubted it. "My fake contract can't be that interesting."

"I'll have you know it's a real contract I'm negotiating, for all intents and purposes, and I've put my law degree to a disgusting amount of use on your behalf."

Jamie rolled his eyes. "Tell me what Ethan had to say that was so interesting."

"Not him. Blake."

"Besides the business card?"

"He asked if I was your boyfriend."

Jamie jerked, the car briefly rumbling over the reflectors before he corrected. "Shit." Blake had said as much during their confrontation, but Jamie had deflected it. Apparently, the punk had pieced together a different truth Jamie wished was true.

Aidan angled toward him. "You wanna tell me how he got that idea?"

Despite the calm tone, Aidan had likely been just as thrown when Blake sprang that question on him. Jamie curled his hands around the wheel, knuckles white. "Press, the freshman shooting guard and Riley's best friend, is gay."

"He's out?"

Jamie nodded. "Blake gave him a hard time after Press showed him up at practice. Told him to mind his place, only with more colorful homophobic language. I stepped in and broke it up. Told Blake that was no way to speak to anyone."

Aidan reached across the armrest and grasped his biceps. "You broke up a fight. You're a coach. That's what you're supposed to do."

"Blake asked if I was 'one of them too.' I didn't tell him no."

Aidan squeezed. "Good. I'm proud of you."

It was exactly what he needed to hear. His partner had his back. "Thank you."

Aidan dropped his hand and retreated to his space. "Talk to me about practice. Anything off? Anyone besides Blake you suspect?"

The rest of the drive was spent curating their suspect list, which Aidan gave to SAC Carr once they were settled in the conference room at the local field office. "The athletic director, eight team members, including Blake and his upperclassmen crew, and one of the assistant coaches, Neil Cashman."

"What about Polk and Turner?" Carr asked. Relatively young for an SAC, the forty-year-old New Yorker wasn't afraid to take on the big names.

"I tend to agree with our source that Turner isn't involved," Jamie said.

"Polk, I'm not sure about yet," Aidan added, just as Renee hustled into the room.

"Apologies for being late."

"We only got here five minutes ago," Jamie said with a smile.

"Agents," Carr said, regaining their attention. "Please keep me posted and let me know what we can do to help. We appreciate your assistance on this."

They exchanged parting handshakes with Carr as Renee took the seat next to Grant. Jamie and Aidan filled them the rest of the way in. "It's a shame this could mar their season," Renee said. "Riley, Press, most of them are good kids."

"Good players too," Jamie said. "I saw no evidence on the court today at practice. I'll watch the game on Tuesday closely."

"So it's not really about the gambling?" Grant asked.

"I tend to agree. I think the identity theft is the driver."

Grant shifted his attention to Aidan. "Do you have an invite yet?"

Aidan shook his head.

"And we have less time than we initially thought," Jamie disclosed. "All the evidence will be wiped after the game Tuesday unless I get access to the program and either copy what we need or deactivate the kill switch."

Grant's and Renee's eyes grew wide. "I can talk to Riley

again," she said. "See if maybe he knows anyone else with an invite."

"I spoke to him after practice," Jamie said. "I let him know who we were and that we were working together. He won't be surprised if you follow up."

"On it."

"You think AD Reynolds is behind this?" Grant asked Aidan. The Charlotte agent continued to impress. He was reserved but sharp, always attentive, and quick to action when Jamie had asked for local detail and research yesterday.

"The guy's a designer suit removed from a used-car salesman," Aidan said, and Jamie tried hard not to look smug. "I told him I might be interested in a little action."

Smug fled the premises. "You told him what?"

"Of the betting kind," Aidan said, palms out. "I also told him you were good with computers. We'll see if he takes the bait, one way or the other, and yes, I think Ethan is more likely calling the shots than Blake."

"Speaking of," Jamie said as he picked up a pen and twirled it around his thumb. "You said he was outside Ethan's office when you left. Did he overhear you?"

"The door was cracked, so I'm betting on it."

Grant groaned. "You just had to go there with the pun . . ." Reserved but with a sense of humor too.

Aidan grinned. "Too good to pass up."

"If Reynolds doesn't get you the invite," Jamie said, "then maybe Blake will, now that he knows you're interested. And we'll know where he is at all times."

"How's that?" Grant asked.

"I slipped him a StickyHeel special."

"A what?" Renee asked.

"See, Agent Walker here is what cyber dorks refer to as a white hat."

"A hacker for the good guys," Grant said.

Jamie rolled his eyes. "He watches Michael Mann movies too."

Aidan cut him a glare then turned back to Grant and Renee. "The business card I gave Blake is actually two, with a device hidden between them."

"Sounds more like Bond to me," Renee said.

"Please don't inflate his ego," Aidan replied, and Jamie fought the urge to chuck the pen at him. "He picked it up at a convention he never attended."

"What's this device do?" Grant asked.

"Tracks and clones." Aidan pushed his phone across the table, app opened.

"That *is* some Bond-level shit," Renee said with a wide smile.

"Language, Renny," Grant chided.

Jamie grinned back, amused at the friends' back and forth.

"Do you know where he is?" Aidan asked.

Renee peered at the screen while Grant used two fingers to zoom and re-center the map. They worked for different agencies, but close as they seemed to be, they worked together like partners, like they had been doing this for years.

"Is that the old depot?" Grant said.

"Yeah, I think so," Renee replied. "Unfortunate but not surprising." She scooted back in the chair, an unhappy look on her face.

Grant wore one to match. "It's the old train depot in downtown Matthews."

"Suburb," Jamie clarified for Aidan.

"When trains stopped running through, it was converted to retail—a post office, grocery store, pizza parlor. By the time we went to high school, those were closed too. Now it's a cluster of abandoned buildings where local kids go to get high, vandalize stuff, and get into trouble."

"We should check it out," Aidan said.

"I can go out there with y'all tomorrow evening after shift," Renee said.

"You might have to go without us."

"Why's that?" Jamie asked.

"What would you say if I could get you a peek at Ethan's computer?"

"I'd say what's the catch?"

"You have to smile pretty for the boosters."

# THIRTEEN

Jamie was not smiling, pretty or otherwise, when Aidan dropped him at the house with ten minutes to spare before Derrick's arrival. Trying not to think about the booster dinner he had no desire to attend or Aidan's dinner date with Ethan, he scurried around the house, starting a pot of coffee, stowing their case files, getting a fire going, and changing out of his dress clothes for the second time today.

The doorbell rang in seven minutes, not the ten he had budgeted for.

Nerves getting the better of him, he struggled to get a T-shirt on over his head as he stumbled into the foyer. He yanked the shirt down and knew instantly it had been a bad idea. All of it. Walking out half-clothed, inviting Derrick over, coming back to North Carolina.

Derrick stood on the other side of the glass-paned door, eyes wide with interest, full lower lip caught between his teeth.

*Shit.*

Aidan was right. Derrick was definitely still interested, boyfriend or not.

No help for it now. Jamie tightened his jaw and opened the door. "Come in."

Hands in his pockets, Derrick stepped past him and into the dining area. "Not much has changed."

"I've been renting it out," Jamie answered. "Coffee?"

"Yes, please."

Derrick disappeared into the great room and Jamie concentrated on fixing their drinks, mundane tasks to rein in his nerves. Nerves that were shot all over again at the sight of Derrick crouched by the fireplace. He looked so delicate and beautiful in the glowing firelight it physically hurt. Angelic, Jamie had always thought, and age hadn't dulled the too apt description. The copper in his chestnut curls shone, his pale skin pinked, and when he looked over his shoulder, the red-gold flames danced in his twinkling hazel eyes.

It was like he had never left, like *they* had never left. Like Jamie had slid right back into his old life, in his old house, with the man he had intended to spend the rest of that life with. But then Derrick stood, and with his sleeves pushed to his elbows, the tattoo on his forearm reminded Jamie of the present. He cleared his throat and held out a mug, careful to keep his fingers out of the way. "For you."

Derrick smiled shyly, accepting the mug and sinking into one of the sofas. "You look good, Jamie."

"Thanks, you too." He sat on the opposite couch, mug cradled between his palms. "You've made some changes," he said with a nod to the tattoo.

Derrick ran his fingertips over the ink. "It was the first thing I did when I moved here."

"And the quote? 'To thine own self . . .' "

"Be true." Derrick glanced up. "You know what it means as well as I do."

"You're out, then?"

He nodded. "I spent enough years hiding who I am. When the CU position opened, I jumped at it. I can be me here."

"And you couldn't at Bob Jones?"

Derrick chuckled, bitter and remorseful. "It was as awful as you said it would be."

He had warned Derrick. Even in the closet, he had suspected the ultra-Christian academy would be the definition of hell on earth for a beautiful young gay man like Derrick. With professorships scarce at the time, Derrick had believed he had to take it and had accepted without talking to Jamie first. Still, he hated that Derrick's experience there lived up to his worst expectations. "I'm sorry."

"Don't be." Derrick leaned forward and set his mug on the table between them. "I'm the one who should be apologizing."

"You don't have—"

"Let me say this, Jameson. I never thought I'd get the chance."

He nodded and took a fortifying gulp of coffee.

"I'm sorry you felt you had to leave," Derrick started.

"I made that choice."

"And I made a choice that put you there, put us there." He stood, rounded the table, and sat a cushion over from Jamie. "We were partners. We should have made that choice together or found a different one to make. I should have loved you enough to see that."

Jamie didn't want to talk of love with Derrick. Nor did

he want Derrick to take all the blame for an end that was both their doing. "I had my reasons too. I didn't want to be an out player in the NBA."

"If I'd decided to teach elsewhere, even high school for a few years, somewhere we could be out together, would you have reconsidered?"

Jamie couldn't say. It unnerved him to think that if he had stuck it out, if Derrick hadn't taken the job at Bob Jones, then maybe he wouldn't have left. Maybe Derrick would have blossomed into the man he was now, and Jamie would have been brave enough to come out as a professional gay athlete. That wasn't what had happened, though. But on a day when Jamie's head hadn't stopped spinning from one extreme to the other—being back in his home, first with Aidan this morning and now with Derrick, a coaching career he had never considered followed by a meeting at the FBI field office where he had been jarred back into agent mode—a heaping pile of what-might-have-beens had him eyeing the stocked bar at the opposite end of the room.

"No issues here or at CU?" he deflected.

Derrick looked like he was going to call him on it but, after a long moment, reached for his coffee again. "No problems so far, even with the political climate being what it is. CU's pretty liberal. Not like Chapel Hill but a far cry from Bob Jones. I'm a faculty advisor for the Gender and Sexuality Alliance on campus."

The last was said with a wide smile and Jamie returned it. "That's great, Derrick. And the professorship, your classes, are going well?"

"Now you've done it." Grinning, he toed off his shoes, settled in the far corner of the couch, legs crossed under him, and regaled Jamie with classroom anecdotes.

Jamie had asked the question intentionally, seeking neutral ground. He remembered how much Derrick loved teaching. Their discussion flowed beyond CU—to their families, old friends, and travel. Curled on the couch, warmed by the fire and coffee, the sense of home crept up on Jamie again.

*Like they had never left.*

Until he glanced at the fire and Aidan's cuff links shimmered on the mantel. He had taken them off and rolled up his sleeves when starting the fire earlier. Following his gaze, Derrick's smile dimmed. He opened his mouth to ask the question, and Jamie beat him to another. "You said you're seeing someone?"

"Yes, but it's not serious. Not like we were." When Jamie didn't rise to the bait, he added, "And you and Ian?"

"Just friends."

Derrick ducked his head and ran a hand through his curls. "Earlier today, he seemed . . . protective."

As uncomfortable as this conversation was, Jamie had agreed to meet Derrick to shore up his cover. Bearing that in mind, he answered with as much truth as possible while preserving the story. "We were friends before I signed with him. He talked me through the decision to return. He knows what's at stake and how nervous I am about my sexuality getting splashed across the headlines."

Derrick drew up his knees and wrapped his arms around his shins. "So when your ex showed up out of the blue . . ."

"He went into crisis mode. It's what he does." Understatement of the year.

"And he's staying here at the house?"

Jamie nodded. "While we finalize the contracts and I get resettled."

"This is for real, then?" Derrick said, eyes brightening. "You're really back?"

"I missed the game, and I missed North Carolina." None of that was a lie, and that sick what-might-have-been merry-go-round restarted.

Derrick ramped up the speed. "Could you play again if you wanted to?"

Jamie hadn't allowed himself to think that far, had blocked the very thought from his mind, but there it was, glowing in the firelight next to the other vestige of his prior life. The life he could reclaim if he wanted it.

He dodged again. "I'm out of practice and getting old."

"Tim Duncan played until he was forty."

"Still a fan, are you?"

"You ruined me for all other sports." It was said with affection, but it reminded Jamie of everything else he had ruined.

He owed Derrick an apology too. "You were a big part of that life, and I am sorry for my part in blowing it up."

"Thank you." Derrick laid his cheek against his knees, face soft and beautiful, inviting. "It's good to have you home."

"It's good to be home."

It wasn't a lie.

# FOURTEEN

Shoulder to the jamb of the great room door, Aidan stood and admired the cut body of his partner. Jamie was dressed casually in jeans and a tee and leaning over the pool table. He struck the cue ball hard. It crashed into the triangle of tightly racked balls, sending stripes and solids scattering, not one falling into a pocket. Two end taps on the floor, chalk on the tip, and Jamie took another shot, hitting the cue ball hard and sending it around the world, knocking the felt-covered inside of each rail without hitting a single other ball.

Add pool to the very short list of things Jameson Walker was bad at.

"I'm surprised," Aidan said, and Jamie muffed his next shot. "I thought mathematicians were supposed to be good at pool."

"The geometry and physics geeks, yes." Jamie circled the antique beauty, hand trailing the wide wooden rail. "The ones and zeroes nerds like me, not so much." He lined up another shot, clipped a ball, and proved his point, pocketing nothing.

Aidan skirted past him, toward the bar, and stopped short at seeing an open bottle of Johnnie Walker Blue. "Special occasion?"

Jamie didn't answer, just whiffed at another ball.

So coffee with Derrick had gone that well.

Aidan poured two fingers' worth for himself, figuring he would need alcohol for this too. Glass in hand, he sifted through the professional-grade pool cues in the wall-mounted rack. He withdrew one and rolled it in his palm, testing its weight and balance. Good enough. He threw back the rest of his whisky and banged the glass down on the bar. "Rack 'em."

Jamie shot him a tired, unamused glare, like all he wanted was to be left alone. Aidan was sure he would refuse the offered game. A beat later, though, he propped his stick against the table, grabbed the wooden triangle, and arranged the balls inside. Mission begrudgingly accomplished, he returned to the bar and took a long swallow straight from the bottle.

"You want to tell me about this special occasion?" Aidan asked.

"Not really."

Time for evasive maneuvers.

Aidan went to the head of the table, lined up his shot, and broke, scattering the balls wide and pocketing none. "Your shot."

Jamie had to surrender the bottle to take it. Steps heavy, he loped over to the table, picked up his stick, and aimed for the hardest shot on the table when a dozen other easier ones waited. He really didn't know what he was doing.

Neither did Aidan with a Jamie like this. Broody, quiet, resigned. He would gladly take the Jamie who had screamed in his face last week over this one. "Pool's not your game?" Aidan ventured.

"No, I just loved the table."

"It's antique?"

"From 1918."

Aidan took another shot and missed, cutting short Jamie's return to the bottle.

"You're missing on purpose."

He didn't deny it, merely shrugged and stepped out of Jamie's way.

"How'd the date with the AD go?" Jamie asked.

"Ethan," Aidan said, and Jamie missed the cue ball. "He knows something. I'm working a potential suspect."

"Working." He took a second shot at the ball, hit it full force, and sent it around the world again.

Aidan's anger rose with each hit rail. What right did Jamie have to be angry at him? He had set a date with Derrick first. "How was coffee with your ex?"

"Why do you care?"

"You're drinking fifty-dollar-a-glass scotch straight from the bottle. Something's wrong. I care."

"It's my house, my whisky, back the fuck off."

"Jamie—"

"And stop that."

Direct hit, right to the gut. It was several long seconds before Aidan regained his breath and words. "Is Derrick going to be a problem?"

Jamie's laugh was colder than the winter breeze outside. "You have no idea." He went for the bottle again and Aidan snatched it away.

"Talk to me, dammit."

"Your shot," Jamie said with a dead-eyed stare. He shuffled behind the bar, moved around bottles, and came back with a Pappy 23.

Now that was stepping over the line. Gut punches be damned.

Aidan lined up behind the cue ball, sank a stripe, then proceeded to run the table, one shot after another, every stripe cleanly into a pocket until there were none left. He tossed his cue onto the table. Jaw on the floor, Jamie didn't protest when he filched the bottle of Pappy. "You are definitely not going to guzzle this. Now talk." Instead, Jamie turned away and Aidan grabbed his arm, drawing him back around. "What happened with Derrick?"

Jamie's gaze shot to his hand. "He bought the cover. He knows how much I loved the game."

"So, is it Derrick you're upset about or being back on the court?"

Chin lifting, Jamie held his gaze another long moment, then all the short-lived fight rushed out of him, and he was back to downtrodden. He surrendered his stick and climbed onto a barstool, propping his elbows on the bar and hanging his head in his hands. "I thought I was doing the right thing. Leaving the game, getting my doctorate, joining the FBI. And I'm good at what I do now."

Aidan returned both cues to the rack, then poured two tumblers of Pappy and slid one under Jamie's nose. "You're damn good at what you do. That doesn't lessen the fact you were damn good on the court too."

"I didn't realize until today how much I missed it."

Aidan swallowed hard, his stomach knotting. Focused on Jamie's fear of exposure, he hadn't considered the possibility his partner might want to reclaim his old life. A life that included the sport he loved, a beautiful home, a beautiful ex-lover. A life that didn't include him.

"You regret your choice?" Aidan asked, fearing the answer. He would never regret it. Jamie's choice had brought them together, for better or worse. It would hurt, if Jamie's answer was yes, but it also hurt seeing him this miserable.

Jamie looked at him with resigned eyes. A hole began to open in Aidan's chest, but then Jamie shook his head and Aidan breathed again.

"No, I don't regret it," he said. "I was unhappy, Derrick was unhappy, the both of us always looking over our shoulders and questioning each other's decisions. It was a bad situation all around. Basketball was all I'd known for so many years. I needed the break. I needed to see what else, who else, life had to offer. And what we do is important."

"Back to my question, then . . . Is Derrick going to be a problem?"

"He's got a boyfriend."

"You're pretty hard to resist, Whiskey."

Jamie stared into his glass. "And yet not enough to hold your interest."

"It's not about that and you know it."

"Doesn't mean I have to like it." He tossed back the rest of his bourbon. "Still fucking hurts."

Aidan curled a hand around the back of his neck, squeezing gently. "Jamie—"

Cold, hard eyes cut in his direction and Jamie batted his hand away. "I said stop it." He tempered the harsh words with a softer, "Please," then added, "At least for tonight. I can't handle it. Not on four hours of sleep, and not with everything else today."

Aidan retreated to his stool, hands clasped in his lap. "I'm sorry," he whispered, the words terribly inadequate.

"Are you interested in Ethan?" Jamie picked up his empty glass and rolled it in his hands. "What you said before we left, about your type . . . tall, blue eyes, built. He's all those things."

*But he's not you*, Aidan wanted to say, but after Jamie's outburst, he held his words and his hands. "I have no interest in him. I'm here to work and back you up as your partner and, if you'll allow me, as your friend. You have a problem, talk to me, please. Do not drown it in top-shelf alcohol. That's not like you, on either account."

"You don't know the old me."

Aidan followed Jamie's gaze to the fully stocked bar.

"Why does a guy who only drinks on special occasions have a bar like that?"

"Renters."

"Renters don't stock top-shelf, and you bought a house with a bar in it."

Jamie's smile was small and sad. "Housekeeping brought it out when I asked them to ready the house. The game room, the bar, the alcohol . . ." He waved a hand at their surroundings. "It was a way to fit in, to distract my teammates if they ever got too close to the truth. And I used to like it."

"What changed?"

"I was hungover the day I got injured."

"Shit."

"Yeah, shit." He reached over the bar and set his glass in the sink, then slid off the barstool. "Speaking of work . . ."

He headed for the door and when Aidan, too jarred by the abrupt change in tone and topic, didn't budge, he beckoned with a head tilt.

Jamie led him down the long hallway to the farthest room at the back of the house. The door was closed and secured by a keypad.

"Did you move the case stuff back here?" Aidan asked. The dining table had been smartly cleaned off for Derrick's visit.

Jamie punched in the code and opened the door. "No, I stuffed those case files in the Tupperware drawer."

Aidan's chuckle turned into a shocked gasp as he took in the half-moon-shaped study. In front of him, three sets of windows jutted out in a semicircle, an oak desk positioned in the open floor space. To the right were two leather chairs and a round matching ottoman scattered with legal files and pens. To the left, a massive television and gaming system. And on the long, straight wall behind him, built-in shelves full of books, movies, vinyl records, sports trophies, and other memorabilia. Aidan studied the awards, his hand running over a wood-and-brass replica of the NCAA championship trophy.

"This is incredible, Ja—Walker." The old name already felt wrong.

Busy behind the desk, Jamie didn't notice his correction. "I know it's risky in a rental, but I didn't want to move all this when I left. I was back here occasionally when I was at MIT and Quantico, and then in an apartment when I first moved to San Francisco. I figured it was safer here behind lock and keypad. Haven't had a chance to move it since I bought the place in Bernal."

Or was he holding out hope of moving back here one

day? Keeping the house and his most prized possessions in it?

"Sorry, I just want to print these out," Jamie said as the printer cranked to life.

Aidan flopped down in one of the oversize chairs. "If our other case files are in the kitchen drawer of doom, what's back here?"

Jamie grabbed several sheets from the printer tray and placed them on the ottoman, then dropped into the other chair.

Aidan pulled the papers closer. When he realized what they were—documents related to KAG Holdings—guilt and apprehension warred for dominance. As intended, the Renaud investigation had taken a backseat to the CU matter. But of course Jamie had pulled double duty and continued to work on it.

"I'm sorry I didn't show you this sooner," he said. "I meant to this morning, but Grant and Renee showed up early, and with everything else today . . ."

Aidan sucked in a breath. Every time they circled back to this case, another shoe from the endless supply in the sky dropped. "What have you found?"

"You actually gave me the idea, or rather, Ian Daley did."

"Go on."

Jamie's hands flew into motion, grabbing the papers and spreading them out on the ottoman. Aidan wanted to smile at the familiar, frenetic debrief, at Jamie's previous despondence fading away, but he held it in, not wanting the reprieve to vanish. "I started digging into Mason West. I found a paralegal at a firm in Palo Alto named Martin Westley. Check out the signatures."

Jamie pointed at Mason West's signature on the KAG formation documents he had unlocked last weekend and at Martin Westley's signature on an SEC filing for a different company. Aidan picked up the two pieces of paper and laid one on top of the other, lining up the signatures. The pen strokes on the *M* and *W* were identical. In fact, all first four letters of the last names matched. "Same person," he agreed. "Which firm?"

"Eldridge Park & Cole."

A bullet ran up Aidan's spine and he shot out of his chair.

"Irish, what's that name mean to you?"

"Gabe worked with Eldridge all the time. So does my family."

Jamie flinched, hard, no doubt as startled as him by the connection, but he recovered quickly. "How could Gabe or your family not? They're one of the big three in the Valley."

"Not helping, Whiskey." He made a valid point. Anyone who worked in Silicon Valley, especially in finance or large-scale commercial transactions, had dealings with at least one, if not all, of the three biggest law firms there, including Eldridge. But Aidan was done with coincidences. "Out of those three, and the countless other wannabes, my dead husband and my family just happen to use the same firm as the terrorist trying to kill me?"

"We don't know for sure Renaud's connected to Eldridge." Jamie picked up a pen and spun it around his thumb. "Maybe it's just where Martin Westley happens to work, and Renaud got to him some other way. Maybe it has nothing to do with you."

"Only one way to find out."

"We can make an approach as soon as we get back."

Aidan wasn't waiting that long. "I have a better idea." He pulled out his phone, scrolled to Danny's number, and dialed. As it rang, he snatched the pen from Jamie's hand to twirl around his own and tossed the phone on the ottoman, speaker activated.

Just before voicemail picked up, Danny answered with a winded, "Hey, big bro."

"You up for some more hapless civilian consulting?"

"Hell yes," he said, while a familiar, exasperated voice, murmured, "Down, boy."

Aidan hung his head, a little exasperated himself and more than a little amused at how tangled his life had become. "You have company, baby bro. If I need to call back later . . ."

"Nah, we're good," Danny replied, a satisfied leer in his voice.

A pop—a palm hitting flesh—preceded Mel's irritated, "For fuck's sake, Daniel."

Wide-eyed, Jamie gasped and stared at the phone like it was poisonous. Aidan laughed, only taking the phone off mute once his hilarity subsided.

"What've you got for me, Ai?" Danny said.

"Boss lady?" Aidan asked.

"He's going to be insufferable now," Mel said. "You might as well proceed."

Aidan had to tread carefully. Danny had heard Renaud's name last September, had seen what the terrorist was capable of when they had faced down a bomb together, but he didn't know the connection went deeper than an isolated terror threat. For his safety and because Aidan needed to tell the whole story to his family in person, when he had all of it, he kept the details vague. "I need you to look into a paralegal at Eldridge."

"Well, what do you know? I've got an appointment with Preston Cole tomorrow. Maybe I'll take my friend, Melissa, who is interested in getting her estate in order."

Another pop, then Mel stole the phone. "Who are we looking for?"

"Martin Westley," Aidan answered. "Works in corporate."

"Profile?"

"Thirty-two," Jamie said. "Comes from money. Law school burnout who traveled for a while before coming home and getting his paralegal certification."

"And a job at one of the Valley's top firms," Mel said.

"Nothing suspicious about that at all."

"What am I missing?" Danny chimed in.

"We'll explain when Aidan gets home," Mel said, in a voice softer than her norm. Maybe Danny wasn't the only one getting serious. "Jamie, pull financials."

"Already on it. Travel records too."

"I'll see what I can do to expedite."

"Mel, be careful," Aidan cautioned. These were two of the most important people in his life. They'd had one close call already. He would rather they not have another, especially when he was clear across the country. "Don't let him know you're on to him."

"Wha—" Danny started.

"We got it," Mel said, then ended the call.

Aidan turned the phone facedown and tossed the pen aside. "Anything else?" he asked, and Jamie diverted his gaze to the floor. "Hey, Whiskey, don't drop back into surly mode. Tell me what else."

"I'm sorry."

"For what?"

"Not having the whole story for you."

Aidan wanted to brush the hair off his forehead. He sat on his hands instead. "You're running point on the CU case, and you still got us a lead on Renaud. That's more of the story than we had yesterday." An ugly, scary story as it was turning out to be, but at least they were getting somewhere. So long as they didn't get buried under falling shoes. "We need to be careful. Mel, Danny, and you."

"I'm not a civilian."

"I know, but you're important to me, so are they, and Renaud's targeted me three times. If any of you get caught in the crossfire . . ."

"And what if that bull's-eye lands on you? You don't think that'll affect me?"

All Aidan wanted to do was reach out and pull Jamie into his arms. Apologize for being a fool. Kiss him. Make love to him right there on the study floor. Promise him he would always be there.

But he couldn't do those things and he couldn't make that promise.

He dug his fingers into the leather chair. "Let's just both try to not get dead."

# FIFTEEN

For as tired as Jamie had been after Sunday's nonstop roller coaster, a good night's rest was elusive. His subconscious plagued his dreams with all the wrong ways the press conference and first practice—and the altercation afterward—could have gone. Spliced among the nightmares were alternating flashes of angelic Derrick by the fire and devilish Aidan appearing in front of him at the airport. And all the half dozen times he'd jolted awake, it was to the phantom feel of Aidan's hand around his neck and his lips against his, as if Aidan had acted on that split second last night when Jamie could have sworn Aidan had been about to kiss him.

When his phone alarm finally woke him for real, Jamie was more tired than when he'd gone to sleep. And he was hard too. A problem he took care of in the shower, his fist shuttling up and down his cock in desperate strokes, only the redheaded Irish devil behind his eyelids as he came with a muffled groan.

He stifled another groan when he stepped out of the

steam-filled bathroom to familiar aromas sneaking into the bedroom and tickling his nose. Familiar sounds trickled in from the other side of the door. Something sizzling in a pan, the gurgling coffeemaker, the angry strains of Irish punk rock. The moment stopped him in his tracks. He and Aidan hadn't shared a morning like this since Galveston. Back in the Bay, Aidan had always left his bed after they'd had sex, never staying the night, never the morning. He hadn't been in Jamie's bed last night, but he was in his home this morning, cooking him breakfast like he belonged here.

And the roller coaster started again.

"Walker!" Aidan shouted. "We need to be out the door in ten."

*Walker*. Not *Jamie*. Like Jamie had asked. He shook his head, jostling himself out of his stasis and slinging water all over the hardwood floor. Whatever was happening on the other side of the door was just Aidan being a good roommate, a good FBI partner. Nothing more. And Jamie needed to be a good partner too.

He dropped his towel, cleaned the water off the floor, and hustled to dress. He snagged a pair of tennis shoes from the bottom of his closet, went to shove his foot in one, and was reminded of what he'd tucked inside. He tipped the shoe up, the Carolina blue leather key chain with its distinctive metal medallion and the single key on the ring falling into the palm of his hand.

The roller coaster picked up speed, resuming last night's ride. His old life in his hand, his new life in the kitchen outside his bedroom door. He closed his fingers around the key chain, an idea coming to mind, a way to at least make these two parts of his life work together.

He finished putting on his shoes, finger-combed his hair,

then started for the kitchen, wallet and keys in his pocket. He found Aidan behind the stove, Jamie's UNC apron over his jeans and sinfully tight Henley of the day.

He flicked off the burner, a slice of cheese melting over what looked and smelled like country ham, pulled pork, and eggs. He glanced over his shoulder at Jamie, and his brown eyes grew wide. "Whoa."

Jamie tried slicking back his hair once more. Not that fiddling with the overlong strands would do anything for the bags under his eyes. "Sleep seems to have deserted me."

Aidan set aside the spatula and reached for the travel mug waiting by the coffeemaker. "Red-eye with a double shot," he said as he held the mug out to Jamie.

Jamie took a sip and groaned, his eyelids fluttering closed. The extra strong brew was exactly what he needed. When he opened his eyes again, Aidan was scooping the meat, eggs, and cheese out of the skillet and onto a toasted sub roll slathered in mustard and a row of pickles.

"You cooked too," Jamie said, obvious about all he had the brain power for until the caffeine kicked in.

"You worked your ass off yesterday, which was a long, hard day for multiple reasons." He left the spatula flat on one side, then folded the other half of the sandwich over it before sliding the spatula out. "This seemed like the least I could do." He tossed the spatula in the sink, then began wrapping the parchment paper below the sandwich around it. "You took forever in the shower, though, so you'll need to eat yours on the go." He handed Jamie the wrapped sub. "Cubano, as best I could make it with what you had in the fridge. Plus an egg because breakfast."

Jamie glanced at his coffee in one hand and the sandwich in the other, warmth seeping into him from each, and from the consideration. "Thank you," he said quietly.

"I just hope . . ."

He jerked his gaze back up. "Hope what?"

Aidan nodded at the items in his hands. "That those make you feel a little more like yourself today."

*Like himself.*

Which he'd decided today needed to be Jameson Walker, past and present. "Did you already eat yours?" he asked as Aidan put the last of the dishes and utensils in the dishwasher.

"Yeah, I'll drive." He wiped his hands on the apron, then removed it over his head. He tossed it on the end of the island as he walked around it. "You got the Jeep keys?"

Jamie balanced the sandwich and coffee in one hand and dug the key chain he'd discovered that morning out of his pocket. He tossed it to his partner, who deftly caught it. Then stared at it with even bigger eyes than he'd stared at Jamie minutes ago. If the red, white, and blue logo hadn't given it away, *Chevelle* in its distinctive script across the medallion would. "This isn't the key to the Jeep."

"No, it's not."

Those wide eyes lifted, the autumn practically aglow, as Aidan gazed at him like Jamie had given him the best gift ever. The sheer joy on his handsome face was gorgeous, second only to seeing that same face in blissed-out ecstasy.

"Don't tease me. You said *never*."

"I need be both Agent Walker and Whiskey Walker today, on the court and at that booster party tonight. The Chevelle will help. But the last thing I need is to wrap it around a tree because I fall asleep at the wheel, so . . ." He nodded at the key in Aidan's hand. "Never say never."

"You're sure?"

He nodded, and in the blink of an eye, Aidan skirted past him, grabbed his coat off the foyer bench, and yanked open the garage stairs door. "I'm going before you change your mind." He disappeared down the stairs and Jamie laughed as he followed in Aidan's excited wake, that warm feeling in his chest growing more intense and comforting him for the day ahead.

# SIXTEEN

The morning's comfort only lasted so long. Monday's practice was an absolute mindfuck. No other word for it. Worse than all of Sunday's ups and downs. Jamie struggled to do his job on the court while Ethan and Aidan observed, his partner never more than a few feet from the AD.

Jamie had been through undercover training at Academy, but seeing an agent as skilled as Aidan put those lessons into practice boggled his mind. All that Aidan Talley purpose and arrogance channeled into suave, charming Ian Daley. Shoulders back, he walked with a casual strut instead of his usual determined stride and his smile, while artificially wide, was no less bright and brilliant. He shook all the right hands and spoke to all the coaches, assistants, and players, spending longer and flashing more bling with Blake and his crew. As for staying in Ethan's orbit, the maneuver gave the impression of interest while allowing Aidan to listen to their suspect's conversations.

Jamie understood all that; didn't mean he liked it.

Nor did he like the prospect of attending Ethan's welcome party. After Aidan dropped him off and went to park the Chevelle, Jamie stood on the sidewalk outside the AD's giant brick colonial, unwilling to enter. Pretending to be a coach on the court was one thing. There he felt like he at least knew what he was doing, like he wasn't a complete fraud. Pretending to be a coach at a party full of donors, swindling them out of their money, was a whole different story.

"I told you to go on inside while I parked the car," Aidan said, rounding the corner at a trot, his pale cheeks rosy. "It's fucking freezing."

The chill outside couldn't touch the cold spreading through Jamie's veins, obliterating the morning's warmth. He stared blankly ahead, up the walk toward the brightly lit house. "I can't do this."

"Yes, you can." Aidan led him off the sidewalk and into the shadow of a huge oak tree. "Marcus, Riley, and Press beat Blake's crew in that scrimmage today. I think they can win it all without them. You want that, don't you?"

Jamie nodded. "They're good. They've got a shot. The whole team shouldn't be punished because Blake's a greedy punk."

"Then we're going to go in there and make that happen."

So certain, in the job and the cover.

"How do you do it?" Jamie asked. "Switch back and forth so easily."

Aidan waved a hand at his smart-casual appearance—windblown auburn hair, checkered scarf artfully draped around his neck, fitted wool overcoat cinched tight. He looked as comfortable in Ian's attire as he did in Aidan's three-piece suits. "Ian's just a cover, like any other cover I've assumed for a case." Stepping closer, he lowered his voice and laid a gloved hand over his chest. "I know who *I* am. Aidan Talley. Widower, son, brother, uncle, godfather, surly Irish expat." He grinned. "FBI field agent and Jameson Walker's partner."

Jamie tried to return the gesture but failed, his smile nearly as weak as his knees, made so by Aidan's words and the daunting situation. "But *Whiskey* isn't just a cover. He's part of me. He—*I*—could have had this life."

Aidan's long, slow exhale formed a cloud of mist in the frigid air between them. "You still can."

Stomach protesting, Jamie closed his eyes and rested back against the tree trunk, heedless of the bark making a mess of his hair.

"Save it for later," Aidan said. "For now, don't think of Agent Walker and Whiskey Walker as two separate identities."

Brow furrowed, Jamie righted his gaze. "But you just said—"

Aidan lifted a hand, stretched it toward his face, then stopped. All day, outside the company of others, Aidan had referred to him as "Walker" and kept his hands to himself, respecting his demand of last night. Jamie fucking hated it. He had needed that space then, wrung out and exhausted as he had been by the too long day full of surprises. And he had needed to get the remnants of anger at Aidan out of his system, but now he needed him close, needed his touch, needed his "Jamie." Partner, friend, lover—whatever Aidan could give—to help steady him while his life spun out of control.

As if sensing his desperation, Aidan let the trailing hand

land on his lapel instead, right over his tattoo, and the heat from his hand warmed through leather and wool, centering Jamie. "You're still Agent Walker," Aidan said, holding his gaze. "But you're going to go in there and do your Whiskey Walker thing. You're going to smile, you're going to schmooze, right through that crowd so we can get to Ethan's computer, deactivate the kill switch, get what we need to close this case and protect your players. Make sure they get a chance." He pressed more firmly, and Jamie lifted his own gloved hand, laying it over Aidan's. "Marcus at the draft, Riley at State, Press during tomorrow's game. Protect and serve."

Laughter bubbled out of Jamie. "That's the LAPD's motto."

Aidan smirked, his autumn eyes dancing.

Jamie rolled his eyes. "Fucking Michael Mann." He clutched Aidan's hand tighter, belying his dramatic annoyance. "Thank you."

Aidan's smirk smoothed into a warm, confident smile. "Ready, partner?"

"Ready."

Aidan's words, even the ridiculous ones, carried Jamie through the next hour. Through Ethan and Chancellor Polk parading him around like a show dog. Through recounting his player glory days with nearly everyone. Through shoptalk with Turner and one of his former Carolina coaches in attendance.

He endured each posturing handshake, each forced smile, each interminable conversation, while Aidan slipped in and out of the main party area, scoping out the rest of the house. He would return to his side every few minutes, whispering that another room or wing of the house was clear. When he disappeared for an extended period, Jamie began to worry until Aidan strolled down the main stairs, arm in arm with Ethan. He had put himself back together well enough for the casual observer, but one glance and Jamie knew exactly what he had been doing with the AD.

His stomach revolted and the roar of blood In his ears muted the surrounding noise. Gazes locked, he was too angry to interpret the message in Aidan's.

"Whiskey," Ethan said, "are you having as much fun as I am?"

Jamie gritted his teeth and forced back the venom on the tip of his tongue. "Tons," he managed, voice leaving no doubt as to the opposite.

Ethan eyed him with alarm, whether for himself or CU's boosters, who were easing back a step, Jamie didn't know or care.

"How about some drinks?" Aidan said, distracting the target of Jamie's rage.

Taking stock of the skittish, perhaps offended, boosters, Ethan quickly put his car-salesman smile back on. "Yes, we'll toast to the finalized contract," he said, loud enough for everyone to hear, then under his breath, only loud enough for the three of them, added to Aidan, "Get your client in line."

As Ethan was swallowed by the excited crowd, accepting congratulatory handshakes and backslaps, Aidan steered Jamie into the foyer.

"Nothing happened."

Jamie glared—at the ruffled hair, dilated pupils, and plumped lips. "I know what you look like when you've been kissed."

"Nothing happened except a kiss," Aidan corrected, and

Jamie growled. He had no right to be angry—they were over—but last night, Aidan had said he wasn't interested in Ethan. "Cover, Walker, remember? Ethan caught me in his office upstairs. I had to pretend I was there to discuss your contract."

"And you celebrated with a kiss?"

"I distracted him with a kiss when he asked if I'd watched him enter his password, which by the way is, bluedevils1, all lowercase."

Jamie wrinkled his nose. "I didn't think it was possible to hate him more."

"Yeah, well, get in line." Aidan wiped the back of his hand over his mouth, and Jamie understood the message in his eyes from before. Disgust, and a commitment to the job in spite of it. "Get upstairs. Third door on the right."

"I'll be back in five, ten at most." He turned for the marble staircase and was stopped short by Aidan's fingers around his wrist.

"Keep your phone in view. I'll text if anyone heads upstairs." Aidan squeezed, heat blistering skin, then with a nod, released his hand and faded into the crowd.

Jamie took the stairs two at a time as he coached his brain back into agent mode. He had limited time to deactivate the kill switch and copy the files they needed, if they were on Ethan's computer. If Ethan was even involved. This whole plan, their investigation, hinged on the AD's complicity. Jamie didn't doubt he was dirty; the question was how dirty.

Steps muffled by the carpeted hallway, Jamie hustled to the study door. He closed it behind him and scanned the room, locating the desk and computer. Before sitting behind it, he opened the interior door on the adjacent wall, revealing an attached bath that led to another bedroom. Perfect escape route. He left the getaway doors open, then returned to the desk, woke the computer, and entered the password Aidan had spied.

Searching through the file directory, he hit pay dirt on the fifth folder. Program files for the gambling portal. He opened the program and smiled when Ethan's username and password autofilled. At a minimum, he was a user. Jamie logged in, then hacked the program's code, neutralizing the kill switch that had been crudely programmed to sync to the countdown clock. It would appear to the coconspirators that their program was still counting down, but the kill switch wouldn't actually activate, fooling them long enough to give him and Aidan a chance to gather evidence and trace the program's source.

That done, Jamie inserted a flash drive and made a copy of the program files. He next searched for the spyware. If buried deep where a user wouldn't normally find them, then maybe the AD was just a victim. Doubtful. If the spyware files were readily accessible, though . . .

Jamie's phone vibrated on the desktop.

**GET OUT, NOW**, read the text from Aidan.

Jamie halted and cocked an ear toward the door. The second floor remained silent. He had at least another minute and an escape route ready. He continued clicking through directories. Nothing, but if the gambling program was there, the spyware ghost had to be as well. He searched every likely file name and extension. He was scanning the results when another text from Aidan appeared.

**INCOMING. GTFO NOW.**

Standing, he leaned over the computer and read faster. Three lines from the bottom—an encrypted file—that had to be it. He copied it onto to the flash drive, ripped the stick out of the computer, and pocketed it with his phone.

The knob turned.

The door was pushed open.

He wiped the computer's history, closed the search window, and bolted for the bathroom door.

"Jamie?"

He froze, one hand on the knob.

*Fuck.*

Jamie turned and laid eyes on the person who kept showing up at the worst possible moments. "Derrick, what are you doing here?"

Dressed in charcoal slacks and a black sweater, his ex looked like an angelic harbinger of doom. Sounded like it too with his next declaration. "I live here."

Jamie struggled for words. "Excuse me?"

Derrick nodded toward the window. "In the guest house, on the grounds. Ethan rents it out." His eyes swept the study before landing back on Jamie. "What are you doing here?"

*Breathe. Think. Cover.*

"I needed to get away from the crowd downstairs."

"It's a bit much," Derrick said with an understanding smile. "Ethan's parties always are."

"I should get back." He started for the hallway door, and Derrick leaned back, closing it.

"You said you needed to get away." He folded his arms and crossed his ankles. "So stay, Jamie, and tell me what's wrong."

Go with the truth, or as much of it as possible. Easier than spinning a lie. That's what he'd learned in Academy. But what if the truth wasn't easy either? He backpedaled to the front of the desk, fingers curling around the molded wood edge. "Being back on the court, back in this life, is harder than I thought." Two days and the second-guessing merry-go-round had spun him dizzy.

"I know what you mean." Derrick pushed off the door, crossed the room, and sat next to him. "Maneuvering through the crowd downstairs was surreal, like a highlight reel past and present. I saw Coach McGhee. First time since the day after you won the second championship. You remember that morning?"

Jamie smiled, recalling everything about that week. It had been the best in his twenty-one-year-old life. The game, the second title, the welcome home party. "It was what, four in the morning, when we landed at RDU?"

"To a crowd of adoring fans."

"I can't believe that many people showed up."

"If they were like me, they hadn't slept the night before."

Neither had he on the flight home, too keyed up from the win. "It was a good night."

"And morning." Derrick peered at him through thick lashes, his eyes hot and cheeks red.

Remembering that morning, Jamie felt his own face heat. Derrick had waited off to the side and Jamie had broken away long enough to bang his boyfriend in the car in a dark corner of the parking garage.

"You haven't returned my texts." Derrick slid closer, their arms brushing. His presence and warmth were so familiar, despite the eight-year absence. "I didn't mean to surprise you tonight."

Jamie had ignored the messages. He didn't need the extra dizzying rounds, and Aidan had been right. Derrick carried a torch, and it was blazing bright tonight. "You could have said in your texts that you'd be here."

"But then you might not have come." He lifted a hand and traced the shell of Jamie's ear with his fingertips—just like he'd done that long-ago morning in the car. Jamie trembled. "And I might not have gotten the chance."

"What chance?"

"To do this."

Delicate fingers curled lightly around his neck and drew Jamie down. His lips met Derrick's in a slow, gentle kiss. Lulled into nostalgia, Jamie expected the kiss to feel like home. Derrick still tasted like spring, even in the dead of winter, and he kissed with the same sweet shyness that had first attracted Jamie. But there was no blinding need, no lingering coffee or whiskey taste, no layers of darkness and light.

It wasn't the kiss he wanted.

Jamie jerked away, then tempered his abrupt withdrawal with a hand on Derrick's face. "I can't."

Luminous hazel eyes stared back at him. "There's someone else?"

Yes, but he couldn't compromise their cover. And he didn't know if there really was. "No."

"Then why not?"

"You have a boyfriend."

"It's casual."

Jamie dropped his hand and turned away. Fuck, he hated that word. Hated the whole concept. And Derrick of all people knew he didn't do casual. Neither had the old Derrick. He might have been in the closet, but he had been a one-man guy.

"Look at me, please."

Jamie turned back, meeting his earnest gaze. "What we had is over," Jamie said. "That was a different lifetime for me."

"Yet here you are, living that life again. Tonight with the boosters, last night at the house, on the court at practice."

"You were there?"

"I might have watched from the tunnel."

Jamie bowed his head, and Derrick laid a hand on his neck. "You love the game, Jamie. You always did. Look how easily you slid back into it and into being home. You belong here." He squeezed and Jamie looked up. "With me."

Just like everything else—the court, the house, Charlotte in general—being back with Derrick had all the trappings of home without the heart of it.

Because there was no Aidan. "This isn't—"

"You're lying to yourself if you think otherwise."

He shook off the hold. "That's rich, coming from you."

Derrick pushed up his sleeves, the forearm tattoo on full display. "I'm not lying anymore." He reached for him again, and Jamie stood, though not fast enough. Derrick grasped his wrist and held him in place. "I want what we had back. I want another chance with you."

"How, when you're fine with casual?"

"Not if I had you."

The conviction in those five words caused the merry-go-round to halt and Jamie to waver. Derrick offered a sure thing, a heart for the taking. No more casual, no more waiting for a chance at love. Love offered freely, given completely, and while things with Derrick had deteriorated at the end, it had been good, comfortable, for most of their relationship. Maybe the blinding need would come later, maybe the spark would reignite. If only Aidan . . .

A noise from the adjacent bedroom loosened Derrick's grip, and Jamie took the out. "I have to go."

Derrick beat him to the door, blocking it with his body. He laid a hand over Jamie's heart, right over the tattoo, and Jamie gasped, remembering Derrick's steady presence beside him at the tattoo parlor all those years ago.

"You decide to stop hiding from what you want, from who you are, I'll be here." He leaned forward, lightly brushing their lips together again. "I'll always be here for another shot with you."

# SEVENTEEN

The instant Aidan had spotted Derrick's chestnut curls bobbing through the crowd of partygoers, he had known things were about to go sideways. Of course he fucking lived here. Leave it to Jamie's ex to be everywhere they least needed him. And now, the conversation he had overheard —the scene he had witnessed—replayed in his head like a horror movie.

He couldn't decide which was worse.

His glimpse, through the open bathroom doors, of Jamie and Derrick kissing.

Or Derrick's casual dismissal of his casual boyfriend.

Had *casual* sounded as awful coming out of his mouth as it had out of Derrick's? Like he was casually dismissing Jamie every time he went out with Nic, Casey, Scott, or any of the other men he had dated the past five months? Aidan didn't mean it the same. With Jamie, he meant the opposite. Keeping things casual wasn't a matter of disinterest. He wasn't waiting for someone better to come along. He was interested, more than he should be, and there was no better man out there than Jameson Walker. Keeping things casual was the only way to protect himself against getting too attached, too lost if something happened to Jamie, by choice or otherwise.

But what had he lost by staying detached?

He couldn't deny Derrick was right. Jamie had slid right back into his old life. There was a spark in his eye, and he was happy on the court, back where he belonged. Aidan had said it himself to anyone who would listen—Jamie behind the computer was a waste of talent. He was a damn fine Cyber agent, but on the court, whether player or coach, he was something else.

That question he had brushed off earlier with a "Save it for later" required an answer. Now. Between Aidan's baggage and the terrorist targeting them, no one could blame Jamie for choosing his old life with Derrick. After everything he'd put him through, it wasn't fair for Aidan to change his mind now and decide he wanted more. He didn't deserve Jamie, plain and simple. If this was the life Jamie wanted, if Derrick was who he wanted, then Aidan had to accept that.

After all, he had done nothing to keep him. Only casually dismissed him.

Disgusted with himself, Aidan paced the adjacent bedroom, waiting for Jamie and Derrick to exit the study. He needed to sweep the room to make sure his partner didn't leave anything behind and then he needed to get the hell out. Ethan would be angry he'd bailed on the contract signing, but Aidan couldn't be Ian anymore tonight, and he couldn't face Jamie. Not when his heart was breaking for the second chance at love he had driven away. He had to get out before he said or did something he regretted.

To Ethan. To Derrick. To Jamie.

The light flicked on. *Fuck.* Not fast enough.

"You're gonna wear a hole in the carpet," his partner said.

"You need to get back downstairs." He avoided Jamie's gaze as he tried to skirt past him. "I'll clean up. Did you get what we needed?"

"All done." Jamie shot out an arm, blocking the bathroom pathway into the study. "And I already cleaned up."

"Great, let's go," he mumbled, turning for the other door.

Jamie yanked him back around. "You overheard me and Derrick."

Aidan's gaze darted up. He must have done a poor job hiding his anger. Jamie, not realizing it was self-directed, responded in kind, his voice low and gravelly like it had been in the hospital room with Nic. "You *saw* me and Derrick."

"I'm sorry," Aidan said. "I was trying to get up here and warn you. It doesn't matter now. I'm leaving."

Faster than Aidan could blink, his back hit the wall and Jamie's body hit his. He pinned him to the wall with his hands around his wrists and a knee between his legs. Aidan struggled against the too-tempting hold. Days without that big body on his and he couldn't stand the heavenly weight, knowing it was about to be torn away for good. He wasn't prepared to face the loss he had wrought.

"Dammit, Aidan, stop."

"Let me go."

Jamie pressed closer. "I know what you saw and heard. Let me explain."

Aidan shook his head. "You don't have to. I've got no claim on you."

"That's bullshit and you know it."

His eyes shot to Jamie's, and the words were out before he caught them. "Don't fuck him." He had no right to ask, yet he couldn't stop himself from making the hopeless, helpless plea. "Don't fuck him, and don't let him fuck you."

"What?" Surprise weakened Jamie's hold, and Aidan snaked an arm free. His hand landed over Jamie's heart, fingers curling into fabric as if he could touch the ink and life beneath. Jamie grabbed his wrist and slammed it back against the wall. "Hypocritical much?" he said, voice and body vibrating with anger.

"I didn't . . ." Aidan swallowed around the lump in his throat. "Since Gabe, it's only been you. The others . . . I didn't."

Jamie gasped, and the tension in his body melted. He crushed Aidan to the wall not with anger but with something else equally hot and strong. His hands trailed down Aidan's arm, branding and burning, and came to rest around his neck. "Why not?"

Aidan closed his eyes, fighting twin waves of regret and desire. "I'm sorry. I'm so sorry."

"For what?"

"For ever saying this was casual. This isn't casual. It never has been." Aidan opened his eyes, staring into wide blue ones swirling with disbelief and hope. "That's why, and hearing him say it . . . I don't mean it like that. I don't."

"Baby." Jamie's strangled whisper floated across his lips.

"I don't mean it at all."

Hands diving into his hair, Jamie clutched the long strands, angled his face, and crashed their mouths together.

Aidan opened to him, opened to everything. He was just as terrified as he had been in that hospital room last week, but he was more terrified of never having this again. It could still be ripped away at any minute, but it wouldn't be because of his own cowardice. He would hold on, as long as he could, as long as Jamie would have him. Aidan let every ounce of need speak for itself, in the way his tongue tangled with Jamie's, the way his nails scraped over his scalp, the way his erection strained against his zipper. He couldn't get enough and didn't think he ever would.

Jamie broke away and Aidan groaned his displeasure until Jamie dipped and ran his hands under Aidan's ass, lifting him. Shoulders hitting the wall, Aidan wrapped his legs over Jamie's hips and rutted their cocks together. The emptiness he'd ignored all these months roared to life with a vengeance. "Jamie, please."

"Shh, Irish," he murmured against his lips. "I've got you." He sealed their mouths once more then spun, hauling them off the wall and moving toward the bed. Aidan's ass had just hit the mattress, his legs spread for a descending Jamie, when Ethan's voice in the hallway cut through the haze of lust.

"Ian! Jamie!"

Jamie tore out of his arms and stood at the end of the bed, glaring at the door like he wanted to commit murder. "Motherfu—"

Aidan scrambled to his feet and clamped a hand over his mouth.

"Ian, Whiskey!" Chancellor Polk repeated from right outside the study. "Where are you? We've got an emergency!"

Glancing between them, Aidan evaluated their respective "problems." His erection was relatively constrained by his jeans, whereas Jamie's created a tent in his dress slacks. "Go stand in front of the window," he whispered. "Look tortured."

"Not gonna be hard." Aidan smirked at the too-accurate word choice, and Jamie grumbled, "Shut it," as he got into position, one arm to the window frame, back to the room.

Aidan adjusted himself, ran a hand through his hair, then raised his voice. "In here."

The breathless AD appeared through door, Chancellor Polk a step behind.

"What's wrong?" Aidan asked.

"We need an attorney," Ethan said.

"What for?"

"Blake. He's been arrested."

# EIGHTEEN

Frat boy ballplayer crashes car through fence while high. Some fucking emergency.

Aidan should have known.

And this was what had interrupted him and Jamie. Granted, what they'd been doing, what they'd been about to do—at Ethan's party, in a house full of people—was about as foolish as Blake's decision to drive high, but after days without Jamie in the way he wanted him most, after admitting to himself and his partner that things between them weren't casual at all, Aidan had been ready to risk it all. Including his heart, even as terrified as he was of letting Jamie in and losing him to an assassin's bullet. Losing him forever terrified Aidan more.

He leaned against the Interrogatio" roo' wall and tamped down his frustration at the interrupted reunion. He needed to get his other head in this game and figure out how to play this incident to their advantage. Jamie had done his job. He'd stopped the kill switch and copied the program. He would be home by now analyzing data and stuffing printouts in colored file folders. Now Aidan had to do his job—get the damn invite.

The arresting officer, who they had waited over an hour for, finished his equally long-winded charge and process explanation and went to retrieve Blake, leaving Aidan alone with Ethan in the drab room.

Ethan hadn't bothered to ask whether Aidan was a criminal law attorney or even open to the representation, but Aidan had been married to a former athlete and watched enough sports television to know this sort of thing was in a sports agent's job description, attorney or not. And if he could use it to gain Blake's and Ethan's trust, then by all means, he could play at being a lawyer for Blake as well as he could for Jamie.

"Is Whiskey going to sign the contract?" Ethan asked.

"Why wouldn't he?"

"Back at the house, he looked like he was having second thoughts."

Second thoughts, yes, but more about murderous impulses and blown covers than his fake contract. "It's a big decision for him."

Ethan tilted his head, considering, and Aidan felt uncomfortably like he was being read in more ways than one. "And you were helping him with that? I thought he'd already made his decision."

Did Ethan suspect something? That he and Jamie were involved? That this was all a cover?

*Cover*, that was what he needed to do, and fast.

Aidan pushed off the wall and sat next to Ethan, checking to make sure the speaker to the observation room was off. "Jamie's my client and my friend. He's uprooting his life again. The party tonight may have been too much, too soon."

"What aren't you telling me?" Ethan tapped out a nervous rhythm on the metal table. He wasn't going to let up without a better explanation.

"There was someone in San Francisco," Aidan said, going with near-truths.

"But he said at the press conference . . ."

"It was complicated; it ended badly."

Ethan stilled. "Did he leave her? The last thing we need is another scandal."

"He wasn't given the choice." Aidan ignored the incorrect assumption. In part to preserve the cover, in part to protect Jamie, and in part because his own mind was hung up on the matter of choice. He hadn't given Jamie a choice when he'd called things off. Had he given him a choice tonight either?

"Mr. Reynolds, Mr. Daley." Aidan's gaze swung around at the familiar voice.

"Renee, thank God." Ethan bolted out of his chair with his best smile on. It made Aidan recoil, Paulson too, but Ethan was too keyed up to notice. "Are you going to let Blake out? He didn't hurt anyone, and his parents will pay for the damage. We need him for the game tomorrow."

Paulson cringed. Riley had likely told her Press was getting the start. She passed off her flinch as surprise at Ethan's sudden approach. "Mr. Daley," she said, looking past Ethan. "I understand you're Blake Whitehead's attorney."

Aidan extended his hand. "Prospective agent. Also an attorney."

She played it with the perfect amount of disdain, withdrawing her hand and putting it in her pocket as if wiping it off. Aidan stifled a laugh. "Ethan, I'd like a word with Mr. Daley."

"Shouldn't he speak with his client first?"

"Ethan," Aidan said. "It's fine."

The AD looked back and forth between them. His decision was made for him when Blake's uncle, dressed in full uniform, stuck his head in the door and demanded his presence. Paulson shut the door behind them, slapped a folder on the table, and sat with her back to the observation window.

She waited for the raised voices outside to fade before doing that whiplash-fast stoic-to-smiling face morph. "Didn't expect to see you here."

"Didn't expect to be here, but Ethan didn't give me much choice. And it doesn't help our case much if Blake's locked up in here."

"I know, Jamie called ahead. I convinced Cap to cut Blake loose, not that it took much effort with the Whiteheads throwing their weight around."

"If your captain has already agreed . . ."

"What am I doing in here?" She braced her forearms on the table, tilting forward menacingly, all the while grinning. "I'm in here to make it look like we're arguing and that you're the one convincing me to let him go."

Aidan shifted forward, matching her argumentative posture and keeping his face stern, in case anyone was watching through the glass behind her. "Nice work, Paulson."

She grinned wider. "More good news." She pushed the folder across the table to him. "Beau and I searched the old depot. There's been more activity than the usual stoner kids," she said as he flipped through pictures. "Especially in the old post office building. A lot of shoe tracks in the dust and a generator and utility light stacked in one corner."

"Check the land records. See if it was purchased recently. Maybe a new owner is getting ready to renovate?"

Paulson shook her head. "In that part of town, I doubt it, but I'll check."

"The usual stoner kids . . ." He tapped the picture of roaches, empties and other drug paraphernalia. "They could've seen something. Did you pick some of these up?"

"Beau took them back to the field office for forensics. I didn't want to tip off anyone here, and he said the feds could run them faster."

"Pictures of the shoes too?"

"Shoes too," Paulson confirmed.

"Good work." He relaxed back in his seat. "Now, do you think we've argued enough that I can break out a victory smile?"

She chuckled. "I think you're good."

He smiled as they stood. "We'll be in touch tomorrow."

Paulson paused with one hand on the door handle. "Ethan said CU needed Blake for the game tomorrow. Who's starting, him or Press?"

"Jamie already benched Blake for going after Press. After this stunt, Blake's ass will be glued to the bench for sure."

"That's what I wanted to hear." She winked, then opened the door for him. "Mr. Daley," she said, loud enough to draw the attention of Ethan and Blake standing a few feet away. "You'll see that Mr. Whitehead keeps his nose clean and pays for all damages."

"Of course, Officer." He shook her hand then returned to his party. "Let's go before they change their minds."

"That's it?" Blake said. "I'm off?"

Ethan shoved him toward the exit. "Shut up before you get into even more trouble." He glanced over his shoulder at Aidan and mouthed *Thank you.*

Outside, Blake blocked him from opening the car door. "I owe you, man." He pulled a card out of his back pocket. "If you're still looking for some action . . ."

Aidan took the offered card and flipped it over. In plain block print were a website address and randomized username and password.

Mission accomplished.

———

Fueled by caffeine and a powerful need for distraction, Jamie ricocheted between three laptops, dozens of files littering the dining table, and his printer in the study. Even with the hyperkinetic activity, his mind rebelled every few minutes, flashing back to the kiss from—he checked his phone—three hours ago.

Each time, conflicting emotions flooded him.

Triumph that Aidan had said all the things Jamie had wanted to hear. That there was nothing casual about them.

Desire that stiffened his cock and would have been quelled if Ethan and Polk hadn't interrupted them.

Anger that the AD and chancellor had quite possibly the worst timing in the world.

Relief that the AD and chancellor had quite possibly the best timing in the world.

Before things went further, Jamie needed to come clean.

About everything. He had wanted the whole story first, but he wanted Aidan more, and he didn't want him back in his bed only for Aidan to discover his betrayal and abandon it forever. That said, if Aidan walked through the front door right now and slammed their mouths together, shoved his body against his, or invited him to do the same, Jamie wasn't sure he could resist.

Paralyzed by possibilities, he guzzled more coffee and threw himself into decrypting the files from Ethan's computer, pushing through his wavering attention span. He cracked the gambling program first, but it only loaded the betting portal. It wasn't until a user logged in with a unique invite code that the spyware downloaded and activated. They still needed an invite. Maybe, though, he could at least trace the gambling program's creator with this much.

The middle computer trilled with an incoming video call from 'anny's number.

Jamie hit Accept, only to have his boss's face fill the screen. Hair twisted in a chignon, makeup perfect, wearing a pink silk blouse, she looked right at home in what appeared to be a luxury yacht's below-deck cabin.

"SAC Cruz," he greeted.

She pursed her lips, about to correct him, when Danny's face appeared over her shoulder. "Ooh, so official sounding." He avoided her backhand and smiled at the screen. "J, good to see you. Though, gotta say, you've looked better."

Jamie raked one hand through his hair and yanked off his dangling tie with the other. "It's been a long few days."

"I'm afraid it's more bad news on our end," Mel said. "Is Aidan there?"

"He's out, case matter. Go ahead and tell me. I'll fill him in."

"Your boy Westley's in the wind," Danny said.

"Turned in a letter of resignation Friday," Mel added, voice resigned.

"Is he still in town?"

"Doesn't look like. We went by his last known address. Cleaned out and no forwarding address left with his landlord."

"Shit."

"That about sums it up," Danny said.

Westley was their best lead on Renaud, and now he was gone. Off the board just like the detectives. Maybe, though, he'd left a paper trail in his legal work.

"We need access to his case files. Or at least a client list."

"Can't," Mel said, while Danny disappeared from view. "Client files are privileged."

"Even if he's gone and his apartment is cleaned out? He could be dead like Nelson and Rollins for all we know."

"We're going to need more for probable cause."

"Or access some other way," he said. "All I need is an open portal and I can hack the rest." Her eyes narrowed, and Jamie defied her warning glare. They were already operating out of bounds. What was one more toe over the line? And if he controlled the flow of information, Jamie could frame the story better for Aidan. "The stakes are too high, and our leads are disappearing too fast for us to wait. We need answers, Mel. I *need* to tell him."

"I've got your back, J." Danny reappeared, waving around his phone. "Just scored a date with the paralegal taking over Westley's matters."

Mel's eyes flared and she whipped her head around, hair coming loose from the violent speed. "You what?"

"Text me what I need to do," Danny said to him. "I'll get it done."

"I'll send you the protocols."

Danny clapped and dodged another of Mel's swings. "Now I'm an official member of the secret society."

She rolled her eyes, and Jamie suppressed a laugh.

"Go up top so I can talk to my agent in private." Despite her irritated tone, Danny braved her wrath for a quick kiss. He departed with a wink, and Mel waited several seconds before turning back to the screen. "Where are you on the CU case?"

"We identified primary suspects, averted a near loss of data, and collected information tonight that I'm in the process of decrypting. If Aidan returns with the invite we need, we should have this resolved in the next couple days."

"Good." Her gaze drifted up, as if checking that Danny was still above deck, then she lowered her voice. "I had lunch with Isabella today."

"That deposit in Tom's account wasn't a mistake, was it?" He had hoped for an accounting error, or a fabricated paper trail to throw them off. He hadn't found anything else amiss in Tom's financials, and there were no calls or texts from Tom's phone near the time of the accident. But by the dejected look on Mel's face, he knew his hopes, and Aidan's fond memories of his partner, were about to be dashed. "What did Renaud have on him?"

"Not on him. On Isabella, or rather the immigration status of her grandmother."

"She's undocumented?"

Mel nodded. "Ninety years old, the last of four siblings

who fled Mexico as teens. She's dependent on her family, who are all in the States now."

"So if deported, it would be to a place she hasn't lived in seventy-plus years and with no one there to care for her."

"Tom adored his wife. He'd do anything to protect and keep her happy, including whatever it took to keep her grandmother here."

Defeated, Jamie pushed the computer away, folded his arms on the table, and buried his head in them. Not only was Tom involved, but Isabella too—one of Aidan's childhood friends. Another person in his inner circle who had betrayed him. Another person at risk.

He lifted his face. "Mel, you've gotta get her into protective custody."

"Already on it."

"There were no calls on Tom's phone, but they were at a pub right before the accident. The call signaling the SUV must have originated from there. I'll request those phone records."

"I think you should wait to tell Aidan."

"Wait? No way." He shook his head, vehemently opposed to her suggestion. "At the rate we're going, by tomorrow there'll be another three people who betrayed him, and then I didn't just lie about one, then two, then three, but six." He swiped an arm out, sending folders flying off the table and onto the floor. "Fuck!"

"Agent Walker," Mel called, her voice strident and commanding, reeling him to order. She held up a single manicured finger. "One day. That's all I'm asking. We know the why now behind Tom's involvement. Danny will get access to Westley's files tomorrow. Let's see if those give us the why behind Gabe's. One more day and we'll have *all* the answers to give to Aidan."

He slumped in his chair and stared blankly up at the ceiling. Could he do it? One more day of lying to the man he was falling in love with? Who was he kidding—was already in love with. Christ, his whole life felt like a lie right now. Which one was the truth? Dizziness overwhelmed him, same as it had on the sidewalk in front of Ethan's house earlier tonight.

"Jamie," Mel said, coaxing, and he righted his head. The panic must have been written on his face. "You and Aidan have a job to do there. Focus on *that* case. Let me and Danny focus on getting what you need for the other one."

He eyed the scrolling decryption on the other computers. It would take time to sort through this and whatever else an invite might open to them. And he had the game tomorrow. Not even considering the matter of their personal relationship, if he told Aidan tonight what they knew about Gabe, Tom, and Renaud, about the lies everyone had been keeping from him, it could ripple out and crater the CU investigation. A case they could wrap tomorrow.

And then they could put *all* the truths on the table.

"Okay," he said. "One day."

# NINETEEN

Aidan barely got the front door closed before Jamie materialized in the foyer. Clothes wrinkled, eyes caffeine-wide, hair sticking in every direction, the supersonic hedgehog came to mind, and Aidan couldn't help but smile.

His grin died with Jamie's next words. "We've got a problem."

He tossed his overcoat at the banister. "Can it wait until after I fuck you?"

Jamie made a tortured groan, and the next thing Aidan knew, he was crushed between the glass-paned door and his partner's hot, hard body. Smashing their mouths together, Jamie shoved his tongue between his lips and Aidan sucked him in farther, greedy for it. Legs spread, he raked his hands down Jamie's back, dove inside his waistband, and hauled him closer, thrusting. Jamie countered, rocking his hips and moaning into his mouth. This is what he had spent the past four hours, the past five months, dying to get back to. If Jamie took him to the foyer floor right now, he would gladly get on all fours for him. Consumed by the devouring kiss, by the firm round globes of Jamie's ass in his hands, by the desperate rutting of their cocks together, he nearly collapsed when Jamie suddenly wrenched away.

He staggered back, heaving. "It can't wait."

Aidan clutched the door handle to hold himself up. Not how he had intended to wind up on the floor. "Are you fucking kidding me? If I had my sidearm right now, I'd shoot you."

Jamie chuckled, palms up and out. "Justifiable homicide." He started to approach again, and Aidan threw out a hand.

"Don't! Not unless you intend to finish what you started."

He kept coming, only stopping when there was less than an inch of tension-filled air between them.

"Jamie," he warned.

His big, warm hand cradled Aidan's face. "I'm sorry." He dropped the softest of kisses on his other cheek and lingered there, nuzzling, a sharp contrast to the fierce mauling of a minute ago. "I just needed to taste you again."

Eyes fluttering closed, Aidan savored the rough scrape of stubble and the lingering tropical scent of his cologne. "You're killing me, Whiskey."

"Not doing myself any favors either." He pulled back and dropped his hand, resigned. "But we've got bigger problems."

Aidan's gaze flickered to Jamie's plenty big problem, to his own, then back to his partner's face, lifting one brow. "I don't see how that's possible."

"Unfortunately, it is." Jamie turned for the dining room

and Aidan followed. "I copied two sets of files from Ethan's computer. The gambling program and an unknown folder of encrypted files I thought were the spyware."

"I take it they weren't?"

Jamie shook his head and sat at the head of the table behind three open laptops, his fingers flying across the keyboard of the far right one. Aidan crossed behind him, stopping to run his hands through the light brown waves, smoothing it down. Putting Jamie to rights was the only way Aidan was going to make it through a serious conversation, and he had craved one last indulgence before all hope of fucking was gone. Jamie shuddered, fingertips lifting off the keyboard, and Aidan smiled. He continued to the chair on Jamie's other side and lifted a teetering stack of folders out of the seat. He tried to discern the order of chaos on the table and seeing none, dropped them in the middle.

"Show me what you've got."

Jamie angled the computer toward him, a spreadsheet opened on the screen. "Anyone's name look familiar?"

He had asked a similar question last week, and for a terrifying second, Aidan expected to see Renaud's, Hamilton's, or Westley's name. To find them connected to this case would be unreal, and at the same time, not at all surprising. After a quick first pass with no sign of their names, he released the breath he had been holding and started at the top again, reading each name. It only took a few to recognize the pattern. They were names any FBI agent who had ever worked narcotics would recognize.

"These are cartel contacts." Aidan examined the adjacent columns. "Why are they listed next to player names? And are those game times and drug weights?"

Jamie nodded. "I think the cartel is communicating

through the program. Coding shipments and deliveries using bets."

Aidan fell back in his chair. "And Ethan knows this? I knew the guy was dirty, but I would have never connected him to the cartel."

"He created this file." Jamie pointed at the screen. "He knows it's going on. Whether he created the gambling program as a means for the cartel to communicate or if they independently found it and used it to their advantage is up in the air."

"He could be tracking info to turn informant. We need to dig deeper into his background."

"Already on it." Jamie tilted his head to the far-left computer, which appeared to be running internet searches at high speed. "Checking our suspect list too for cartel connections. I hope the kids aren't involved to this level, but . . ."

"We know Blake uses. We have to check." He pulled out his phone. "And we're going to have to call the DEA in on this."

Jamie's hand covered his, pinning it and the phone to the table. "Not yet, please. If we call this in now, CU will be crawling with DEA agents by morning, and our gambling and identity theft case will be the least of their concerns. Even further down that list will be the rest of CU's season."

Aidan's chest tightened at the earnest look on his partner's beautiful, weary face. Whiskey Walker, *Jamie*, the coach, was trying to do right by his players. "You're still trying to save them the tourney bid."

"They don't all deserve to go down for this, and I don't want them caught in the middle of a cartel skirmish.

Besides, we don't have anything prospective to give the DEA."

Aidan glanced back at the spreadsheet. "All of these are for past shipments?"

He nodded. "We need to get into the gambling program to see what's lined up for the next game. If I can hack it, I can manipulate the where and when, and deliver the cartel to the DEA on a silver platter, without compromising CU's season or my players."

"In that case . . ." Aidan lifted a hip, reached into his back pocket, and withdrew the invite from Blake. "Get to work."

Jamie snatched the card from him. "You couldn't have led with this?"

"I'm sorry, but someone had his tongue down my throat two seconds after I walked through the door."

"You baited me."

"True." Aidan smirked but the expression was run askew by a yawn.

"Go get some sleep," Jamie said. "I'll get the gambling program up and running, place a few bets, and we'll see what damage it does by morning." He positioned the card in the groove between the keyboard and screen and typed a combination of commands that loaded a separate desktop, one displaying a picture from Halloween of them dressed as their *Destiny* warlocks.

Aidan pushed out of his chair and stood behind Jamie, messaging his shoulders. "You need sleep too."

Jamie lolled his head back, tired eyes gazing up at him. "Once I've got everything running on autopilot."

"Fresh coffee, then? And Oreos?" Bending, Aidan stole a kiss, keeping it short in deference to their mutual lack of self-control. He turned for the kitchen, but Jamie stayed him with a hand around his wrist. "I do intend to finish what I started once everything's on the table."

Smiling, Aidan shook loose the hold and headed into the kitchen. "I believe the line is 'dope on the table.' "

His partner's faintly repeated "everything" echoed behind him.

# TWENTY

Ravenous and reenergized after a night of hacking, Jamie started on breakfast as soon as he woke from his power nap, making a riotous mess of his oversize kitchen. At first glance, a stranger might assume the game room, with its fully stocked bar and antique pool table, was his favorite in the house. But as rarely as he drank, and as poorly as he played pool, he would gladly trade the game room for his kitchen. He had upgraded his kitchen in San Francisco too, but that one was half the size. He liked taking advantage of the extra elbow room while he could.

Eggs and country ham close to ready, he tilted up his head and hollered, "Irish!"

Moments later, a hassled yet bright-eyed Aidan appeared over the upstairs railing that was open to the vaulted-ceiling kitchen. He looked like he was about to tell him what for, but then his brow furrowed. "You didn't sleep?"

"A little." Jamie shrugged and turned back to the food sizzling on the griddle. "I'll catch another nap later today."

Aidan thundered down the stairs and reappeared around the left side of the kitchen. He sidled up next to him and slid a hand across his back. "Smells good."

Jamie wasn't sure if he meant the food or his neck, where Aidan had buried his face, nuzzling. He smiled and leaned into the intimate touch. "I haven't gotten to cook much this trip. We haven't had time, with schedules and whatnot." Aidan's shower-fresh scent tickled his nose and other parts south. He wanted to reach a hand back, grab Aidan's hip, and haul him against his backside. Turn them, swipe the mess off the kitchen island, and let Aidan fuck him right here.

"I've missed it too," Aidan said, interrupting his spiraling fantasy.

*Focus.*

Jamie cleared his throat. "You didn't tell me what happened with Blake."

With a parting nip, Aidan removed his face from his neck and bumped his hip, knocking him over the few inches needed to get to the plates and coffee mugs. "Driving while high. Crashed his car into a fence."

"You and Renee were able to get him off?"

"Mostly Renee. Thanks for calling ahead. If I'd had to deal with Blake and his shit any longer . . ." Aidan reached around him, snagged a piece of ham with his fingers, then immediately dropped it. "Ouch, that's fucking hot."

"No shit." Jamie's over-the-shoulder grin died when Aidan put his burned fingers in his mouth and sucked. *Fuck.* Blood rushing to his face, Jamie whipped back around. "Renee said she had more evidence."

Aidan launched into a recap of Renee and Grant's findings at the old depot, and Jamie breathed easier, libido crisis averted. Plates loaded, Aidan carried them to the table, and Jamie followed with their mugs and a basket of homemade biscuits out of the warming oven.

"Speaking of findings," Aidan said, "Mel texted that Westley was in the wind."

"I spoke with her and Danny last night." Pausing, he took a bite of a steaming biscuit then flapped a hand in front of his mouth to cool it off.

Aidan laughed. "You think you'd learn by now."

"Yes, but I'll get to seconds before you make a dent in yours."

Rolling his eyes, Aidan steered them back on course. "You were saying about Mel and Danny?"

"Your brother and I are exploring alternative means of acquiring information."

Aidan waved his fork in the air. "I don't want to know." He jutted his chin toward his laptops and files. "What've you found so far?"

"The gambling and identity theft is more far-reaching than we thought." He grabbed the middle laptop and set it between them. "I logged in with the invite and created an account using Ian Daley's identity." He loaded the gambling site, logged in, and moved the cursor around, showing Aidan the various features. "You've got all the usual bets on games—points, spread, score. Then, in fantasy mode, there are bets on individual players—shots, assists, steals, fouls even."

"Pretty attractive for getting students hooked."

"With the popularity of fantasy sports, it's a system many of them know already."

Aidan pushed his plate aside and began clicking through the site. He stopped on the window with bets and dollar amounts. "Except there's real money involved here."

"And more." Jamie resumed control of the computer and, with a few keystrokes, opened another of those programs he wasn't supposed to have. "Spyware on the spyware." It ran much like a diagnostics window, monitoring the spyware's activity. "This is the information the spyware already extracted on Ian Daley."

Aidan whistled low.

With the monitor window open so Aidan could see it in action, Jamie placed a bet on one of tonight's other DII games. A pop-up window appeared. "When a user places a bet, the program asks you to confirm certain information to prove your identity. All in the guise of limiting access to registered users and protecting its secrecy on the dark web."

"My ass."

Jamie grinned, thinking what a nice ass it was.

"Focus, Whiskey." By the sly smile on his lips, Aidan knew exactly what Jamie was thinking. Playing innocent, he grabbed a biscuit and gestured for Jamie to carry on.

He entered Ian Daley's billing zip code in the pop-up window, the spyware captured it, and the monitoring window displayed the activity.

"Why would someone give them all their information?" Aidan asked.

"It collects it in pieces. For someone focused on the gambling—getting tips, sure bets, all the things the site offers—they're not necessarily going to put it together right away. Especially not a gambling addict or a student more concerned with scoring extra cash."

"What else do they have on Ian Daley?"

Jamie pushed the computer away and dug into the rest of his food. "They're a phone number away from having everything they need to get Ian's bank account and credit card info."

"And if I were to log in from my phone?"

"Then they've got it."

Aidan handed him Ian Daley's phone. When Jamie turned it over, a text from Ethan, inviting Ian to dinner after the game tonight, was displayed on the screen. His appetite withered and he set the plate aside.

"Just hit ignore," Aidan said.

Easier said than done. He and Aidan hadn't talked about where things stood between them. Aidan would have fucked him last night if he hadn't pulled away, and he was affectionate this morning, more so than after Galveston. Last night at Ethan's, he had said things weren't casual between them, but he hadn't said he was done being casual with everyone else.

And Jamie also had his secrets, ones that could destroy Aidan.

Before he lost his breakfast, he turned his attention back to the phone, opened a browser window, and entered the gambling site address. The site hitched briefly—the spyware activating—then resumed loading. He logged in, placed a bet, and when prompted for Ian's middle name, he entered it. "Just a matter of time."

"There it is." Aidan pointed with his fork at the monitor window, which showed the spyware aggregating Ian Daley's data. "Any luck tracing its origins?"

"Not yet. It would help if I could get directly into the system, especially the spyware."

Aidan stood, grabbed their plates, and carried them to

the sink. "I'll drop again to Ethan that you're good with computers. Get you access to his."

Following him into the kitchen, Jamie leaned a hip against the counter and crossed his arms. "You need to be careful, especially if he's connected to the cartels. We need to get eyes on him."

"I'll set it up with Paulson and Grant. Let them know about the cartel tie. Did you find anyone else connected?"

"I'm still running the searches on Ethan. No connections with team members, and no bets yet on tonight's game. I'm also keeping an eye on the other DII match ups."

"So even the kids involved don't know the full extent?"

"That'd be my guess."

"What about any on-court evidence they're throwing games?"

"I still haven't seen any, but with Blake riding the bench tonight, we'll see if anything different shakes out." Once Aidan dried his hands, Jamie handed the phone back before he dunked it and Ethan's text in the water. "I need to go."

He turned to leave, and Aidan grabbed his arm. "We need to talk."

"And I need to get to campus. We've got a team meeting this morning, a lunch Ethan set up with more boosters where I'm supposed to sign my contract, then game prep. You can have the Chevelle today; I'll take the Jeep."

"Well, when you put it that way." Aidan released his arm, only to lift his hand and wrap it around his neck, hauling him in for a deep kiss. Jamie's irritation at Ethan faded as he tasted the declaration in Aidan's kiss. "We'll talk after," he said once they came up for air. "Now go get a Ravens win."

"Someone becoming a fan?"

Aidan smiled and slapped his ass. "Of their hot-as-fuck assistant coach."

———

Press started the game in Blake's place. Even if Jamie hadn't already stripped Blake of the starting position, his near-arrest last night had sealed the demotion. The punk shouldn't have been here at all. He should have been suspended. But because no charges were filed and because they needed Blake close for their investigation, the senior warmed the far end of the bench.

Much to Jamie's delight, Press ran with the opportunity, literally. Midway through the second half, he was still in the game and the Ravens' leading scorer, against King no less, their toughest Conference Carolinas opponent. Press, a largely unknown variable, was a major advantage for CU this late in the season. The ten-thousand-strong crowd was likewise pumped, cheering louder with each shot Press swished through the net.

If they could win this game, they would clinch the division championship and a spot in the tourney. King was keeping it close, though. The Tornado signaled time out, and Coach Turner called the Ravens to the bench.

"Press, you good to keep going?" he asked.

"Yeah, Coach." A little winded, but the kid, bouncing with excitement, could barely hold his leg still long enough for Neil to rewrap his calf, which had cramped at the half. He might have been amped up on adrenaline, but his body wasn't used to playing this hard for this many minutes.

Blake joined the huddle. "I can take a turn, Coach."

"Press said he's fine," Jamie replied.

Blake opened his mouth to protest, and Turner cut him off. "I'm saving you for the final minutes and for Saturday against Belmont."

Blake conceded, appeased for the moment.

Belmont Abbey, situated just north of Charlotte, was their biggest rival. The rivalry game was CU's last of the season. It could go either way, no matter how good one team was versus the other. All bets were off. They couldn't depend on winning against Belmont to clinch the division and tourney birth; they needed the win tonight.

"All right, King's defense is limiting us to one shooter," Coach said. "We need a work-around so we can open up the lead."

Coach was right. While allowing Press to flourish, the traps were stifling Marcus. CU was in the lead, but with only one player getting open looks, King was able to keep the score close.

Jamie's gaze snagged on Riley, standing next to Press. "How about a two-point set? Let's put Riley on the floor with Marcus." Every head turned to him, including Riley's, who looked both excited and scared half to death. "King will have to split their attention. Should break the traps."

It was a risky move in a big game, pulling one of their defensive players to put in Riley, who didn't get as many minutes handling the ball, but Press could pick up the defensive slack if Marcus was also shooting. King might get a few more shots, but CU would get even more.

"You up for it, kid?" Coach asked Riley.

"Yeah, Coach," Press answered for him. "Put him on the floor. Played together our whole lives. We can do this."

"They pulled it off in scrimmage yesterday," Jamie added.

"All right, we'll go with Whiskey's plan," Coach said, and when play resumed, Marcus and Riley were both on the floor to handle the ball.

Jamie remained standing, too nervous his first big game call would crater CU's season. He needn't have worried. Press and Riley were so in sync that within a minute, CU had stretched their lead from four to ten on two three-pointers from Marcus, the point guard finally getting looks at the basket.

"Jamie," called a voice behind him.

Twisting, he was surprised to see Renee, dressed down in jeans and a Ravens sweatshirt, straddling the row seats an elderly couple had last occupied.

"Thanks for putting him in the game," she said with a nod to her brother.

Keeping one eye on the game, Jamie turned one to her and lowered himself into his coach's chair. "We needed a distraction to break up their defensive traps."

"Speaking of distraction . . ." She leaned closer and lowered her voice. "I got those land records you asked for." She didn't say what property, but he knew she was referring to the depot. "Purchased six months ago by the Polk Family Trust."

"As in Chancellor Polk?"

Renee nodded. "Executor. Found something else interesting too. There's a subfloor to the PO building." The same place where they had found evidence of activity.

His gaze flickered up ten or so rows to where Aidan sat next to Ethan. Catching his glance, Aidan zeroed in on Renee, and his eyes widened. Next to him, Ethan shifted in his seat, putting Renee right in his line of sight. Before the AD spotted them, Aidan crossed his legs toward him and stretched an arm out across the back of his seat, redirecting his attention. Jamie breathed a sigh of relief while contemplating Ethan's murder for the second time in as many days.

Probably not a good career move either way.

"We need to get back out there, full scope," he said to Renee, meaning with a warrant. He continued to talk low and vague in case anyone managed to hear them over the game and crowd. "And we need to bring the executor in."

"Working on the former. Not sure if we've got enough PC."

"Let's see if the goods you and Grant gathered get us there."

"Beau might have some pull with the bench. I'll ask when we're on AD duty tonight. I've got a morning shift, but I'm off by two."

"We'll plan to head out then, assuming we get the paper. I don't have practice until four."

"What about the traffic?" She was good at this doubles-peak, disguising her question about the drugs and cartel.

"Not a problem with tonight's games. Two tomorrow, though." His eyes flickered up again to where Aidan was whispering something in Ethan's ear, hand on his knee, keeping him distracted. "I should be able to provide alternate directions."

"Excuse me, miss." The older couple reappeared at Renee's side. "These are our seats."

Renee smiled up at them, big and bright. "I'm so sorry. I wanted to get Whiskey Walker's autograph," she said, covering brilliantly. "Just one sec."

She shoved a program and pen at him, and Jamie scribbled his signature. "Always nice to meet a fan."

"Go Heels and go Ravens!" She ducked out between him and the couple, blocking herself from Aidan and Ethan's view, if they were even still looking.

Endeavoring to keep his homicidal tendencies in check, he ignored the possibility of what they might be doing and turned back to the game. He checked the scoreboard again. Six more points, Riley with four of them. The distraction had worked, better than they'd hoped. King, however, looked to be catching on, shifting their defense. After another minute, and two King baskets, Coach substituted a defensive player in for Riley, who collapsed on the bench.

"Good job," Jamie said. "The decoy worked."

"That a decoy too?" The boy's brown eyes were aimed into the stands. Jamie didn't have to look to know what he referred to. "Heard things, Coach."

"What sort of things?"

"Mr. Daley bailed Blake out of some shit last night."

"What sort of shit?" Jamie wondered how much had filtered down to his players.

"Don't know the details, but I heard Blake would have been arrested and charged if Mr. Daley hadn't sweet-talked some cops."

"You know the reasons."

"But—"

"I know it sucks, Riley. Just remember, Blake's the one ruining his own future."

"There's more."

Jamie's eyes narrowed. "What else?"

"I overheard Blake say Mr. Daley asked to get in on some action."

"Again, you know why."

Riley's gaze drifted back into the stands. "That looks like action all right."

Jamie looked. He shouldn't have. Aidan's hand was farther up Ethan's thigh as Ethan whispered in his ear. Jamie righted himself, simmering. He and Aidan needed to have that talk ASAP and set some ground rules. As far as he was concerned, casual in all forms was off the table if this thing between them moved forward again. Giving Aidan the benefit of the doubt, that he was leading Ethan on for the sake of the case, they also needed to determine if it was still the best strategy. His agent and his AD cuddled up at a game could bring all the wrong attention. The threat of exposure reared its head. Adrenaline tickled Jamie's feet, sped his heart, and whispered "Run."

He ignored the instinct, locked it down, and shifted his focus to the job at hand, to the court where King's defensive set had changed again. "Your number's up," he said to Riley. "You worry about your game. I'll worry about mine."

# TWENTY-ONE

Rapid-fire keystrokes were Aidan's first clue this wasn't going to be pretty. The heavy, furious way Jamie attacked the keys of his precious computers was a dead giveaway of his bad mood. As were his ramrod-straight spine, stiff shoulders and empty bottle of Blue sitting on the table by the computers. Surly Jamie was back, and this was bound to get ugly.

Aidan took a fortifying breath, wishing it was scotch instead, and braved the dining room. "Celebrating the win?"

"Forgetting the sideshow," Jamie replied, not sparing him a glance. "We have work to do." His voice was flat, cool, and anger rolled off him in waves.

Rather than poke the angry bear, Aidan detoured to the kitchen and the far more welcoming scent of coffee. "What else have you found?"

"All of Ian Daley's credit cards have been cloned."

"Shit, that was fast."

"Also, they're not running the programs on the campus servers."

"It's someone who lives off campus, then?"

"Or a student who lives on campus using a place off campus."

"We might have a way to find that out." He returned to the table, a mug for himself and one for Jamie. "They want to bring you in."

Jamie took the offered mug and sipped. "What do you mean?" he asked, tone slightly warmed.

"I let slip again to Ethan that you're good with computers. He's got a 'network issue' he needs help with. It'll get you access to his computer again."

Jamie set aside his mug. "I said servers, *plural*." All trace of warmth gone, Jamie's gaze was ice cold. "We're looking for a setup that's bigger than Ethan's home computer."

"Well, if you get into his computer, maybe you can find out where it leads. You haven't found that yet with your access, have you?"

Jamie sneered. "Thanks for the vote of confidence." He shoved back from the table, stalked through the kitchen, and fled into the game room, flipping on lights as he went.

"Hey!" With all the blinds open, Aidan's exclamation echoed loudly in the huge room surrounded by windows. "You just told me whoever is running this scam is doing so from off campus. I got us a possible in."

"And I told you it's bigger than just Ethan." Jamie grabbed a stick from the wall rack, and with no setup whatsoever, leaned over the table and struck the cue ball. It crashed into the tightly racked others, solids and stripes scattering, not a single ball falling into a pocket.

"Based on his one computer." Aidan snagged the cue he

had used the other night and leaned a hip against the rail closest to Jamie. "Maybe he's smart enough not to run it from his home computer."

"He ain't too bright if the gambling program is still on it." Jamie didn't offer him a turn. He hit the cue ball again and missed all but the rails. "Besides, we've got a better lead on the servers."

"Go on."

"Renee learned who owns the depot."

"That's why she approached you at the game?" At the arena, Aidan had had to cover fast when Ethan nearly spotted Paulson and Jamie. A revolting few minutes had followed as he took drastic measures to distract the AD.

"It's owned by the Polk Family Trust."

Aidan's cue hit the floor, the crash of wood on wood making his ears ring. "What?"

"And the post office building has a subfloor."

Meaning Blake might have been there the other night for more than just a high if the servers and other hardware were belowground and out of sight. Neil Cashman, the coaching assistant on their suspect list, who Aidan had observed shooting Jamie death glares all night, might have been with him. "We need to get out there."

Jamie circled the table and lined up his next shot. "Renee is drawing up the warrant. Grant will find a judge to push it through and schedule an interview with Chancellor Polk."

"Good," Aidan said. "But we should follow up on the Ethan lead too."

Ignoring the shot, Jamie straightened, propped his cue on the rail, and headed for the bar. Aidan caught him by the biceps before he wasted more top-shelf booze. "What's your problem?"

Reversing, Jamie wrenched free, pivoted around him, just like he did on the court, and took up his cue again. "My problem"—he struck the ball hard to no avail—"is that you told me yesterday this wasn't casual, and then today you're practically making out with another man in fucking public. And you had dinner with him, didn't you? That's where you've been the past few hours."

He eyed another shot, but before he could bend to line up, Aidan, taking his life in his hands, wedged himself between the rail and Jamie. He seized the cue and shoved it up so as not to get struck in the gut.

"I don't want Ethan."

"That's not what it looked like at the game. Even the players noticed."

"Good, the cover's holding."

Jamie's eyes blazed and his knuckles around the cue turned white.

Aidan slid his hand down the stick and covered Jamie's. "You have to be okay with this. You have to be able to separate work from reality."

"And what's reality?" His entire being shook, from his body to his voice. "How am I supposed to tell the difference when a week ago you were dating Nic, Casey, Scott, me, and God knows who else?"

"That wasn't reality either. That was me running scared."

Aidan pried the cue from his hand and tossed it to the floor next to his. He grasped Jamie's chin between his thumb and forefinger, caressing the underside of his jaw until his partner began to melt. He closed the distance between them. "This is reality," he declared, then did what he had dreamed about all day. He crushed his lips against Jamie's and set about finishing what they had started last night. He would leave no doubt who he wanted, in his life, his bed and his heart.

Lips sealed, he shuffled them back to the pool table. Taking the hint, Jamie boosted himself onto the rail, and Aidan stood between his legs. He ran his hands up the insides of Jamie's thighs, fingers tracing through denim the crease where legs met hips, his thumbs skating either side of his zipper, teasing the erection hardening behind it. Jamie's head fell back on a groan and Aidan kissed, licked, and nipped across his stubbled jaw to where intoxicating cologne and man mingled. Fuck, that smell did wicked things to him.

Jamie's hands tangled in his hair, holding him there. "How do I trust this reality?"

"It's you I want." Aidan shoved his dick against his thigh, proof positive. "Those nights in Galveston with you were the best since . . ." Memories of Gabe strangled his words. He gulped another shot of Jamie's scent, re-centering his universe. "No night's been as good since we returned. Not without you."

Jamie tugged his head back so their gazes locked. His eyes weren't cold anymore. The thin ring around the molten center was cobalt, swirling with so much love and heat it scorched Aidan's soul.

"What are you saying, Irish?"

He needed to give Jamie the choice. "I'm ready to take a shot at something real. But if you want your life here instead, if you want Derrick . . ."

"Aidan—"

"You're at home here," he talked over him. "You're at home on the court too. You're sacrificing your happiness for a man past his prime who comes with a hell of a lot of baggage."

Jamie lifted a hand, palming the side of his face. "You are far from past your prime, Aidan Talley." His thumb caressed his cheek and Aidan's eyes fluttered closed. "And I love you. I think I have since that night we danced at the Tavern. I know I have since I saw the real you in the airport." His fingers ran through his red hair and gave a tug. Aidan opened his eyes. "I don't want him. I only want you. You're my home now."

Still scary.

And everything Aidan wanted. Everything he needed.

"I'm yours, Whiskey."

He barely got the nickname out before Jamie claimed his mouth. So full of love, the kiss would've driven last week's Aidan to the airport. Now it drove him farther into Jamie's arms.

"You know . . ." Jamie's lips curved into a smile against his. "This pool table would look a lot better if you were on it with me."

Aidan smiled, remembering how he had said the same about the bathroom floor in Galveston. He wasn't about to argue now. "I couldn't agree more."

Reaching around Jamie, Aidan used one hand to sling balls into pockets, clearing the table, then pushed his partner back off the rail and onto the black felt. Smirking, Aidan clambered up and laid out over him. "Better?" he said with a downward thrust of his hips.

Even that didn't wipe the grin off Jamie's face. Fuck, he was gorgeous, stretched out and flushed beneath him. The smile splitting Aidan's face hurt, but it was the best kind of hurt. He didn't think he would ever smile this big again after Gabe. He was thrilled to be wrong.

"Come here, baby." Jamie curled a hand around his neck and brought their grinning mouths back together.

Aidan dove in—tongue, hands, hips—savoring every part of Jamie he could reach. When it wasn't enough, he wished for a button-down and instead fought the damn Ravens polo off over his head. "I can't wait for you to get back into fucking dress clothes."

His partner's raucous laughter died the instant Aidan sunk his teeth into the tattoo, getting as close as he could to the second most intimate part of him. Jamie rolled his hips, grinding their cocks together, and broke Aidan's worship long enough to yank off his shirt and sweater, tossing them onto the growing pile of clothes on the floor.

Skin to skin, Aidan shuddered and lost the rhythm of their rocking hips. Jamie wrapped his legs over the backs of his and guided the motion, relieving Aidan of the need to think. His body had already clouded his mind with sensation. The taste of warm, salty skin; the rough, enticing abrasion of Jamie's chest hair against his nipples; his cock straining for Jamie's firm grip; the emptiness inside him demanding to be filled.

Aidan levered up and stole another kiss, then trailed his open mouth across Jamie's cheek to his ear. "I need you."

Jamie plunged a hand inside his boxers and traced a finger along his crease. "I want—"

Aidan shoved back into the touch. "I know what you want. You're going to come inside me tonight. I want it all."

"Oh God." Jamie bucked off-rhythm, the sharp jolt to Aidan's cock utter torture.

"Too many clothes." He sat back and jutted his belt and fly forward. "Work fast, Whiskey."

Seconds later, they were both naked, but before Aidan could stretch out beside him, Jamie yanked him forward by the ass and positioned him over his face. Jamie took one, of his balls into his mouth, then the other, sucking, rolling, teasing, before that talented tongue licked up the underside of his cock, circled the tip, and guided him inside.

It fucking felt amazing. And fucking looked amazing too from this angle, watching as he thrust into Jamie's mouth. His blue eyes slitted, long burnished lashes fluttering. His high cheekbones thrown into sharp relief by suction. His full lips spread around his cock.

Jamie's hands clutched his ass cheeks, hard enough to leave bruises, and forced him to tilt forward. Straddling his face, Aidan gripped the pool table rail and pounded deeper.

"Fuck, that feels good."

More intoxicating than the velvet slide and rough suction, though, was when Jamie pulled off and craned his neck, looking up at him with wanton need and naked pleasure. Desperate to satisfy his desire but unwilling to lose Jamie's mouth yet, Aidan righted himself and reached back, grasping Jamie's erection already leaking precome. Aidan's fist glided down the length of him, and Jamie groaned around his cock, catapulting Aidan's orgasm closer. He pumped faster, and Jamie sucked harder, matching his rhythm.

Together, in sync, back where they were supposed to be.

But Aidan wanted Jamie inside him when he came, wanted to feel that life pulsing into him. "That's good, that's good." He pulled up and out, whimpering at the loss. "Get inside me, now."

"Stuff's in—"

"Don't need it."

Jamie scooted out from under him and braced himself on an arm at his side. "Aidan—"

"No one else, Jamie. I'm negative."

His face softened. "So am I, but if it's been since Galveston . . ."

Their first time together, the first time he'd had sex since Gabe's death, Aidan had been tight, and Jamie had had to coax him open. His body would resist again, but not his mind. The obstacles of guilt and fear were gone. He coasted his hand over Jamie's hip and ran the flat of his palm up his still-slick erection. "I'm ready, and so are you."

"Just in case." He tilted his head to the side pocket on Aidan's other side. "Stuff's in there."

Aidan grinned as he plucked a condom and lube from the pocket. He tossed the condom packet to the floor but kept hold of the single-use lube. "When did you do this?"

"When you were trapped at the station with the frat boy squad." He snatched the packet from his hand. "But there's something else I want first."

Jamie moved from beside him, and Aidan, on his hands and knees, feared he was going to leave him on the table and grab the condom again, but then his ass cheeks were spread, and a curled tongue speared his hole. Aidan lost all tension in his arms and sank to his forearms, his forehead pressed against the black felt, as Jamie licked and teased his rim. He added a slick finger, the searing pressure overwhelming, but then his other hand smoothed over his backside and his muscles relaxed, drawing him in.

"Fucking hell, that's it." He shoved back, riding Jamie's finger, until it wasn't enough. "More," he begged, and

Jamie obliged with a second and third, stretching and coaxing. "Yeah, that's it."

Jamie draped himself over his back and whispered in his ear. "You're gorgeous like this, Irish. Skin so red I can barely see the freckles. A sheen of sweat coating you. I can smell you too, leaking from your cock." And fuck if he wasn't painfully hard and pearling moisture too. Jamie rubbed against his backside. "And I can smell me on you. I can smell us." He bit the back of his shoulder and smoothed over it with his tongue.

"Need you, Jamie, all of you." Aidan turned his head and Jamie gave him the kiss he sought, their tongues tangling. "Please," he panted, openmouthed. He needed more. He needed everything.

"All right, baby." Jamie peeled off, his hand retreated, and cold emptiness swept over Aidan, but only for a second before Jamie's cock nudged his hole, the promise of the end of emptiness a breath, a thrust, away.

He half keened, half growled, and Jamie pushed in.

"Fuck!" Aidan cursed the burn, then groaned a long, drawn-out "Yes" when pain gave way to bliss. Jamie bare inside him was perfect, terrifying, everything.

Jamie was all he would ever want.

"Talk to me, Irish," Jamie said, lips against his shoulder, body draping his.

"I love you," Aidan gasped out, and Jamie froze. He hesitated only a moment before repeating, "I love you."

Jamie wound his arms around his body and levered them upright so he was spread over his thighs, back to chest. One hand over his heart, Jamie's other reached for his cheek and turned his face. When Aidan looked into his eyes, all the blue was gone, his pupils blown wide. "I love you too."

Hearing the words, in that sex-roughened Southern drawl, sent another wave of desire crashing through Aidan. "Make love to me, Whiskey."

And he did, holding him by the chest and cock. Lips locked, thrusting up into him, Jamie pounded and stroked him to orgasm, coating chest and hand, before emptying inside him with another whispered "Love you too."

Filled and sated, Aidan sagged into his arms.

Jamie held him tight. "Sleep in my bed tonight."

"Well, I sure as shit ain't sleeping on this pool table."

The body behind him jerked, then shook, and after a moment, Aidan realized Jamie was laughing, his face buried in the crook of his neck, muffling his hilarity.

Aidan nuzzled the sweaty curls at his temple. "What's so funny?"

"You said *ain't*," Jamie managed between wheezing breaths.

Aidan rolled his eyes. "Fuck me."

Jamie fell to his side laughing, and Aidan fell with him, in more ways than one.

# TWENTY-TWO

Jamie woke with a start, heart pounding, stomach knotted, convinced he was being watched, certain there had been a flash of light behind his eyelids.

He held his breath, listening for any noise outside the open bedroom door. He looked left, right, up, down. Nothing but the ruffled red hair of his partner tucked beneath his chin, silent but for Aidan's light snores tickling his chest.

Had it just been a dream? A publicity-related nightmare?

His phone came to life on the bedside table, lighting the vaulted-ceiling primary with an eerie glow. That must have been the light that woke him. Detangling from a dead-to-the-world Aidan, he reached for the phone.

A text from Mel lit the screen. **Westley files downloading. Call me ASAP.**

The knot in his stomach expanded, creeping up his throat, making breath hard to come by. He slipped out of bed before his hyperventilation woke Aidan. He grabbed jeans and boxers off the chaise in the corner, tugged them on, pocketed his phone, and tiptoed out of the room, pulling the door closed behind him. Retrieving a laptop off the dining table, he returned to the study, closed the door, and settled behind the desk. He logged into his remote server and opened the Project Angel file. The subfile labeled "MW2" had tripled in size.

The program he had written for Danny was, ironically, derived from the CU spyware. All Danny had to do was make an excuse to check his email on the replacement paralegal's laptop and download the program. Once she logged into Eldridge's VPN, it would skim and copy to Jamie's server, with a carbon copy to Mel, all files tagged by Westley or anyone else at the firm that mentioned Gabriel Cruz, Eric Hamilton, Pierre Renaud, and any of the Talleys.

He plugged in his earbuds and dialed Mel. She picked up after the first ring. "Jamie."

"Where do I start?"

"With Gabe's intake form," she replied, voice wrecked.

"His intake form? He was a client too?"

"White-collar consult. He knew he was in trouble."

He scrolled through the files—corporation charters, leases, shipping and passenger manifests—until he found the intake form, a ghost of a document that had been deleted. He opened it and read while Mel painted the broader picture.

"My brother was ambitious, on and off the field. When he retired from football, venture capital was a natural fit. He was good with numbers and good with people. A natural-born schmoozer."

"A perfect fit for Silicon Valley."

"Maybe too perfect. He made a name for himself as someone who worked fast. And sometimes loose. When a French émigré with business interests here and abroad contacted him about making investments and creating holding companies, he went to Morocco, met this potential client, and came back with a whale on the line."

Jamie sank back in the chair and closed his eyes. "Renaud."

"He didn't do his due diligence. By the time Gabe figured out he was laundering money for an international terrorist and that the holding companies he'd created were being used as leverage, he was in too deep."

"What tipped him off?"

"When Renaud went behind his back, to his own inside man, Martin Westley, and put all the companies under one umbrella."

Everything clicked, and Jamie cursed himself for not seeing it sooner. "KAG Holdings. Katie, Aidan, Gabriel. He turned it around and used it as leverage against Gabe."

"Renaud set up bank accounts for KAG Holdings."

"We didn't find any."

"Because Gabe closed them as soon as he learned they existed. Before that, there were payouts to a Caymans account. The beneficiary was Katie."

Aidan's niece, their goddaughter.

"Aidan was the trustee," she added, a final dagger.

Elbows to the desk, Jamie covered his face with his hands. This was both better and worse than he had imagined. Gabe hadn't intentionally allied with a terrorist, but his negligence had cost him his life and had serious implications for Aidan and possibly also Katie, the closest Aidan had to a child of his own, born the same day as his and Gabe's wedding. "Fuck, this is going to kill Aidan."

"It almost did."

"The accident?"

"All the accidents. December before last, Gabe went to one of the white-collar attorneys at Eldridge. The aforementioned consult. He told her everything. She opened a file and created the intake form. She put all her notes in it, including her suggestion that Gabe tell his FBI husband everything."

"And Martin Westley shuttled the file to Renaud."

"Looks like it. Renaud's been taking out anyone who knows since."

"The attorney?"

"Climbing accident at Yosemite."

Jamie ran the list of potential victims in his head: Aidan, Mel, him, Danny, Kevin, maybe Isabella, maybe even Katie.

"Christ, Mel, we have to shut this guy down. Do we have any idea what he's after?"

"No, but I'm hoping the answers are in the rest of Westley's files. Maybe we can piece together what Renaud is doing by his legal and corporate moves."

"I have to tell Aidan."

She sighed heavily, and Jamie recognized it for the concession it was. "Do you want me there? I can catch a flight first thing in the morning."

Would he like the backup? Yes. Someone to tell Aidan he was ordered to keep silent? Yes. Did he want a witness to the destruction of the most important relationship in his life? "No," he answered. "I need to do this now, and I need to talk to Aidan, alone."

"Do I need to assign someone else to your current case?"

"No," Jamie replied without hesitation. "This is my—our—case. We're invested." With the players, CU, Renee, and Grant. "We'll solve it regardless."

"Jamie—"

"I'll handle it," he snapped, then immediately regretted the sharp tone directed at his boss and friend. "I'm sorry."

"It's fine," she said, weary and exhausted.

"No, it's not. You're doing your job, which can't be easy right now." He couldn't imagine what she was going through. This was her family too—Gabe, her brother; Tom, her colleague; Isabella, her friend. They had betrayed her, same as they had betrayed Aidan. "I'm sorry, Mel. If you need to be here with Aidan, I'll wait."

"Go ahead and tell him," she said. "Report in after. Solve your case there. I'll work through the rest of these files. See if I can find the thread, and we'll follow it when you get home."

She disconnected, and Jamie ripped out his earbuds. He palmed his phone and drew back his arm, ready to launch it into the shelves across the room. He wanted the glass and metal trophies to shatter, to crash against the hardwood floor, same as his heart was shattering for his partner. For the relationships, the love, past and present, he was about to destroy.

He didn't let it fly, though. The noise would startle Aidan awake, put him on edge, and Jamie had to handle this delicately, had to contain him or else the collateral damage to their present case would be too great.

Had to kiss him, had to make love to him one last time before betrayal poisoned what they had only just begun.

The phone vibrated in his hand.

He turned it over, expecting another text from Mel, then shot to his feet, nearly dropping it in horror at what he saw on-screen. Derrick's beautiful, angelic face beaten to a bloody pulp. One eye was swollen shut, his lower lip was busted, and cuts on both cheekbones oozed blood. His curls were in disarray, as if he had been woken and dragged from bed, and his white undershirt was dappled with spots of red. Jamie dragged his fingers down the screen, futilely seeking to comfort him.

Beneath the picture, a text came through from the same unfamiliar number. **Come quietly or your boyfriend won't survive the next round.**

Next round? They hadn't beaten Derrick enough already? Boyfriend?

Another picture appeared. A shot through the bedroom window, time-stamped twenty minutes ago, of him and Aidan in bed, his sex-and-sleep-tousled partner draped across his chest.

The flash he had seen behind his eyelids.

Another text followed. **And don't tell your other boyfriend. We're watching.**

Then a slew of more pictures.

Of him and Aidan.

On the pool table, Aidan straddling his face, dick between his lips.

Aidan splayed on all fours over him, thrusting into his mouth.

Jamie behind him, head flung back in ecstasy.

Aidan spread across his lap, Jamie's hand wrapped around his cock, the two of them kissing over Aidan's shoulder.

They had left the blinds open.

And someone had been watching.

**Come with us or everyone will know Whiskey Walker is gay.**

Incontrovertible evidence . . . and with his FBI partner.

His stomach lurched, his head spun, and his legs were two seconds from giving out.

Derrick, beaten, kidnapped, in danger.

Aidan asleep in the front room, under someone's watchful eye, in danger of losing his job if those pictures came to light.

Him, in danger whether he stepped out the front door or not.

Fuck. Jamie shot out an arm, clutching the desk corner for support.

*Focus, Walker*, Aidan's voice rang inside his head.

Solve for *who*.

The text called him "Whiskey Walker." And it had to be someone who knew about his past with Derrick. Aidan had told Ethan, Derrick's landlord, he was good with computers. It stood to reason this was more likely connected with the case here than with Renaud. If it was connected to CU, this could be his chance to get direct access to the servers running the gambling and spyware programs. And if he could get into the servers, he could lead Aidan, the FBI, and the DEA right to them and the drugs.

He had to go. Everyone—Derrick, Aidan, himself—was in more danger if he refused.

But he needed to leave Aidan a message. Unsure whether his cover was intact, he texted back, **He'll look for me if I don't leave a note**. That would be true of a boyfriend, sports agent, or FBI agent.

**Tell him you left with Derrick. No more. We're watching.**

Jamie's gaze darted around, looking outside for a camera and inside for hidden devices.

**Clock's ticking.**

He grabbed a scrap of paper and scribbled a note, praying Aidan would read between the lines. Standing, he dug Aidan's cuff links out of his pocket and placed them and the note on top of his keyboard. He ducked into the laundry room for a T-shirt, then stopped in front of the bedroom door. Every fiber of his being wanted to push it open, whisper his plan to his partner, and kiss him goodbye in case, God forbid, he never came back. But he couldn't do that under the watchful eyes of his would-be kidnappers. This goddamn house and all its windows. He settled for bringing his fingers to his lips and pressing them against the door with a whispered "I love you."

He slipped out the front door into the darkness, and two big bodies were immediately on him. One tied his hands, the other blindfolded him. It was unnecessary. They had already ensured his compliance by threatening those he cared about.

"What'd you drop on the note?" the one on his right asked, voice muffled.

"A pair of cuff links. He gave them to me. It'll sell the story that I've left him."

"Do it," the other one said. "And ditch his phone."

A needle pricked Jamie's neck, and within seconds, his already blackened world began to grow darker. He sagged between his kidnappers, on the edge of consciousness, remembering the first time Aidan had given him the gold and emerald clovers in Galveston. To hold in trust while he had flown solo, leaving Jamie behind for his safety and to provide backup. He was betting on Aidan to trust their love, to understand Jamie had just done the same, to realize he needed his partner at his back now more than ever.

# TWENTY-THREE

Aidan rolled over in the king-size bed, searching for the heat he had missed the past five months. His back met cold sheets, his arm flailed through empty air, and his eyes popped open. Looking left, all that remained of his lover were rumpled sheets and a dented pillow. He levered up and listened for signs of life.

Silence.

Nothing but the pitter-patter of sleet outside on the copper bay window roof.

"Jamie?"

More silence.

He slid out of bed and winced as his body protested the previous night's activities. He hadn't been so well worked over since Galveston. Judging by the muted morning light outside, they had just enough time to do it again before the real world intruded, if only he could find his wayward bedmate. He snagged a pair of gym shorts off the chaise and went looking.

Opening the bedroom door, he tried a call of "Whiskey,"

to no response.

Down the short hallway, he keyed in the code on the study room door and stuck his head in. An open laptop but otherwise no Jamie.

Apprehension crept up his spine and tightened in his chest. He tried to rationalize the fear away. Maybe he went out to get breakfast and didn't want to wake him. Jamie usually preferred to cook, but it had been late when they'd finally fallen asleep. Aidan's blood heated, remembering the hours of kisses and lazy caresses. He really needed to find Jamie.

He ventured into the kitchen. No sign of him there either. Not even a pot of coffee, fresh or otherwise. If Jamie had gotten up in the middle of the night to work, he wouldn't have done so without caffeine. Hell, he wouldn't have stepped out the door this morning without a dose.

Rationalization became more difficult. Maybe Jamie had to leave in a hurry to meet Paulson and Grant. But if it was the case, why wouldn't he have woken him? He hurried back to the bedroom and grabbed his phone, dialing Paulson.

"Good morning," she answered brightly.

"Where are you?"

"In Beau's cruiser, outside Ethan's abode."

"Is Jamie with you?"

"No," she replied.

Grant came on the line. "What's wrong, Agent Talley?"

Apprehension no longer crept—it zinged up his spine, down his limbs, all the way to his fingers and toes, as a heavy knot formed in his gut. He rushed to the garage door and down the stairs. Both cars were still here. He put a hand on the Jeep's hood, then the Chevelle's. Both cold.

He slapped the garage door opener and ran outside, heedless of the drizzling sleet as he searched for his partner or any signs of forced entry.

"Aidan, what's wrong?" Grant repeated.

"Jamie's gone."

"Gone where?" Paulson asked.

"I have no idea. I'll call you right back." He hung up and dialed Jamie's number on his way back inside.

Then stopped.

A faint ringtone trilled near the front of the house. He ran directly up the hill between the walkway and the front of the house, bare feet squishing over cold, wet grass. When the ringtone died, he hit call again. Following the fading noise, he dropped to his knees under the bedroom window and pawed through the spindly hawthorn bushes and soaked pine straw until he saw his own face, cracked and split, staring back at him from the fractured glass of Jamie's cell. He picked it up, and it fell the rest of the way apart in his hands, his only lead gone.

"Fuck!" He gathered the remains of Jamie's phone and hustled back inside.

He closed the garage door and dialed Paulson. "Has Ethan moved?" he asked as soon as she picked up.

"No, the house is quiet, and his Beemer is parked in the drive."

He dumped Jamie's shattered phone on the kitchen island. "And Derrick?"

"No sign of movement there either."

"Where are we on the warrant?"

"Woke the judge an hour ago," Grant said. "Should come through any minute."

"Get another patrol on Ethan and get here as soon as you can."

He hung up, trusting his orders would be followed, and climbed the stairs to his room, the fear coursing through his veins as cold as the pellets of ice that had pelted his skin. He had just gotten Jamie back; he couldn't lose him now.

Fingers trembling, he dialed CU's athletic department. No staff was in yet, according to the overnight security guard who answered.

"Not Coach Walker?" he asked through his chattering teeth.

"His badge hasn't been used."

"Okay, thank you."

He cranked on the shower, turning it all the way to hot, and dialed Mel as warm steam filled the marble bathroom. "Aidan," she answered, voice scratchy.

"Jamie's been taken," he said as he stripped off the soaked gym shorts.

"Taken?" He vaguely registered an airport PA announcement in the background. Good, she could get here faster.

"Kidnapped. He's gone. Both cars are still here, and he's not on campus or with our local contacts." His voice rose, octave by octave, with every word, echoing shrilly off the marble walls. He was seconds from losing it, panic whiting out the edges of his vision. "I found his phone smashed outside."

"Aidan, calm down." Her order was muffled by his heart pounding in his ears.

"What if it's Renaud?" he said, putting words to his worst fear.

"It's not Renaud."

"How do you know that?"

"Because I've got a line on Renaud, and he's not in North Carolina."

Aidan threw out a hand, grasping the vanity. "You what?"

"I'm headed there now."

"Where the fuck is *there*? I need you here, now."

"Aidan, focus," she commanded.

Chest aching, he remembered all the times he had told Jamie the same thing the past week. He had to live by his own advice, had to do the same, if he was going to find him.

"I talked to Jamie three hours ago," Mel continued. "That's your window. Work with it."

"You talked to him? About what?"

"Find your partner, Agent Talley. Coordinate with local. I'll send backup."

She hung up, the line going dead, and Aidan stared down at his phone.

Furious, scared, betrayed.

Pain cut through him, the loss he had feared too close to bear, and that hole in his chest began to tear open again, right where his new world used to be.

No. Where it could still be if he only focused.

He tossed the phone aside, ignoring the clatter it made against the marble, and hurried into the shower. Warm water poured over him and he braced a hand against the steam-slicked wall, closing his eyes and taking a deep breath to steady himself.

He could do this. He could find his partner and bring him home.

Not *could*. *Would*. His heart and world depended on it.

# TWENTY-FOUR

Jamie swam toward wakefulness. His eyelids were heavy and uncooperative, and his limbs felt like lead weights. Moving them, much less lifting them, was too herculean a task. Last night shouldn't have leveled him, even if it was the best sex of his life. He had counted on sore knees and thighs, not waking up a rag doll.

"Jamie! Jamie, wake up!"

*Wrong voice.*

And wrong place.

There was no plush mattress beneath him and no warm body draped across his chest. The air was cold, and the floor beneath him hard and unforgiving.

*Floor.*

Jamie forced open his eyes and stared at an unfinished ceiling. Exposed wiring and duct work wove between metal and wood beams, barely visible in the storm-muted light filtering through transom windows. He turned his head left. Nothing but drywall, freshly plastered and patched. He rotated it right. A similar unfinished wall . . . and Derrick.

"Oh, thank God." Derrick lunged forward, only to fall back onto his ass. His arms were bound behind him and tied to a floor hook near his hip, severely limiting his movement.

Mustering his energy, Jamie shifted his own arms and found them similarly restrained. The binding was too tight to do more than recline against the wall. He closed his eyes and willed the nausea and pounding headache to subside, the reality of his situation and the memory of last night rushing back to him. Given his size, they must have double-dosed him.

"What are you doing here?" Derrick said, his whisper as loud as a bullhorn.

"I got a text." He eked one eye open and, when the world didn't spin, opened the other. "It was a picture of you—bound, gagged, and beaten."

The bruises on his ex's face were more livid in person than they had appeared on his phone. Derrick winced as he readjusted, indicating more bruises in places Jamie couldn't see.

"There was a noise outside my place last night. I thought it was the neighbor's cat wanting in. I opened the door, and someone jumped me."

"They used you as leverage to get me here."

"Why'd you come?"

"They threatened to hurt you."

"Jamie." Derrick's voice was soft, tinged with more than just fear.

"They also threatened to tell the press about us."

"Are you saying there is an us?"

"Christ, Derrick, no." At the kicked-puppy look, Jamie regretted his retort. Not because it wasn't true, but because he had delivered the blow when Derrick was beaten, scared, and couldn't fight back. And because his ex wasn't the only reason he had gone willingly into his kidnappers' hands. But that was besides the point. Right now, he needed a location he could feed to Aidan. "Do you have any idea where we are?"

"No, it doesn't look familiar, and I was out when they brought me in."

Squinting, Jamie took in the room anew, observing it through an agent's lens. By the location of the windows, they were in a basement. The old post office at the depot? He couldn't tell from this angle. He needed to see outside, but bound as he was, that was impossible.

The depot would be the first place Aidan searched. Meanwhile, he had to figure out how to play the situation and how to send Aidan more clues if they weren't at the depot. Shifting, he pressed his ear to the wall and listened. A hum as familiar to him as his favorite song reached his ears. Hard drives, several server racks' worth, and computers. They, whoever the coconspirators revealed themselves to be, had brought him in after all.

"Jamie, what are we going to do?"

"Shh." Approaching footsteps carried through the wall. "Someone's coming."

Blake was first through the door, Neil a step behind.

Across from him, Derrick gasped.

Neil regarded him coolly.

"You two know each other?" Jamie asked.

"I was fucking him," Neil said. "Before he decided to get back with you."

And there was motive and an explanation for the other assistant's hostility.

Jamie's head whipped to Derrick. "You told him about us?"

"He didn't have to," Neil said. "He mentioned his ex was a former baller, and I saw him lingering outside the auditorium the day you were introduced. After what happened in the locker room with Press, I put it together."

"This whole thing?" Jamie didn't buy it. From what he had seen, neither Neil nor Blake was smart enough to pull this off. Turned out he was right. The two parted, and a third person stepped between them. Jamie clenched his jaw to keep it from hitting the floor.

"Nah, Coach." In the dim lighting, Marcus's grin appeared more maniacal than genuine. "These two fools thought Derrick would be leverage enough. I wasn't sold. I saw how you and Mr. Daley kept sneaking looks at each other during practice and the game. We just needed a few compromising shots, and boy, did you put on a show last night. Neil got a phone full of 'em."

He tossed a stack of pictures on the floor. More of him and Aidan. Anguished, Derrick looked away. Jamie couldn't. "How'd you get into the neighborhood?"

"My parents live there," Neil said. "Security let us right through."

As his mind replayed the past few days, searching for clues he had missed, something else in Marcus's words registered. He had called Aidan "Mr. Daley," called him "Coach." Their covers held. They didn't know this was a sting.

"We hear you're good with computers," Marcus said. "Need you to do us a favor."

Ethan had fed them that information; the AD was definitely involved.

"What sort of favor?" Jamie asked.

"Just a little programming."

"You could have asked."

"Well, see, what I need you to do is illegal, but your boyfriend here—"

"He's not my boyfriend."

"Right," Neil said. "That would be Ian." His words were aimed directly at Derrick, as were the pictures he kicked his direction.

"You left the game to protect that secret." Marcus jutted his chin at Derrick. "Figure you'll help me out to keep that one," he said with a nod to the photos.

"Jamie, you don't have to this," Derrick said.

Oh, but he did. The stakes were higher than any of them realized. His and Aidan's lives, reputations, and careers would be ruined if those pictures saw the light of day. With evidence like that, there would be no plausible deniability.

"What do you need me to do?"

————

Grant's Bureau-issue sedan spit gravel as he swung into the depot lot and parked next to Paulson's truck. Aidan gripped the door handle, fighting his instinct to charge inside after his partner. They had agreed on a limited tactical approach and ordered FBI backup to hold a block away. The tracker he had put on Blake was in there. Until they determined whether cartel operatives were also on-site, they didn't want to spook anyone or provoke a gunfight.

Seeing Chancellor Polk with a suited stranger in front of the run-down post office, Aidan reconsidered that decision.

He hadn't taken charge of this rescue in spite of his shredded insides to have to deal with legal posturing. He'd done enough of that already this week.

"Lawyer with her?" Grant said.

"That'd be my guess." He pushed open the door, opened the umbrella he had swiped from Jamie's closet, and made his way across the parking lot, flanked by Grant and Paulson.

"What's the meaning of this?" Polk asked.

"You've got the warrant," Aidan said. "I assume your attorney has read it and explained it to you. Evidence of drug use was found on the premises."

"And how did you obtain said evidence?" the suit said.

"By walking in the open front door," Paulson replied. "Since the Polk family purchased this property six months ago, they've done nothing to secure it. No locked gate, no boarded windows, no door locks. This place is a nuisance that attracts vandals and drug dealers. It's a threat to public safety."

"Why's the FBI investigating a minor drug matter?" the attorney asked.

"Does this have something to do with"—Polk paused, glanced at her attorney, then back to Aidan—"the other case?" So she hadn't told her attorney about the gambling and identity theft. If she were involved, she would have asked him to cover her ass, to come up with a credible defense. The attorney's responses so far indicated he was in the dark.

Aidan kept his response vague. "The evidence collected puts the primary suspect in our other investigation at the scene here."

"Evidence being DNA on a smoked roach?" the attorney said.

"And imprints in the dust that match his shoe size and tread," Paulson added.

"Maybe he's a druggie," Polk said.

"Maybe," Aidan replied. "But we still need to look around. We have legal authorization to do so."

"This place is set for demo in a month. The fences are going up next week. I'd heard there was a problem, but I didn't—"

"Chancellor," the attorney said. "I'd advise you not to say more."

Polk's worried gaze bounced around to each of them and finally landed back on Aidan. "I had no idea it was connected to the other matter."

Aidan believed her, but he didn't have time to placate her right now. Jamie could be in there. He needed to get inside. "Chancellor, if you want this case over and done with, you need to let us through."

"We can challenge this, Liz," the attorney said. "If they're after something else—"

"Let them through."

Aidan didn't wait for the attorney's go-ahead. Shoving past them, he shut and discarded his umbrella outside the doorless front entrance and drew his gun, holding it down in front of him. "We go in silent," he said. "Hand cues only and tread lightly. Where's the entrance to the subfloor?" he asked Paulson.

"According to the plans, back right corner, in the floor. There were boxes there last time. That's why I didn't see it."

"I'll go left, Grant right, Paulson through the middle. We converge at the subfloor door."

They nodded, and Aidan led them inside before breaking left. The lack of boarded windows provided enough light to maneuver and to see evidence of recent foot traffic. The faint odor of pot lingered, and scattered roaches, cigarette butts, and empty forties littered the floor.

He met Paulson and Grant at the subfloor door and helped push the boxes aside. Beneath them was a locked in-floor hatch. Aidan withdrew a lock pick set from his coat pocket and unlocked it in under a minute.

"Nice work," Grant whispered.

Aidan nodded and lifted the hatch door. It swung open without a squeak. A good sign; it had been kept up and recently used. As they descended the steps, the smell of pot faded, and a humming sound reached Aidan's ears. They swept their flashlights around the basement. Cleaner than upstairs, it was free of roaches, bottles, and dust. Grant tapped his arm and indicated a hallway to their right. At the end, a light flickered from under a closed door.

Aidan signaled to move, and he and Paulson fell in behind Grant.

The hum grew louder, and battle-ready adrenaline surged through Aidan. Jamie could be behind that door. He would get him back safe, close the case, and they would go home, together. Jamie's house in Bernal Heights flashed in his mind.

*Home.*

Grant paused outside the door and pressed his back against the wall. Aidan recognized the hum as a generator, maybe two. Powering servers and computers? Shouldn't he also hear those?

No voices either.

Maybe Jamie and the others were farther back.

Grant motioned him forward. "Go in soft."

Gun aimed down, ready to draw if necessary, Aidan pushed the door open and shouted, "FBI." The call was swallowed by silence.

And crushing disappointment.

But for the generator and hanging utility light, and his business card tossed in the corner, the room was empty.

No servers, no computers, no Jamie.

———

As soon as Marcus untied him from the floor, Jamie could have escaped. Marcus and Blake, and Neil too for that matter, were large guys, but Jamie was taller and had at least thirty-five pounds on Blake, the biggest of the three. Add FBI combat training, and Jamie could disarm them, even groggy from the drugs.

But could he do so before one of them got to Derrick? He didn't want to risk it. Not with the way Neil roughly handled his ex. A chance to get back at Derrick was the carrot used to secure Neil's cooperation. Jamie didn't want to test him.

This was also the opportunity he and Aidan needed. Jamie would have direct access to the gambling and spyware programs, and he had identified at least three conspirators. He would get them to admit what they had done, those confessions would be witnessed by Derrick, and once he had access to the programs, he would redirect the cartel-coded bets and feed all the evidence they needed to his remote server. Once Aidan found him, they would have everything they needed to close the case.

He only hoped that in putting his plan into action, he

wasn't also putting Derrick in more danger than he could get them out of.

Marcus led them into the server room down the hall from where they had been held. Bigger, but with the same unfinished drywall and exposed ceilings. Four server racks, two desktop units, the same as Ethan's, and a generator were arranged along the far wall. Marcus pushed him toward the computers, and Neil shoved Derrick to the floor in the opposite corner.

"Hey!" Jamie said. "Take it easy."

Marcus intervened. "Go easy, Cashman. We ain't trying to hurt anyone here."

Once Neil relented, Jamie asked Marcus, "What is it you want me to do?"

Marcus explained the gambling program and spyware, and Jamie continued to play like this was the first he'd heard about it. Marcus wanted him to tweak the spyware so it retrieved more than just the registered user's information. He wanted all the user's contacts so they could sell more information to third parties.

"This is illegal, Marcus. How can you gamble on the sport you love?" he said, appealing to the player he had grown fond of the past few days.

"I'm not the one placing bets."

"No, you've just set up a framework where others can, and used it to steal personal information to sell to third parties. That's theft and fraud." He couldn't let on about the drugs without blowing his cover, but they needed to understand the situation was very serious.

"Under NCAA rules, I can't even deliver a pizza. And we're DII, in a city full of bankers and more rich people by the day. Sue me, us"—he gestured to Blake—"for wanting a little extra cash in our pockets. We've earned it."

Jamie knew the rules. They sucked for a lot of kids. But most schools had legal means of helping student athletes who needed extra financial assistance. "There are other ways, Marcus."

"And what would you know about that?" Marcus threw his arms wide, and for the first time, Jamie glimpsed the desperate kid buried beneath the wide smile. "You were recruited out of high school to UNC and offered a full ride."

"If I make this change, if you start collecting more information and selling it to third parties, we're talking felony fraud with serious time."

"Good thing you're not a fed anymore."

"And good thing we have those pictures to keep you quiet," Blake added.

"You're also going to install a better kill switch," Marcus said. "I don't trust the one Blake programmed. It already malfunctioned once." Because Jamie had tampered with it. "I want all traces of the programs erased the day after the Belmont game, or with a single click in case I need to kill it sooner."

Jamie had no problem with that demand. A foolproof kill switch, one a hacker like him couldn't get in and disconnect, was at the top of his list. In fact, he planned to activate it before the other changes went into effect.

"Can you do that?" Marcus asked when he didn't immediately respond.

"Yeah, I can do that."

"Good. Get to work."

"And no funny business," Neil said, knocking Derrick over and kicking him in the ribs.

Jamie twined his feet around the legs of his chair to hold himself in place. The urge to take Neil out grew by the second. He met Derrick's eyes, held his gaze until he stopped trembling, then started making the changes Marcus requested.

He tested each change made—using Ian Daley's account.

# TWENTY-FIVE

Aidan stormed into the house and threw his sopping coat at the banister. Missing wide, it landed on the foyer floor. He kicked it out of the way as he barreled through to the study. The depot had been a dead end; they were back to square one. Paulson was on her way to check Blake's apartment, then campus, while Grant, after dropping him off, was headed to pick up Ethan and bring him into the field office for questioning. Aidan wasn't fucking around any longer.

He was two steps around the corner, headed down the short hallway, when he froze. Feet paralyzed by hope and fear, he stared at the open study door. He was sure he had shut it before he left. Was Jamie back? Were his kidnappers here, after something else? Had Renaud tracked them to North Carolina?

A shadow fell across the study floor, and Aidan, kicked into motion by instinct and training, flew back around the corner. Flattening himself against the wall, his hand shot to his sidearm as he waited and listened.

He sniffed the air, detecting traces of Old Spice, not his

partner's cologne. His stomach plummeted in disappointment while his muscles tensed to strike.

He peeked around the corner. The shadow grew bigger, creeping toward the door, and the unmistakable click of a safety coming off ripped through the silence. Aidan drew his gun, holding it cocked in front of him.

"Talley, is that you?" called a familiar Boston accent.

Aidan lowered his gun and fell back against the wall. "Fucking hell, Byrne."

The other agent came around the corner, and his dark eyes grew wide as saucers.

Aidan realized he probably looked a shock, sopping wet in jeans and one of his sweaters. Not the three-piece suit Byrne was used to. "Sorry, rough morning." Aidan smoothed the wet hair off his forehead and remembered it wasn't just overly long and unruly. It was red. And he hadn't checked his accent.

"It's part of the cover." He grabbed Byrne's pistol by the barrel, switched the safety on, and handed it back, butt first. "What are you doing here and how did you get in?"

"I've got a spare key." He holstered his weapon. "Cruz called. She said you needed a K&R assist. For Jamie. Didn't believe her then. Believe her even less now."

"How do you figure?"

Byrne lifted his other hand and held out a folded piece of paper. "Found this in the study, on his computer."

Aidan knew with absolute certainty he wasn't going to like what that note said. He should tell Byrne to tear it up, avoid it like the land mine he sensed it was, but any information about his partner's whereabouts was better than nothing. He unfolded the note and read the last words he expected.

*Derrick needs me. I'm sorry. —Walker.*

Aidan changed his mind. He much preferred nothing. He dropped the paper and it fluttered to the floor, landing on his booted foot. He kicked it off, violently.

What the fuck? Needed him how? And why had Jamie signed it "Walker"?

Aidan thought they were past that. Jamie had demanded "Walker" when he had needed distance, when he had been torn between his past life and the present one. But last night Jamie had said he didn't want Derrick, that he only wanted him, that he was his home.

That he loved him.

Had Jamie changed his mind? Was that why he was sorry?

Had Aidan read everything so wrong?

Jamie hadn't been kidnapped. He had left. Derrick made a final plea, and Jamie went running. Back to his ex. Back to his old life. Aidan had seen this coming yet ignored it in favor of his own skewed reality. A fantasy where Jamie loved him, gave up all this—a beautiful house, an unburdened man, and an assassin-free future coaching the sport he loved—because *he* was Jamie's home.

And now Aidan had lost his.

Fantasy shattered, the hole in his chest that had started to form that morning tore wide open, and his legs gave out.

He would have hit the floor, except Byrne was there, shoving his shoulder underneath his and dragging him into the study. He dumped him in the chair and sat on the ottoman across from him.

"Talley, talk to me."

"I thought things between us had changed. I changed."

"You've changed?" Byrne said, skeptical.

"How much do you know?"

Byrne crossed his arms, every bit the surly Bostonian Aidan recalled from cases pre-Jamie. "Enough to know you've been an ass the past five months."

"I deserve that." Aidan met his gaze head-on. "I'd also add *fool.*"

"Yes, you were. And you're not now?"

Aidan pressed his hand to his aching chest and stared out the window. "I told Jamie I loved him."

Byrne gasped in surprise. "And he said it back?"

Aidan nodded. "But with the shit I've put him through, it wouldn't be a shock if he changed his mind and chose Derrick. Jamie's been home five days. He looks comfortable in his old life. And Derrick still wants him."

"No surprise there."

"Derrick loves him, and he's uncomplicated and beautiful."

"Last I spoke to Jamie, you two were off. I didn't know things had changed." The tension in Byrne's shoulders eased. "He didn't leave with Derrick."

"How do you know that? The note—"

"Jamie's the most loyal man I know, and he's head over heels in love with you."

Aidan's eyes widened. "He told you?"

Byrne smiled, something Aidan was still getting used to. "He wouldn't risk another job he loves if he didn't love you more. And if he knew the feelings were returned, he wouldn't betray you by leaving with Derrick. No matter how much of a foolish ass you've been."

Aidan exhaled in relief and dragged himself up on the offered life raft. If this man, Jamie's best friend and confidant, believed he hadn't left with Derrick, then maybe Aidan's reality wasn't a fantasy after all.

"And you're calling him Jamie."

"It's the cover."

"No, it's not." Byrne clasped his forearm. "Coffee, then tell me who you think kidnapped our boy and why so we can get him back."

Over two mugs each, Aidan laid out the chain of events he had pieced together, and when he got to the end and considered the newly found note, he realized how it fit in. "They used Derrick as leverage to get him out of the house."

"Very likely." Byrne dug into his pocket, and Aidan's gold and emerald cuff links spilled out of his fist onto the dining table. "He left those with the note on top of his keyboard. What's he trying to tell us?"

Aidan picked them up, turning them over in his hand as he put himself in Jamie's head. His mind flashed back to the first time he had given Jamie the cuff links, when he was about to lead a team into the field and had to leave Jamie behind.

For his safety. To run comms. To hack what they needed.

"You said you found these and the note on his computer?"

"Right on the keyboard."

Aidan cracked his first smile of the day. "I know what he wants us to do." He pushed out of his chair and ran for the study. "Jamie was kidnapped for his hacker expertise. He's programming."

"What are you thinking?" Byrne said.

"He's leaving clues"—Aidan nodded at the computer—"in here?"

One corner of Byrne's mouth hitched up. "Jamie would do that."

"And I think I may know how." He woke the computer, opened a web browser, and entered the address for the gambling site.

And hit a wall.

"What the hell?"

Byrne came around the desk to his side. "What's wrong?"

"I'm blocked from the site. Why would he do that?" He pulled Ian's phone out of his other pocket and tried getting at it that way. "I can get in here, but this isn't what I need to see."

"What are you looking for?"

"Whenever we tested the gambling site, Jamie had a monitoring window open that showed everything the spyware captured. Spyware for the spyware, he called it."

Byrne pointed at the top corner of the screen. "This is his official work user, isn't it?"

Aidan nodded.

"He's not supposed to have that software. It's going to be on his remote server."

"What remote server?"

"Hit the drop-down on the user."

Aidan clicked on the other user, only to be hit with the black box of doom. "Fuck!" Rather than pushing the laptop off the desk, he took his frustration out on the note, tearing it in half and throwing the bits on the floor. "It's fucking encrypted."

"Of course it is. Fucking hackers." Hands behind his head, Byrne took up the daily pacing. "Who do we know who can crack it?"

"Kevin, he's a hacker contact we made last year." Aidan reverted to his phone and dialed. "No answer," he said after trying twice. He shot off a text, then racked his brain for another option.

"Has anyone you know actually been in his system?" Byrne said.

When he put it that way, an option Aidan didn't like at all came to mind. But with Kevin out of reach, he was the best and only option left. Aidan scrolled again through his contacts, found the one he was glad for the first time ever he hadn't deleted, and dialed.

"Agent Talley," Oscar Torres answered. "I hear your partner wised up and got out of the Bureau."

The delight in his voice made Aidan want to reach through the phone and strangle the former agent who had made no bones about his interest in Jamie last fall in Galveston. "It's a cover," he said, restraining himself.

"I should have known he'd never leave you, even if he can do better."

Aidan ignored the too timely dig. "I need to get into Jamie's encrypted remote server."

"Have Jamie grant you access."

"Jamie's been kidnapped," he replied, patience waning.

"Six-five, 250, that same Jamie?"

"Yes, that Jamie. Now, can you help or not?"

"Why do you need access? What's on his hard drive?"

Frustrated, Aidan ground his teeth together and Byrne snatched the phone from his hand, putting it on speaker. "Torres, this is Agent Cameron Byrne. I'm a friend of Jamie's and a K&R specialist. We think Jamie may be leaving clues as to his whereabouts through spyware that's on his remote server. We need your help to find him."

Byrne's agent voice brooked no argument, and Torres wisely changed his tune. "I know the program. He keeps it off his primary mainframe since it's not Bureau sanctioned. We used it in Galveston. If he hasn't changed his setup, I can get in."

The doorbell rang.

"I'll get it," Byrne said to Aidan. "Work with Torres."

He disappeared down the hallway, and Aidan returned his attention to the phone. "We've got to find him, Oscar. Tell me what to do."

Torres fed him commands to type into the terminal box, and before Byrne was back, Torres was in Jamie's system and driving, entering decryption commands at lightning speed.

"These boys say they're looking for Coach Walker," Byrne said, returning with two unexpected visitors. "Security let them through since one of them had police clearance."

"That's right," Riley said. "My sister."

Hacking in Torres's capable hands, Aidan stepped out from behind the desk. "Riley, Press, what are you doing here?"

"Coach Walker didn't show up at practice today," Press said.

"What's going on?" Riley asked.

"How much does he know?" Aidan asked Riley.

"Enough to be here with me."

"Was there anyone else missing from practice today?"

"Marcus, Blake, and Neil."

Aidan considered for a moment whether to bring another person into this, but he didn't have time to waste. Press had gone to Riley about the ring in the first place. He already had some knowledge of it. Right now, Aidan's top priority was finding Jamie, in which case, four brains were better than two. "We think they've taken Jamie and are forcing him to tweak the system programming."

"Any idea where?" Riley asked.

"No, we think Jamie may be leaving a trail, but we have to crack the encryption on his computer first."

"I've got it," Torres's tinny voice called from the speaker, and Aidan rushed back behind the desk. The black box had vanished, replaced by the Halloween picture Aidan remembered from yesterday morning.

"All right, we're looking for a program he's labeled 'Hunt.' " Jamie and his ridiculous naming conventions. Magnum, Hunt, he was sure there was a Bourne and Bond here too. Torres directed the cursor to the D drive directory and scrolled through the list of folders. Aidan recognized many of the case names—tagged with Project—except one, Project Angel. A case Jamie had worked before they were partnered? But it had been opened earlier today. By whom, if Jamie was working elsewhere? He added that to the after-Jamie's-rescued list. He moved down the list and found Project Hunt. "Got it."

The monitoring box appeared. "That's it," Aidan said. "Thanks, Torres."

"Text me when he's safe."

"Will do." Aidan hung up and tossed the phone on the desk.

He opened a browser window, typed in the gambling site address, and logged in once it loaded. The monitoring box came to life. And not just fresh login life. There were entries from the past hour. Changes made to the handful of bets next to familiar cartel names. And new bets made using Ian Daley's login. With each one, the spyware collected more than just his information. All the contacts from Ian Daley's phone and accounts were being copied. That was what they wanted Jamie to tweak.

He looked again at the bets Ian Daley had placed. Unlike the cartel's bets on other teams, Ian's were on the Ravens' next game.

M. Smith, leading scorer.

B. Whitehead, leader in assists.

N. Cashman, leader in fouls.

Final score, 103-87.

He understood Jamie's first two clues. Marcus Smith was the ringleader. Blake Whitehead was his number two. N. Cashman had to refer to Neil, the other assistant coach. But leader in fouls? Fouls were penalties. And Neil didn't seem to like Jamie.

"Hey, guys." He called over Press and Riley. "How's Neil's temper?"

"Short," Riley said.

"He's the loose cannon, then."

"Who's Neil?" Byrne asked.

"Neil Cashman," Riley answered. "Another assistant coach."

"He's not a player?" Byrne said.

"Jamie programmed him in for a reason," Aidan said.

"He's also the chancellor's grandson," Press added.

"Her what?" Aidan was sure that hadn't been in Neil's file.

"Illegitimate. Her son got a girl pregnant in high school. CU lore."

"They were at that depot," Byrne said, and Aidan nodded. "They've moved."

"Do the numbers 103 or 87 mean anything to you?" he asked Press and Riley. "An address, maybe?"

"You got a pen and paper?" Press said, and Aidan handed him both. Press wrote the numbers down, first as Aidan had said them, and then, after staring at the paper a few seconds, he moved the eight over with the first three. "It's an address. 1038 Seventh Street."

"What's at that address?"

"A factory building," Riley said. "We had a team party there last month."

"Who owns it?"

"The Polk family."

Aidan's phone vibrated, displaying Grant's picture. "What've you got?"

"Ethan slipped his tail."

Aidan's breath hitched, fear slamming into him. "I know where he's headed."

# TWENTY-SIX

Jamie entered the last lines of code on the kill switch and prepared to put the final nail in the coffin of this operation. Marcus was right to have him update it. Blake's existing version, while adequate to shut down the program, left traces on the dark web and in users' cache files. It wasn't the complete wipe Marcus wanted. Neither was the kill switch Jamie programmed. His was a true self-destruct. The minute the updated spyware tried to extract additional information from anyone other than Ian Daley, the kill switch would activate and terminate both programs, wiping them completely.

He didn't want the framework out there on the dark web, and by now, he had the evidence they needed for their case collected and copied to his remote server. Plus, he had redirected all the cartel bets to allow enough time to brief the DEA and send units to the drop locations he had coded.

"All done." He pushed back from the desk. "Spyware and kill switch updated. All you have to do is hit Enter, and the new programming goes live."

"He's much faster than you," Marcus said to Blake. He stepped behind the desk and stretched an index finger toward the keyboard.

Jamie slid a hand over the keys, blocking him. "Are you sure you want to do this?" He also wanted that kill switch activated, but if Marcus hit Enter, at the first bet made and the new spyware activated, he would double his jail time. Jamie liked the kid. He didn't think his love of the game or his encouragement of the younger players was a front. The intimidation was all Blake. Jamie made a last-ditch effort to save Marcus's future. "You don't have to do this."

"You're a good coach, Whiskey. You can fix things on the court, like Press's shot. But you can't fix everything outside the arena."

He knocked Jamie's hand away, but before he pressed Enter, the door crashed open, blasting the doorknob through the drywall behind it.

"Step away from the computer." Ethan, disheveled and drenched from the rain, stood in the doorway, holding a gun trained on Jamie.

"What the hell, man?" Blake took several steps back. "Coach made the program upgrades you wanted."

The AD stalked into the room, his wild eyes and gun locked on Jamie. "No, he was making a copy of everything and transmitting it to his partner."

"His partner?" Marcus said.

"He's still a fed. This has been a sting from the beginning."

"Are you sure, Mr. Reynolds? He seemed like a coach to me."

"That's his partner." Ethan cut his eyes to the pictures on the floor. "I planted a bug on Ian, aka Special Agent

Aidan Talley, last night. Your grandmother called," he told Neil, who had yanked Derrick off the ground and held him by the shirt. "They raided the depot two hours ago."

"Good thing you had us move everything here."

Jamie guessed Ethan had given that order after he'd found Aidan snooping in his office the night of the party. Ethan had been the true ringleader from the start.

"That's not the point," he spat. "After she called, I listened to the recording from the bug. His *partner* didn't buy that he left with Derrick. He called in the cavalry, some kidnap and rescue hotshot from Boston."

Aidan had believed in him, in them, and Cam was there to assist. A smart move, especially if this situation continued to deteriorate.

"Fifteen minutes ago, they figured out *this* location," Ethan ranted on. "They're on their way."

Marcus kicked the pictures. "I thought feds couldn't . . . what's the word . . . fraternize."

"Who the fuck cares?" Ethan shouted as his gun arm swung wildly. "This is about us, not them. You're going to jail. I'm going to die."

"Die?" Blake stepped back another few paces until his back hit a wall.

"Yes, die!"

Jamie had liked his odds against three kids. He did not like his odds against a desperate adult with a gun who was running scared from the cartels. "Guys," he said to his players. "There's more going on here than you realize. You should get out."

"You can hit the kill switch," Blake said. "End it right now."

Ethan's attention and gun arm rotated back to Jamie. "You've copied everything already, haven't you?"

"I made the adjustments Marcus requested."

Ethan didn't buy it. His body tensed, and Jamie prepared to lunge to disarm him, but then Ethan dove the opposite direction. He grabbed Derrick out of Neil's hold, yanked him back-to-chest, and held the gun to Derrick's head.

A chorus of shocked reactions rang out.

Derrick's betrayed "Ethan!" pained Jamie the most. If he got Derrick or any of these kids killed, he would never forgive himself.

Jamie raised his hands. "Ethan, let's calm down and talk this through."

"Man, we didn't sign up for this shit," Blake said.

"Destroy the copies," Ethan ordered. "Destroy the system. Do it now or he dies." His finger tensed on the trigger, and he pressed the gun's muzzle harder against Derrick's temple. "And you're going to put those other bets back how they were last night." Ethan must have checked the cartel bets against his log. He wasn't just a hapless monitor looking to turn informant, or he would have asked for witness protection instead.

Jamie had to offer, though, for the sake of getting everyone else out alive. "Put down the gun, Ethan, and turn State's evidence. We'll protect you."

"State's evidence?" Marcus said. "What the fuck you into, Reynolds?"

"Yeah," Blake said. "I thought we were just skimming bets and selling information. What's he talking about?"

"Boys, it's better if you don't know." Jamie had to lock this down before his players became unwitting targets and before the increasingly jumpy AD pulled that trigger. "Ethan, no one has to die."

"That's where you're wrong. Do as I say, or I kill your ex and put a second bullet in your boyfriend's brain as soon as he arrives."

Derrick's eyes were locked on Jamie's, wide and scared, the hazel made bright by tears. "Jamie, please," he whimpered.

"All right, all right. I'll do it." He'd taken two steps toward the computer when alarm sirens rent the air.

Doors banged open upstairs, windows crashed in, and red and blue lights cut through the narrow transom windows.

"Fuck, cops!" Blake made a break for the door, and Ethan aimed at the runaway.

Torso bent, Jamie charged into Ethan's chest, forcing his arm and shots up, bullets pinging around the wood rafters and ripping through the exposed duct work, sending splitters and insulation raining down around them.

"Everybody get down!" Jamie shouted as he wrestled a still-soaking Ethan to the ground. Fighting him tooth and nail, getting his right arm free, the AD got another round of shots off at the door.

"Get back!" Cam shouted, as Aidan hollered "Jamie!" over him.

And then Ethan was curling the gun around, toward his own head. He must have thought death by his own hand would be better than death by cartel.

"Ethan, no!" Jamie lunged the length of his torso and wrapped his fingers around Ethan's wrist, slamming it down, just as he pulled the trigger. The bullet went sailing past the AD's head, in front of Jamie's eyes, into the drywall near where Derrick had been knocked down in the chaos.

For a second, Jamie feared he had been hit, but then Derrick screamed and scurried on hands and knees the other direction. Jamie slammed Ethan's wrist against the floor again, finally knocking the gun loose. He swept the pistol clear and flipped Ethan over, pinning him down with a knee and elbow to his back.

"Jamie!" Cam called, followed by Aidan yelling, "Whiskey, where are you?"

"Down here!" He held out his wrist to Marcus, who was crouched beneath one of the desks. "Get this tie off me so I can bind him."

Marcus skittered over and undid the wrap. Jamie tied it around Ethan's crossed wrists, then started to rise.

"Not another move," a sinister voice said behind him.

Ahead of him, Aidan and Cam stood in the doorway, guns drawn, gazes aimed behind him. Jamie glanced over his shoulder, and his stomach hit the floor.

Derrick was backed up against the wall, and Neil held the gun trained between his eyes. "They promised me you," he said. "I didn't really care about computer programming, or the Ravens, or my cut of the money. All I cared about was making you feel the same pain I did. You cast me aside for him." Neil glared at Jamie. "For the great Whiskey Walker."

Tears streamed down Derrick's face. "Neil, I'm sorry."

Aidan stepped forward, Neil clicked off the safety, and Jamie threw out an arm. "Irish, no."

He held Aidan's frightened stare. Aidan's primary objective, as his partner and so much more, was to get him out of this situation alive. Jamie, however, didn't want anyone else in this room to get hurt either, especially Derrick. He hadn't properly cleared the gun, and he hadn't gotten them out when he had the chance earlier. Derrick would not die for his mistakes.

*Cover*, he mouthed to Aidan, then slowly stood.

"Neil," he said, turning. "It's me you want."

"Jamie, no," Derrick pleaded.

Ignoring him, Jamie inched forward, the opposite direction of Aidan and Cam. With Neil's attention diverted, Marcus and Blake hustled out, while Aidan and Cam moved into the blind spot. "You want to make Derrick hurt?" Jamie said, continuing the distracting ploy. "Then it's me you want."

"Jamie, no, please." Derrick shook his head back and forth, trembling against the wall where Neil held him pinned. "I did this. Not you."

"Didn't I? I came home to CU and you. I tried to pick up my old life where I'd left off."

"He's right," Neil said to Derrick. "You'll hurt worse if I take away your precious Jamie."

His gun arm wavered, and Jamie made his move. Trusting his partner had his back, he dove toward Derrick, shielding him as shots rang out again. Bullets whizzed past and bits of plaster and drywall exploded, coating their bowed backs and heads. Eyes shut tight against the flying debris, Jamie listened as bodies collided behind him. A struggle punctuated by grunts, a deafening crack, a howl of pain.

Cam shouted, "Clear!" and Jamie's heart stopped. It wasn't Aidan who'd made the call. Had he been hit? Was that his howl of pain? Was his partner—his lover—down because he had chosen to save his ex? Had he chosen his old life at the expense of his new one after all?

*Not again, not now, not yet.*

The cascading heartache and regrets vanished an endless second later when Aidan returned, "Clear!"

Jamie unfolded from over Derrick's body, shook the plaster dust from his hair, and opened his eyes. He got a fleeting glimpse of terror-stricken autumn eyes before Aidan dragged him into a crushing embrace.

"What part of 'not get dead' didn't you understand?"

Choking on a half laugh, Jamie wrapped his arms around his partner and buried his face in his neck, whispering hoarsely, "I love you too."

# TWENTY-SEVEN

The DEA agent at the far end of the conference table did not look happy. Jamie couldn't see why. He had just delivered them a huge bust, gift wrapped and tied with a big red bow.

"We could have used more time," the agent said.

"I gave you more time. The delivery was set to occur"—Jamie glanced at the wall clock—"right about now. I pushed it out to midnight. That's four more hours than you originally had."

"You wouldn't know about it at all, if not for Agent Walker," Aidan added.

"If we could have kept the program running—" the agent started.

"No," Jamie said. "Every time the cartel used that program, my players were in danger, more than they knew. That couldn't continue."

"Take the bust," Aidan said. "And take the credit for it. We're out."

On the way to the field office, they had agreed they didn't want to be involved beyond their case, which was solved. Let the DEA handle the cartel. They didn't need another target on their backs.

"What happens to Ethan?" Aidan asked.

The AD was downstairs, pacing a holding cell.

"If he'll agree to testify against the cartel, we'll put him in protective custody."

"He committed a crime," Jamie argued. "He manipulated those students and put them in harm's way without their knowledge."

"We'll make sure he serves his time, one way or the other."

Jamie didn't trust the vague answer, but he would trade it for another. "And you'll note CU's cooperation in the event of an NCAA investigation?"

"Of course, Agent Walker."

A round of stilted handshakes later, the agent left, and Cam slipped in, carrying a plastic take-out bag. Jamie, however, didn't smell any food.

"Pictures are gone," he said, voice low.

"All of them?" Aidan asked.

"I burned the hard copies from the scene."

"And the ones on Neil's phone?" Jamie asked.

Cam set the bag on the table and pulled back the handles. Inside were latex gloves and three plastic evidence bags containing cell phones. "They all swear the pictures are only on Neil's, but I figured you'd want to be sure."

Jamie hated to think of anyone, much less his best friend, seeing those photos, but Cam, a consummate professional and accomplice, hadn't made a single lewd comment about the indiscretions on display or his and Aidan's lapse in judgment at fucking with the blinds open. It shouldn't have been an issue with neighborhood security and the large lots, but it had been careless, just like his failure to clear the gun.

Aidan clasped Cam's shoulder, the two of them sharing a long look, before Aidan glanced back at him. "I'm going to step out. Make sure no one steps in."

Jamie waited for the door to close, then snapped on the gloves and dumped the phones on the table. Cam handed him Marcus's first. "Quit beating yourself up."

Jamie checked all the possible places for photo files and, finding none of him and Aidan, turned the phone back off. "I fucked up, with the gun and this." He waved the phone in the air.

Cam shot him a devilish smirk. "I wasn't going to say anything about your sudden exhibitionist tendencies, but damn, brother, impressive."

Jamie chuckled weakly as he checked Blake's device. A lot of dick pics, but none of his or Aidan's. He swapped it for Neil's, finally hitting pay dirt. He deleted the photos and checked the history to make sure he hadn't sent them anywhere. Only a networked printer. Jamie made a mental note of the IP address so he could hack in later and delete the last remaining trace.

"Nobody died, Jamie," Cam said, serious again. "You saved Derrick, Ethan, and those kids, even though two tried to kill you, and you handed the DEA a major bust. It was a rough case for a lot of reasons. But you came through all right. Better than," he said, a smile in his voice. "I'm happy for you."

Jamie handed the cleared phone back, and Cam zipped it in the evidence bag. "Thank you, for rescuing my ass and for having my back. I owe you."

"Yeah, you do." He dropped it in the take-out bag with the others and stood. "I'm going to get these back into evidence, then head out. My ASAC called. I'm on the last flight out to Chicago." His voice had dimmed, taking on the quality Jamie had heard in the phone call last week.

"How old?" he asked.

"Ten."

Jamie pulled his best friend into a hug. "You call me anytime."

They met Aidan in the hallway and after, seeing Cam out, headed into what Jamie hoped was the last meeting between them and bed.

Jamie sat at the open end of the table, Aidan to his right, Renee on his left. Across from her were Coach Turner and the university's general counsel. And at the other end of the table were SAC Carr, Agent Grant, the Charlotte Mecklenburg Chief of Police, and an NCAA rep. Grant had started the debrief while he and Aidan were finishing up with the DEA and Cam.

"And Derrick Pope?" Carr said. "Why was he there? How was he involved?"

Derrick sat with Riley and Press in Carr's office, each in line for questioning.

"They used him as leverage to secure my cooperation," Jamie said.

"You two are friends?"

"Agent Walker and Derrick know each other from Carolina," Aidan said.

Jamie laid a hand on his arm and met his guarded gaze.

He had also thought about this on the ride to the field office, longer if he was honest. It was bound to come out in the details of the case, and he owed it to the three people sitting in the SAC's office. And to the man sitting beside him. He was tired of hiding and given the chance to make something good out of this mess, Jamie took it.

He withdrew his hand and braced his forearms on the table. "Derrick and I more than knew each other. He was my boyfriend. The coconspirators found out and threatened to expose me."

"Expose you?" the chief said.

"I'm gay. They threatened to tell the press about my past relationship with Derrick and about my current boyfriend."

Aidan flinched, the motion so subtle those around the table wouldn't notice. But Jamie did. He hoped it was a good, surprised flinch and not a what-the-fuck-did-you-just-do flinch.

"We'll add blackmailing a federal agent to the charges," Carr said.

"I'd ask you not to," Jamie said.

"With all due respect, Agent Walker, it's my—"

"I know it's your call," Jamie interrupted. "But between kidnapping, assault, fraud, and violations of gaming laws, you've got more than enough to charge them with. I don't plan to keep my sexual orientation a secret, but I also don't want it to be the focus of this bust. I took this case to protect the integrity of the game, and that should be the message of tomorrow's press conference. More practically, you have no evidence of the blackmail." At least not as of two minutes ago, thanks to Cam. "I'd also like to protect Derrick's privacy as much as possible. I owe him that much."

Carr nodded and turned to CU's counsel. "Given Chancellor Polk's connection to the crime scenes and one of the accused, I'd recommend she sit out the press conference tomorrow."

"She's taking a leave of absence. Coach Turner will speak on CU's behalf."

"Good, and Chief, will you be representing CMPD?"

"I think Detective Paulson can represent our interests." Grant and Renee smiled, and Jamie was pleased for her. She had been an excellent local resource and deserved the promotion. Maybe she would get the chance to work with her friend more often now. They were a good team.

"When will the NCAA make its ruling?" Jamie asked before the meeting adjourned. "Aside from the individuals downstairs, there's no evidence the rest of the team was involved or that any games were affected. The Ravens should get to play tomorrow and in the tourney. They've worked hard for that."

"Your opinion is noted, Agent Walker," the NCAA rep said. "We'll wait for the DEA, FBI, and CMPD to issue their findings. Then we'll process the matter through usual channels. We won't make any statements yet. The remaining Ravens can continue to play until we do."

Turner exhaled a big breath, and Renee and the chief smiled. Jamie too.

"All right, then," Carr said. "We're set for ten o'clock tomorrow." He stood and extended a hand to Renee. "Detective, thank you for your assistance." Next, he turned to Jamie. "Agent Walker, great job as lead on this investigation. I'll put a commendation in your file."

"Thank you, sir," Jamie said.

As the crowd dispersed, Turner lagged behind. "Walker, can I have a word?"

"Sure, Coach."

Outside in the hallway, Turner leaned back against the wall. "I feel like such a fool. I suspected Blake was involved, and I'm not all that surprised about Reynolds, but I wouldn't have guessed Neil. Definitely not Marcus."

Jamie patted his shoulder. "It wasn't about the game or the gambling for Neil. He had his own reasons. As for Marcus, I missed that too. Some people are better actors than others."

"Like you?"

"I'm sorry if you felt not disclosing my sexual orientation—"

"I don't mean that." Some of the tension in Turner's shoulders eased, and he pushed off the wall. "Who you love is your own business. I meant coaching. From . . . what did Agent Grant call it, the 'debrief' . . . it sounded like none of the guys figured out you were still a fed."

Jamie bowed his head. "Because it wasn't all acting."

"My offer stands, Whiskey. You ever decide you've had enough of this"—he motioned at the general surroundings —"there will always be a place for you on CU's bench. And if you need to be somewhere else because of that boyfriend, whoever he is, then I'll make a call."

"Thanks, Coach."

It was a hell of an offer, a future path he hadn't considered until this past week. A dream job for a player who couldn't, or in his case, wouldn't play anymore. It was a chance to get back on the court and mentor students in the game he loved. But did he love the game more than his job at the FBI and the man he worked with there, the man he loved?

Before he could answer, before he could get back to that

man, he was confronted with a different one. In his way, as he had been the entire week, was Derrick, standing outside the conference room. Hair askew, eyes red, face still blotchy, he looked too much like he had that day eight years ago when Jamie left him in a hospital parking lot. At least this time, he hadn't been the cause of Derrick's tears.

"How're you doing?" he asked.

"I've had better days."

"Haven't we all."

Derrick swiped at his cheeks and ran a hand through his hair, mussing the curls up even more. "Agent Grant said he had some questions for me."

"You'll need to give a statement. You can have an attorney present."

"How much—"

"They know you're my ex."

Derrick's bloodshot eyes widened. "You told them?"

Jamie's gaze flickered down to his tattoo. "To thine own self be true."

He lifted a hand, then hesitated. Jamie nodded and Derrick laid it over his chest, over his tattoo. "I'm sorry for trying to force you back into this life. Seeing you in action today, you're good at what you do here too."

Jamie covered Derrick's hand with his own. "But you weren't wrong. I miss the game, and I miss home."

Hazel eyes cut to the main conference room. "You'd miss him more, though, wouldn't you?"

The notion was inconceivable. Less than a week apart, even while working together, had been hell. Now, Jamie couldn't imagine, yet it was a very real possibility once he told Aidan the truth about Project Angel. He swallowed around the lump in his throat. "Yeah, I would."

"He's out. He won't hold you back like I did."

"You were my first love, Derrick."

"And you mine." Derrick gave his chest a pat, then slid his hand out from under Jamie's. "But he's your last."

# TWENTY-EIGHT

They didn't make it to the bed.

Aidan parked the Chevelle in the dark garage, waited for the door to close, then clambered over the console into his partner's lap, claiming the mouth he had missed since waking up alone that morning. He had considered pulling into one of the dozens of deserted parking lots they had passed on the way home, but they'd had enough captured-on-film moments for today. The second they had privacy, though . . .

"Baby," Jamie groaned against his lips.

It was a tight, uncomfortable fight. Aidan's knees were wedged between Jamie's thighs and the console on one side and the door on the other, his head hitting the roof when he levered up to yank his jacket and shirt off. Jamie's elbow banged the passenger window as he did the same. But Aidan couldn't go another second without him.

He wanted—needed—to touch every part of him. Needed that confirmation of life and love that was worth the risk of losing it. How did he ever think he could go without this, without Jamie?

Diving in for another kiss, their tongues tangled as Aidan wove his fingers through Jamie's hair, nails raking across his scalp, a moan rumbling in his wake. Jamie clutched at his shoulders, fingers digging in, leaving bruises, until one hand fell away and hit the seat lever, rocking them horizontal.

Jamie arched, exposing his throat, and Aidan nipped a path to the spot behind his ear, licking and sucking at his second favorite spot on his lover's body. "Need you, Whiskey. Here. Now."

Jamie palmed the back of his head, holding him there, as his hips lifted off the seat, grinding their erections together. "Right here, baby."

Aidan shoved his hips down, pinning him back to the seat. He dragged his cock along the length of Jamie's and smirked as his partner's long arms dropped away, limp, and his eyes rolled back in his head. "I'm driving this time," Aidan said with another thrust of his hips. "And this car better find its way home."

"Home?"

He kissed his way down to Jamie's tattoo, his favorite spot, and lavished it and the too big heart beneath with all the love he felt for this man. "My house, yours, I don't care. As long as it's in the garage of wherever we sleep."

Jamie's hands captured either side of his head and jerked him up, bringing them face to face. "Irish, what are you saying?"

He leaped, hoping that huge heart and those big hands would catch him. "I don't want to sleep apart ever again. If I'm your home, you're mine too."

Gorgeous blue eyes stared back at him, made brighter by the tears pooling at their corners. "I'll have it on a car carrier tomorrow," he said, voice thick, before he sealed their mouths back together.

Need urgent, their hands collided in the middle, frantic to undo buttons and zippers. Aidan knocked Jamie's out of the way and got both their flies loosened. He nudged Jamie's boxer's down, and his erection bobbed between them. Aidan had a momentary twinge of regret that the space was too cramped to bend down and suck it or to turn so Jamie could slide inside him. But then Jamie pulled Aidan's cock free of his boxers, lined it up against his own, and grasped them in his fist, pressing their hard flesh together, and Aidan had no further regrets.

"Who's the driver now?" Jamie whispered hotly in his ear, and Aidan happily surrendered the wheel, his pleasure kicked into overdrive.

He thrust into Jamie's fist and chased after his kiss. He didn't have to ask twice. Jamie sucked his tongue deep, teeth clashing, while he used their combined moisture to smooth the slide of his fist over the length of them. Hot, wet, firm, and tight, Aidan drowned in sublime pleasure, the two of them held intimately together by Jamie's sure, dependable grip. His partner had caught him and more, awoken that resilient beast in his chest and lured his heart out of hiding with the promise of a second chance at love.

Bracing one hand on the door and the other on the head-rest, Aidan held on for the ride, groaning into Jamie's mouth. His fist tightened and Aidan thrust faster, his climax barreling toward him. When Jamie's other hand glided inside his sagging pants and over his ass to tease his hole, the train jumped the tracks, the last of his restraint shredding. Eyes slipping shut, open mouth skating over Jamie's jaw and down to his neck, Aidan rammed into his partner's sure hold and came with a shout. With panted grunts that bathed the side of Aidan's face, Jamie stroked twice more and groaned out his finish, adding to the warm mess of love and life between them.

Arms weak, Aidan collapsed, and Jamie caught him against his body, running his clean hand up and down his side, the cozy touch causing Aidan's heart to swell. He returned the gentle caress, threading his fingers through Jamie's hair, down his neck and over his shoulders.

"I was afraid I was going to lose you today."

"You're not going to lose me, Irish."

"How can you be so sure? I don't exactly have the best track record."

Jamie lifted a hand and palmed his cheek. "I'm sure because you've got my back," he said, voice full of confidence, gaze full of love. "You can't lose me, Aidan, and I can't lose you either. We'll do whatever it takes to come home to each other every night. No one's losing anybody. I promise you."

He tangled their fingers and lifted their clasped hands, kissing Aidan's knuckles. The last time Aidan had done this, it was an ending. Now, Jamie mimicked the gesture as a new beginning. "Partners, Irish, always."

Lowering their hands, Aidan leaned forward and brushed his lips, sealing the vow. "Partners, Whiskey, always."

# TWENTY-NINE

Out of the khakis and Ravens polo, sharply dressed again in a G-man suit, Jamie stood in a shadowed backstage corner of CU's auditorium. "You sure you don't want to come on stage?"

Aidan, outfitted again in a three-piece suit, the whole picture devastating with his red hair, shook his head and leaned a shoulder against the wall. "Take your moment in the spotlight. This was your case."

"You're my partner. I couldn't have solved it, much less survived it, without you."

"You're the one they care about. And this isn't just about the case." Jamie lifted a brow, and Aidan reached for his hand, entwining their fingers. "You didn't get to leave the game on your own terms last time. You should get to now."

Turner called the crowd to order, and Jamie straightened. Aidan patted down his suit lapels and tweaked the clover cuff links he had insisted Jamie wear. "You remember what I told you last time?"

Jamie grinned. "Go charm the pants off 'em."

Aidan leaned forward and lowered his voice. "Save the boxer-dropping charm for me." He kissed his cheek, lingering there. "Just smile pretty for them."

"I can do that." Jamie pulled back, meeting the autumn gaze of his partner. His lover. He prayed those eyes would still look at him with the same love once his betrayal was revealed. He had decided to save it for the familiar surroundings of home. One more day. One relatively peaceful day with Aidan, happy and in love, before he cut the rope on his own guillotine.

Aidan turned him around and slapped his ass. "Go, Whiskey."

He winked over his shoulder, then followed the path to the stage, stepping out from behind the curtain and standing beside Renee and Grant.

Turner cleared his throat and began. "Several weeks ago, we were alerted to an illegal gambling and identity theft operation at CU. Cooperating with CMPD, we called in the FBI, and as of yesterday, they broke the case and those responsible are now in custody. Unfortunately, several members of our basketball team were implicated and suspended from the team. The Ravens will play out the remainder of our season, compete in the tournament, and hopefully bring home a trophy. We'll leave it up to the NCAA to determine what happens from there. We are sorry this happened, but as soon as I and the administration were made aware of the situation, we took steps to shut the illegal activity down, and no serious injuries or lives were lost in the process. On behalf of CU, I'd like to thank CMPD and the FBI for their diligence and hard work in resolving this matter. I'll turn this over to them now."

Renee and Grant recapped the case, answered several

minutes of questions, then Grant motioned him forward. "Agent Jameson Walker led the team on this case and was a model agent in bringing it to a successful conclusion. Agent Walker would like to say a few words."

Stepping behind the podium, Jamie flashed his charming smile, and Aidan, standing in the wings, smirked back. "Okay, so I need to ask your apology for telling a little fib." He laughed, and the crowd laughed with him. "As Agent Grant said, I was undercover in my role as a coaching assistant to determine who on CU's basketball team was involved in the illegal activity. That's not to say I didn't enjoy my time back on the court or that the Ravens, as a whole, are not to be commended for their hard work, drive, and spirit. At no time did I observe any evidence of the players, including those implicated, throwing any games. This was an unrelated act of a few individuals, and I'd urge the NCAA to consider not punishing the innocent Raven players who worked long and hard to get here."

He paused, summoning the courage for this next part. In his periphery, Aidan gave an encouraging nod and Jamie swallowed hard, ready to step forward. Step out. These words were important, and maybe they would count for something with Aidan in the days to come. "The Ravens and CU accepted me into their family, and for the brief time I was here, I lived a dream I hadn't fully realized. Today, I finish things the way they should have been finished eight years ago. I'm leaving the game on my own terms. I'm doing so to return to a job I love and my home in San Francisco, where there is a special someone waiting for me, and I can't wait to get home to him."

Jamie sucked in a breath, held it.

A wall of silence, one second, two seconds, and then a

tidal wave of sound blasted him. Mics were shoved forward, questions were shouted, and a "Whiskey" chant broke out in one section of the auditorium. He scanned the crowd for the source of the commotion, reached the mezzanine, and saw Press and Riley leading the Ravens basketball team in the chant, clapping along with his name.

Because he had said *him*. And because they supported their coach.

He moved away from the podium, smiling, smug in his pride for his players and for the auburn-haired man grinning in the wings. He hurried to him after Turner's final remarks, and avoiding the press gathered out front, they slipped out the backstage door.

In the deserted utility parking lot, Aidan pressed him up against the Chevelle, stealing a quick but thorough kiss. "I'm gonna have to fuck you in the car again before we leave for the airport."

Jamie dug out his keys and dropped them in Aidan's palm. "All yours, Irish."

"You or the car?"

He grinned. "Both."

"Not so fast, lovebirds."

They startled apart at the familiar yet unexpected voice.

"Baby bro, you look awful." Aidan stepped toward Danny with open arms, while Jamie hung back, trepidation working its way up from his gut.

"Love you too, Ai," Danny said, returning the embrace.

"No, but seriously. What are you doing here, and why do you look like you just got off the red-eye flight from hell?" The description was accurate. Eyes red, hair ruffled, suit wrinkled, Jamie had never seen the usually dapper Danny look so disheveled.

"Because I just did." Danny half hugged Jamie on the way to resting back against the car. "Six fucking hours, in coach."

"Don't you have your own plane for that?"

"Someone stole it."

"Stole it?" Jamie said.

"Who?" Aidan asked over him.

Jamie already knew. Aside from Aidan, there was one other common denominator among them—the woman who pulled the strings of all their lives.

Grimacing, Danny confirmed his suspicion. "Your boss, my girlfriend."

Aidan staggered back. "Mel?"

"That's the one." Hurt, betrayal, and worry laced Danny's voice.

"Where's she headed?" Jamie asked.

"She flashed her badge and paid the hangar crew not to tell me. I had to pay them more." He withdrew a folded piece of paper from his coat pocket. "Flight manifest says Antonio Maceo Airport."

Aidan snatched it out of his hand. "Santiago de Cuba. Why's she headed to her uncle Robert's place?"

When mentioned together, the place and name reminded Jamie of a document he had seen the night before last. In Martin Westley's files. "What's Robert's full name?" he asked, dreading the answer, his apprehension turning to fear.

"Roberto Gabriel Marcelo," Aidan answered. "Gabe was named after him."

Jamie covered his face with his hands, muttering "Fuck!" behind his fingers.

Aidan ripped them away, forcing him to meet his gaze.

"Tell me."

"Right before I was taken, I was reviewing Martin Westley's files. There was a lease of property just outside of Santiago de Cuba. To EH Consulting."

Aidan's eyes widened, realization dawning. "Please, no."

"The property's owned by Roberto Gabriel Marcelo."

"What are you saying?" Danny asked.

Aidan's gaze never broke from his. "Mel's going after Renaud, the terrorist who tried to kill us in Galveston." His voice faded, his eyes closed, and his forehead creased in tortured anguish. "Or . . ."

Danny clutched his arm. "Or what, Ai?"

Aidan's breath hitched, his shoulders shook, and Jamie drew him forward, into his arms, holding him tight. He kissed Aidan's temple, whispering assurances he didn't believe, then met Danny's dark, confused eyes over the top of his partner's head, giving him the terrible possibility Aidan couldn't bear to speak.

"Or she's been working with Renaud the entire time."

———

Reviews are an invaluable tool when it comes to spreading the word about great reads. Please consider leaving an honest review for *Cask Strength* on your favorite review site.

**Thank you for reading!**

# ACKNOWLEDGMENTS

*First Edition Acknowledgments:*

Many thanks to my editor, Deb Nemeth, and the entire Carina team for their continued enthusiasm and support for this series; to Kristi Yanta, for the late night plotting sessions and invaluable insights; and to my beta readers, Tera, Victoria, Morgan and Michelle, for their speedy reads and helpful feedback.

Thanks also to D.M. for the technical advice and to the hubster for confirming sports bits. Cheers to my sprint buddies and writing groups—Chelley, Jess, Natasha, Alyson, Annabeth, Sarah, Megan, the Menlo Le Boule SVRWA crew and the Sassy Bitches—who kept me on track and on deadline. I cannot thank you enough!

And finally, readers, thank you so much for continuing to read and enjoy Aidan and Jamie's story. One more to go and the ride only gets rougher for Agents Irish and Whiskey. Buckle up!

---

*Second Edition Acknowledgments:*

Cate Ashwood + Wander Aguiar + Matheus R. make auburn-haired Aidan magic with this *Cask Strength* cover. I could not be happier! Thanks again to Adam and Sandy for the editing, to Kim and Rachel for beta reading, and to Nina and the VPR Team for getting the word out. And thank you, readers, for coming back for more!

# ALSO BY LAYLA REYNE

For the most up-to-date list of titles and a helpful reading order, please visit www.laylareyne.com.

*Agents Irish and Whiskey:*

Single Malt

Cask Strength

Barrel Proof

Tequila Sunrise

Blended Whiskey

*Trouble Brewing:*

Imperial Stout

Craft Brew

Noble Hops

Final Gravity

*Fog City:*

Prince of Killers

King Slayer

A New Empire

Queen's Ransom

Silent Knight

*Perfect Play:*

Dead Draw

Bad Bishop

King Hunt

*Soul to Find:*

Icarus and the Devil

*Changing Lanes:*

Relay

Medley

Freestyle

*Table for Two:*

The Last Drop

Blue Plate Special

Over a Barrel

*Standalone Titles:*

Dine With Me

Variable Onset

Sweater Weather

What We May Be

# ABOUT THE AUTHOR

Layla Reyne is the author of *What We May Be* and the *Agents Irish and Whiskey*, *Fog City*, and *Perfect Play* series. A Carolina Tar Heel who spent fifteen years in California, Layla enjoys weaving her bicoastal experiences into her stories, along with adrenaline-fueled suspense and heart pounding romance.

You can find Layla at laylareyne.com, in her reader group on Facebook—Layla's Lushes, and at the following sites:

BB bookbub.com/authors/layla-reyne

facebook.com/laylareyne

instagram.com/laylareyne

tiktok.com/@laylareyne

9 781962 010030